Endorsements

"*Red Ink* follows a variety of characters on opposite sides of the world and shows their different spiritual journeys. It's a beautiful and sometimes brutal story about the power of unconditional love, of ultimate sacrifice, and of the faithful, unshakable allegiance of several believers toward their one true God. Though there are many players in this novel, their lives intersect in an unseen tapestry of faith that is crafted by the loving hands of a merciful God. This is a life-changing story that is not to be missed."
—**Michelle Sutton**, author of more than a dozen novels, including *It's Not About Me, Danger at the Door, In Plain Sight*, and *Never Without Hope*

"*Red Ink* is a timeless portrayal of God's love and grace, reaching beyond the human boundaries of race, gender, and generations."
—**Kacy Barnett-Gramckow**, author of Moody Publishers' "Genesis" Trilogy

"*Red Ink* gives readers a candid and realistic look into religious persecution, but with hope and grace. Macias brings surprising redemption to her characters and their stories."
—**Mary DeMuth**, author of *Life in Defiance*

"My heart was pricked as I read Kathi Macias's latest novel. *Red Ink* is a story that reminds us that God's Word is worth everything . . . and prayer changes things! A must-read."
—**Tricia Goyer**, author of 25 books, including *Dawn of a Thousand Nights*

Red
Ink

They took her child,
her family, and her freedom
—but not her faith.

Book 3 in
the "Extreme Devotion" series

Kathi Macias

New Hope
PUBLISHERS
Birmingham, Alabama

More New Hope books by Kathi Macias

No Greater Love

More than Conquerors

Mothers of the Bible Speak to Mothers of Today

*How Can I Run a Tight Ship When I'm Surrounded by
Loose Cannons? Proverbs 31 Discoveries for Yielding to
the Master of the Seas*

Beyond Me: Living a You-First Life in a Me-First World

New Hope® Publishers
P. O. Box 12065
Birmingham, AL 35202-2065
www.newhopepublishers.com
New Hope Publishers is a division of WMU®

Library of Congress Cataloging-in-Publication Data

Mills-Macias, Kathi, 1948-
  Red ink / Kathi Macias.
    p. cm. -- (Extreme devotion series ; bk. 3)
  ISBN 978-1-59669-279-4 (sc : alk. paper) 1. China--Fiction. I. Title.
  PS3563.I42319R43 2010
  813'.54--dc22

                                        2010011638

All Scripture quotations, unless otherwise indicated, are taken from the New King James Version. Copyright © 1982 by Thomas Nelson, Inc. Used by permission. All rights reserved.

Interior design: Sherry Hunt
Chinese script: Kai Chin Bishop

ISBN-10: 1-59669-279-0
ISBN-13: 978-1-59669-279-4

N114127 • 1010 • 5M1

To my beloved husband, Al, and to all the offshoots of our love: children, grandchildren, and great-grandchildren...

To those who continue to share God's love and mercy behind bars, in gulags and prisons, while chained and suffering, including and especially Li Ying, who inspired this story...

And to Zhu Yesu, who holds us safely in the palms of His scarred hands.

Chinese Language Notes

PRIMARY CHINESE CHARACTERS

Yang Zhen-Li [sounds like Yang J'un Lee]. Yang is her surname, the same as her father's, *Yang Hong*. Chinese women generally do not take their husband's surnames, but retain their own family name. Both one- and two-word first names are common in China. *Zhen-Li* means truth, as in John 14:6.

Zhou Chi [sounds like Joe Chirr]. Yang Zhen-Li's husband. Father of *Zhou Chan* [sounds like Joe Chan]. His sister is *Zhou Ming* [sounds like Joe Ming].

Mei [sounds like May]. Means beautiful. A fellow prisoner of Zhen-Li.

Yin Xei [sounds like Yeen Shay]. Wife of Yang Hong and mother of Yang Zhen-Li.

Tai Tong. A prison guard.

CHINESE PHRASES

Yesu; Zhu Yesu Jidu = Jesus; Lord Jesus Christ

Tian Fu; Qin Ai de Tian Fu = heavenly Father; dear heavenly Father (to begin prayer)

Qin Ai de Shen = dear God

Shengjing = the Bible

xiu chi = social shame

baba = Daddy

jiao hui = church meeting

jia tin jiao hui = family or house church

shen = god (generic)

Ni hao ma? = How are you?

ping an = peace

xiexie = thank you

Ni zen me le? = How are you doing?

Zen me le?; Zen me yang? = What's up?; Are you OK?

Hai ke yi = I'm OK, so-so.

Ming bai le = I understand.

ping' an ye, sheng shan ye = silent night, holy night

Shang Di = Most High God

dixiong = brother (as in Christian brother)

Prologue

Y ANG ZHEN-LI WAS NEARING THIRTY BUT AT TIMES FELT TWICE that old. Her back was becoming permanently bent forward from the heavy pails she carried daily, one attached on each end of the thick bamboo rod that stretched across her shoulders, mirroring the heaviness of her heart. There had been a time when she'd been acclaimed as a beauty, but she could scarcely remember why... or imagine that it would matter.

She tried to fight the encroaching darkness, tried to hold fast to what she knew was true, but the constant lies and propaganda were taking a greater toll even than the physical labor and abuse or the burning, gnawing hunger. If her situation didn't change soon, she knew she would never live long enough to see her husband or son again. And with nearly eight years of her ten-year sentence left to serve, the possibilities of her emerging from prison alive grew dimmer by the day.

For to me, to live is Christ, and to die is gain. She forced herself to focus on one of the many Scripture verses she'd had opportunity to memorize between the time she accepted *Zhu Yesu* as her Savior and her arrest by members of the Public Security Bureau (PSB) on charges of teaching religion to children, including giving them papers containing religious writings. Even before her arrest, her parents had written to her—warned her, begged her, threatened her—and finally had her kidnapped in an attempt to convince her to go along with the government rules, especially the one limiting each family to one child. After all, she already had a healthy son. Why would she want another baby when they could scarcely afford to feed the first one? But though her abductors had forcibly aborted her second child, they had not succeeded in convincing Yang Zhen-Li to abandon the faith she had adopted before marrying her Christian husband. If anything, the ordeal had only strengthened her resolve to take a stand for the meaning of her name—Zhen-Li, "Truth"—and spurred her to begin actively sharing the good news of Yesu every chance she got. As a trained teacher, that quite naturally included talking with children about the gospel, a practice expressly forbidden by the government. And she did so without restraint or reservation.

Now she was paying the price. Separated from her family and sentenced to ten years of hard labor and "reeducation," Zhen-Li struggled to survive against pain, exhaustion, and bitter loneliness. Worst of all were the times she felt God had abandoned her. It wasn't enough to know in her mind that He promised never to leave or forsake her. She needed a visible reminder—soon—if she was to continue to remain faithful behind these prison walls.

Chi's heart squeezed with pain.

Chapter 1

ZHOU CHI, AFFECTIONATELY KNOWN BY FELLOW MEMBERS OF their modest house church as Brother Zhou, struggled within himself each time he left his four-year-old son, Zhou Chan, with his older sister, Zhou Ming. Yet he was grateful for her loving care of the boy. Chi had no choice but to go to work in the fields and try to earn enough money each day to feed himself, his sister, and his only child, but it had been so much easier when Yang Zhen-Li was still there to run the tiny household.

Yang Zhen-Li. Chi's heart squeezed with pain as he mounted his beat-up bicycle with the bent frame and nearly tireless rims to make his way to the nearby farm where he had found temporary employment. Though the morning light was just beginning to pierce the darkness, Chi had been up for more than an hour, praying for his family, particularly his beloved wife, who was enduring the unimaginable for her faith. How he continued to beg Yesu to allow him to take her place in the prison camp, but God had not granted his petition. And why should He? Chi knew he had not been a faithful follower of Yesu, though he'd had the privilege of being raised in a Christian home. His halfhearted, lukewarm acceptance of his parents' faith had broken their hearts, though they had been encouraged when their soon-to-be daughter-in-law, Yang Zhen-Li, joined their Christian faith so she and Zhou Chi could establish a godly home of their own. But Chi had continued in his mediocre commitment, careful to maintain a low profile and not arouse the suspicions of the government. He contended that it would be easier to register as a member of the state-approved TSPM (Three-Self Patriotic Movement), the only Christian churches approved by the government. Though the TSPM churches were closely monitored and regulated, they offered a safe place for believers to meet together and to worship. But Zhen-Li had resisted, convincing him instead to remain in their little house church, though it was technically illegal to do so. Now, his faithful wife behind bars, the brokenhearted husband and father, who wished only to trade places with his beloved Zhen-Li, continued to labor in the fields and to care for his son as best he could, even as he pleaded with God to protect Zhen-Li long enough for her to return to them.

His sister's arrival on the scene, just days after Zhen-Li's arrest, had compounded Chi's pain but had also eased his concern over what to do with little Chan during the workday, particularly now that Chi's parents were no longer alive. Chi had despaired over how to care for Chan, and then Zhou Ming's husband had been caught in the melee of a raid on a nearby house church and accidentally killed by the bullet from a warning shot that ricocheted off the wall. The terrified widow had fled to her brother's home, not knowing that he, too, had just suffered a tragedy of his own. And so the two siblings had banded together to help raise Zhou Chan as best they could, even as they prayed fervently for Zhen-Li's release.

Bumping down the muddy, rutted road, Zhou Chi continued to pray as he tried to ignore the rumbling in his stomach. As a peasant farm worker, Chi was among the poorest of the poor; as such, he was occasionally unable to provide sufficient food to go around. That had been the case this morning, and so Chi had eaten only enough to get him through the day, leaving the rest for his sister and little Chan. God would have to give him the strength to do his work so at the end of the day he could bring home the necessary food for an evening meal for all three of them.

Julia hoisted herself to her feet, thankful for the added support of her familiar walker. She felt rested and refreshed after her afternoon nap, brief though it had been, since she'd spent most of the time in prayer. The routine at the assisted living home had become second nature to her during the five years she'd lived there, and she looked forward to the quiet time in her room each day following the noon meal. Though a couple of the home's ten residents refused to go to their rooms to take naps, Julia had heard from the caretakers that those who stubbornly stayed in the family room after lunch nearly always fell asleep in their chairs.

Julia smiled. Not only did she not mind the solitude of her room in the early afternoons, but she rather looked forward to it. It gave her a chance to recharge her physical batteries for the rest of day, and it also gave her the peace and quiet she needed to spend time alone with God. Though she had once considered herself a morning person who always had her prayer and Bible study before breakfast, her routine had changed drastically when she broke her hip nearly six years earlier. Until then she'd had no problem living alone, though she had often wondered if the old two-story clapboard home she and Joe had bought soon after they were married was a lot more house than one old lady needed. Still, the extra room had been nice when the children and grandchildren came to visit.

The thought of Joe and her former life turned her mood melancholy, as it always did. Her beloved husband had been dead for nearly twenty years now, killed in a car accident just when he and Julia thought they were finally going to be able to enjoy their retirement years together, and possibly make a second missions trip to China. Now even the dreams of traveling together had long since faded away, while the memory of Joe's face or the sound of his name flitting through her mind continued to bring back the pain of his death as if it had been yesterday.

Sighing, she pulled herself back from the edge of depression that always seemed to beckon at the reminder of Joe and the life they'd once shared. Instead of allowing herself to peek over the side and risk falling off into an abyss of sadness, she consciously switched her focus to the many undeserved blessings God had given her over the years. Though her marriage to Joe had been cut short by the accident, they'd shared more than forty years as lovers and best friends, raising four children in their small, pleasant California beach town of Carpinteria, and having the joy of seeing all of them make the choice to serve God in their individual lives as well as in their own families. It was more than many people ever experienced or could hope for, so how could she dare feel cheated because she had to live her final years on earth alone?

Her smile was back, as she glanced in the mirror above her dressing table. "You silly old woman," she scolded. "Have you ever really been alone? Of course not! God is your Husband now, and He's never left you, not even for a moment. Your kids and grandkids visit when they can, and you've got this new family here at River View Manor—wonderful cooks and caretakers, a dear prayer partner, and a whole crowd of lost souls who need Jesus." She laughed and shook her head. "What a missions field! You've got your work cut out for you, Julia Crockett! And from the looks of some of those old folks out there, you haven't much time to get it done. So what are you doing standing here, talking to yourself? Let's get busy!"

With another chuckle, Julia pushed her walker toward her private bathroom a few steps across the room. There was just enough time to wash her face and pat a few short gray curls into place before heading out to greet her fellow residents and see what God had in store for her this afternoon.

The guard named Tai Tong was only in his late twenties, but his dedication to the party and efficiency at carrying out his orders had quickly gained the approval of his superiors, practically assuring him of a successful career with multiple promotions.

His rock-hard muscles and persuasive tactics hadn't hurt either. Most of the prisoners, and even many of the other guards, feared him. Even his wife and son cowered when he entered the room, though they obeyed him without question.

Tong smiled at the thought. Respect was important to him, even more than to most Chinese. He would rather die a slow and agonizing death than to be publicly shamed. And so he followed every rule, excelled at every undertaking, and tolerated nothing less than complete compliance from those beneath him—whether prisoner or family member. It was a lifestyle that had served him well so far, and he saw no reason to change it. Compromise was simply not an option. If anyone under his authority failed to grasp that fact, he would do whatever was necessary to reeducate them.

The prisoner named Yang Zhen-Li seemed poised to become his next student. He had heard that despite their efforts to punish her crimes and correct her thinking, she continued to pray and to speak of Yesu to any who would listen, including the prisoner who had told Tong of Zhen-Li's indiscretion. As a result, Tong would watch Yang Zhen-Li more closely than the others. If the report was true, she would pay dearly.

Zhen-Li watched as Mei nearly
collapsed onto the cold cement.

Chapter 2

THE PRISONER KNOWN ONLY AS MEI, WHO HAD RECENTLY BEEN placed in Zhen-Li's formerly solitary cell, reminded Zhen-Li of a wounded bird—a lovely, frail little thing whose wings had been so badly broken that she would never fly again. Zhen-Li supposed the young woman was close to her own age, and her heart ached for her, imagining what must have happened in the girl's life prior to her arrest and in the years following. For in her brief talks with Mei, Zhen-Li had learned that the seemingly helpless wife and mother who cried nearly all the time for her family—an action Zhen-Li could understand only too well—had somehow managed to survive in this horrible place for more than four years. It was a thought that chilled Zhen-Li, as she considered her own ten-year sentence. Would she hold up as well as the fragile Mei?

Zhen-Li watched as Mei nearly collapsed onto the cold cement that served as their floor, as well as their bed. They each had one thin gray blanket infested with lice and smelling of urine and sweat, but they gladly wrapped themselves in them when the cold night wind blew through the barred window above their heads. It was especially difficult when the guards washed the cell floors with icy water, which failed to evaporate overnight and made sleeping nearly impossible. Tonight, however, they had been spared the watery invasion, and the two young women snuggled up close to one another for warmth.

"*Ni zen me le?*" Zhen-Li asked. "How are you?"

"*Hai ke yi,*" Mei answered, her shivering body contradicting her words. "I am...all right."

Zhen-Li wanted desperately to comfort her cell mate. In the past few days since Mei had come to share Zhen-Li's tiny cubicle, Zhen-Li had begun to wonder if perhaps Mei was the answer to her prayer for encouragement and companionship, a visible reminder that God had not abandoned her. Since Mei had joined her, the two had exchanged slight amounts of information about their previous lives but little or no details regarding their charged "crimes." Any such conversation among prisoners was strongly discouraged and could even be punished by extended solitary confinement, cut or deprived food rations, and/or physical punishment. As a result, most prisoners limited their conversations to the most basic of "safe" topics, none of which included the discussion or propagation of what would be considered religious teachings. Zhen-Li, however, saw no way to encourage or comfort her new friend without speaking to her of the love and forgiveness of the Lord Jesus Christ, *Zhu Yesu Jidu.* She had broached the subject a couple of days earlier, and though Mei had seemed surprised, she hadn't rejected her words, brief though they were. Perhaps it was time to try again.

Carefully, Zhen-Li reached out from under her blanket and laid her thin hand on Mei's even thinner shoulder. "It is all right," she whispered. "*Tian Fu,* our heavenly Father, knows where we are. He knows our broken hearts and our pain. He knows where our families are and that they have needs as well."

Mei turned her head toward Zhen-Li, her wide, dark eyes shimmering like deep, wet pools as she nearly hissed her reply. "Why, then, does He not do something to help us? If He sees our pain, does He not care? Is it possible He even delights in our suffering?"

Zhen-Li nearly recoiled at the harshness of the response. She had judged Mei to be a gentle soul and had not expected such a reaction. Still, she was nearly certain now that the young woman had no personal knowledge of or meaningful relationship with God or she could not say such a thing. Zhen-Li had not known God for long—slightly over five years, having accepted Yesu as her Savior just before marrying Zhou Chi—and her Bible instruction had been sporadic since few in their poor village or the surrounding areas owned a complete Bible, or *Shengjūng*, of their own, though many had pages torn from a complete set of the Scriptures, which they lovingly read and reread daily. Yet despite her limited Bible knowledge, Zhen-Li's encounter with the living God had been so real that nothing or no one could ever cause her to doubt His existence, His love, or His goodness. It was that very truth that had driven her to proclaim the gospel to her friends and neighbors, and even to the children who lived nearby, though she knew it was forbidden to do so. When she had been blessed to receive a book for children from the pastor of their house church, containing the Christmas story of the birth of Yesu, she had painstakingly made handwritten copies of the story and bound the pages together to distribute to the little ones she ran across, even as she daily read her own copy to little Chan before putting him to bed at night. It was that same truth of God's goodness and love that had driven her to proclaim the gospel that she now clung to as she struggled to survive day by day, hour by hour—and at times, minute by minute. How much more difficult all this would be if she, like Mei, had no such personal knowledge of a good and loving God!

Zhen-Li's heart ached for her cell mate, as she lightly squeezed the girl's shoulder. "I have little wisdom and few answers for you," she said, "despite the sacrifice of my parents to send me to a state-approved school so that I might obtain a good education. But one thing I do know. Tian Fu is good. He loves and cares for us, and He does not delight in our pain. I do not understand why He allows us to be here when it is within His power to release us, but I know He has His reasons—and they are always right."

Mei appeared unconvinced, though she did not fire back with bitter retorts or probing questions. Zhen-Li waited, praying silently for wisdom, until she realized Mei's eyes had fluttered shut and her breathing deepened. The exhausted little bird had fallen asleep, and Zhen-Li prayed that the words she had heard about a faithful and loving God would touch her heart even as she slept.

★★★

Chi's muscles ached from a long day at work, as he lay on the thin mat that served as his bed. He tried not to dwell on how it had been when Zhen-Li lay there next to him, the warmth of her body touching his, the sweet sound of her steady breathing, as they rested peacefully, knowing their little Chan also slept soundly on a smaller pad just a few feet away. Chan still slept on that same mat, though not as peacefully as before, often awakening during the night to cry for his mama. "Baba is here," Chi would croon, gathering his son into his arms, but though his words comforted the boy, Chi knew it wasn't enough. Even his sister's presence did not make up for the lengthening absence of Zhen-Li, who had been gone now for slightly more than two years.

Two years, Chi thought. *Only two years! It seems so much longer. How will Chan and I manage for eight more? And how will dear Zhen-Li survive such a long ordeal? Will she ever come back to us? Or will she die there, tortured and murdered by those evil men?*

Hot tears flooded his eyes, and he covered his mouth to muffle the sobs that longed to escape from his aching throat. He couldn't bear to let himself imagine what Zhen-Li might be experiencing, even now, at this very moment. And it was all his fault. All of it! If he'd left her alone, safe and secure under her parents' party-member protection instead of insisting she convert to Christianity and marry him, his beautiful Yang Zhen-Li would be sleeping safely in her own bed, possibly teaching school somewhere and...married to someone else.

The memory of Han Bai, the up-and-coming PSB officer Zhen-Li had planned to marry before meeting Chi and no doubt one of the forces behind her arrest and severe sentence, stabbed him through the heart. Yet he knew he would gladly have given her up to another man if she could have been spared the awful fate she now endured.

Would you really, My son?

The voice echoed in the recesses of his still-aching heart, and he knew God was challenging his faulty thinking, asking if he would truly spare Zhen-Li this temporal pain in exchange for eternal damnation. *Qin Ai de Tian Fu,* Chi cried in his mind. *Dear heavenly Father, You know I wouldn't want her to be separated from You for eternity! No, it's not that at all. It's just—*

The echo continued, shaming Chi with the unconditional love that permeated every word. *Then trust Me, My son. Leave Zhen-Li in My hands, and I will care for her. It is you and the depth of your own love for Me that should concern you most.*

Chi felt his eyes go wide. *But, Tian Fu,* he protested silently, *I've known You since I was a child. What are You trying to tell me?*

The voice was silent, and after a moment, Chi released the tears he had been holding back. This time he cried not so much for his wife, whom he missed so desperately, but rather for the depth of love he knew she had for Zhu Yesu—so much deeper than his own, and so much more fearless.

✶✶✶

Yin Xei could not sleep—again. Her husband, Yang Hong, did not share her malady. It seemed he fell into bed each night and slept without moving until morning, while Xei tossed and turned and fought with the demons that appeared determined to destroy her.

Images of a young Zhen-Li tormented her—the sweet, obedient, bright child who had done so well in school and brought her parents such pride, despite being a girl. Xei never dreamed her precious only child would one day turn on her, denouncing and disobeying the Communist State by her words and actions, marrying a poor peasant, and even adopting his foreign religious beliefs.

Xiu chi! The shame. It had nearly killed Xei and her husband too. She had thought things could not get any worse, but then Zhen-Li had written to tell them that though they had not planned it, she was pregnant for the second time and had no intention of aborting the child. Xei and her husband had been horrified. Surely Zhen-Li understood the implications of such a decision! Even if she were allowed to continue with the pregnancy, she would never be able to register the child or receive any sort of assistance for it. Their poverty would only increase, as would the accompanying *xiu chi*. And more shame was something Xei and her husband could not tolerate. When their letters of warning had no effect on their wayward daughter, Xei's anguish was intensified when an enraged Hong had Zhen-Li kidnapped and the baby aborted. He had assured his wife that these drastic measures would bring Zhen-Li to her senses and restore her to her parents'—and the party's—good graces. Instead she had returned to her husband and son and immediately begun flaunting her religious beliefs. Within months word reached the Yang household that their daughter was involved in illegal activities, teaching the children of her village about Yesu. It was rumored that she had even printed and distributed religious books to the children, filled with stories to beguile and deceive those who read them. How could her daughter have been so foolish? Did she not understand that such illegal writings were penned with the blood of Chinese rebels? And where had she gotten these stories? No doubt from foreigners with beliefs like the man she had married.

The very memory made Xei's cheeks burn with xiu chi. That her own daughter would openly break such important laws was more than she or her husband could be expected to bear. As loyal party members, Xei should rejoice that her daughter had been arrested and would finally learn not to betray the government or shame her family. But Xei's heart did not rejoice. In fact, each time she thought of Zhen-Li, languishing in that awful prison, the pain nearly crushed the breath out of her. To make matters worse, she would never forget the look on the face of Han Bai, the officer who had arrested Zhen-Li and then come to report to her parents that their daughter was in prison. Though the man said no more than necessary to convey the facts, Xei saw in his eyes the glimmer of satisfaction that comes from sweet revenge. For this had been the man who had hoped to marry Zhen-Li before she spurned him for a Christian peasant. Xei had no doubt that Zhen-Li's arrest was at least partially instigated by this rejected suitor, though he himself had soon after married and been transferred to another part of the country. For that Xei was grateful. She told herself she wanted her daughter to be reformed through her prison stay, but she certainly didn't want her unnecessarily tormented.

Shaking off the thought, she refocused on her grandson. If only she could bring him home to live with her, then perhaps she could endure her daughter's incarceration. But Hong would not allow it. He was so angry with his daughter that he refused even to consider bringing her son to live with them, despite his wife's pleas. And so the boy would grow up in poverty, destined to follow in the traitorous footsteps of his Christian parents. Xei's only hope was to continue to try to convince her husband to take the child from his father and give him a chance to be raised in a proper manner.

It was a slim hope, but it was all Xei had left.

The young woman's eyelids rolled and she moaned, obviously lost in a private nightmare.

Chapter 3

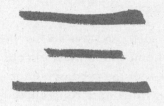

ZHEN-LI LAY AWAKE MOST OF THE NIGHT, LISTENING TO HER new friend breathe and silently thanking God for the gift of another human being so close beside her.

She is sad, Yesu, she observed. *Everyone here is sad, of course. But Mei even more so. What is it that torments her? What can I do to help ease her pain? I am not wise enough to know, Zhu Yesu, and certainly not strong enough to do anything. My own faith is so weak, and I fail You daily. Forgive me, please, and give me a courageous heart that will not dishonor Your name. Make me a shining light that will draw her to You, even when I do not know what to say.*

Mei's sigh interrupted Zhen-Li's petitions, and Zhen-Li turned her head to gaze at the young woman with the broken heart. Zhen-Li did not know the entirety of Mei's history, but she had seen enough to be certain that it was a tragic one. The young woman's eyelids rolled and she moaned, obviously lost in a private nightmare but one no doubt similar to some Zhen-Li herself had on occasion. This place was one that would quickly kill your dreams and stoke your nightmares, sucking out all hope if not for the source of hope Himself. For Him, Zhen-Li was eternally grateful. She prayed she could help Mei find that same hope to sustain her in the midst of what would otherwise surely destroy her.

Tai Tong nodded a curt good-bye to his wife and stepped from their small, modest home into a blast of cold air, compounded by the lingering darkness of the predawn hours. It had proven to be an especially harsh winter, and Tong cursed every day of it. The only good thing that came from it was that he could use the frigid temperatures as leverage against some of the more resistant prisoners. Though most immediately complied with every command from the moment they entered the prison's walls, terrified to do otherwise, there were always some who felt compelled to challenge them.

Tong was an expert at driving that sense of challenge out of the shameful scum, once and for all. He even took pride in the creative ways he found to accomplish this task, one of them being to strip the prisoners of their ragged clothing and leave them outside in the cold until they could no longer feel their extremities and groveled at his feet, begging to be allowed to put their clothes back on and come inside. The combination of discomfort and shame was usually enough to wear down even the most obstinate of prisoners.

There were always exceptions, however, with the religious criminals and prisoners of conscience heading the list. Thieves and murderers were an easy lot to train and discipline, as they liked their comforts and would sell out anyone for an extra blanket.

My job would be a lot easier if they were all like that, he thought, *but a lot more boring too.* His boots crunched on the cold, packed dirt as he walked toward his place of employment, a picture of Yang Zhen-Li rising up in his mind. He felt his jaw clench at the thought. Perhaps today he would deal with her as she deserved and silence her rebellious tongue forever. But first he would make her beg for mercy, for that was Tong's greatest reward for the faithful service he provided to his country. And he did it so very well.

***

Zhou Ming kept a close eye on four-year-old Chan as he played on the riverbank beside the cold, polluted stream where she scrubbed her meager pile of dirty clothes. The water was so foul and the air so full of grit from the distant factories of Beijing that she wondered if the clothes would indeed be cleaner or dirtier when she was through. But she was determined to try. Her brother had taken her in when she fled the scene of her husband's demise, even though Chi himself had just suffered such a great personal tragedy that he seemed scarcely able to speak without weeping. And little Chan had cried almost nonstop for his mama, though he seemed to be doing a little better with the passing of time.

Ming had never had children of her own, and now that her husband was gone, she was determined to help Chi give his only child as normal a life as possible. Ming wasn't even sure what that might be, but she knew that raising the little boy to love and worship Zhu Yesu Jidu must be at the center of it. Though it was technically illegal to hold or attend a *jiao hui* — a house church meeting or assembly — unless it was under the umbrella of the registered and approved State Church, and an even greater crime to give any sort of religious instruction to a child under eighteen, Ming knew it was her responsibility to defy the law and teach Chan about Yesu. And so, softly and carefully, even when it appeared they were alone, Ming taught little Chan to sing songs to Yesu and to pray in His name. She also had several pages of the Scriptures, torn from an old Shengjing that had been owned by her parents and then passed on to her before she married and left her family's home.

"Keep these with you at all times," her mother had urged. "If you ever have to flee for your life, you will have some of God's written Word with you. Because we have only one Shengjing in our family, I will give pages to your brother as well. Your baba and I will also carry pages with us. That way, if one of us is ever stopped and the pages confiscated, the entire Shengjing won't be lost. But above all, memorize what is written in the Shengjing, for then no one can take God's words from you."

Ming had never realized how true her mother's warnings would prove to be until she had witnessed her husband's death, accidental though it may have been, in the midst of the nightmarish raid on their house church. She'd been forced to turn and run as fast as she could, with no thought or chance to take anything with her, escaping only with the clothes on her back and the Word of God tucked inside her clothing—and in her heart. It was all she had to offer, and she would share it freely with anyone who would allow her to do so. At the top of that list was her little nephew, her only brother's son, whose care he had entrusted to her. She would not dishonor that trust in any way.

Julia was up early, sitting in a rocker on the wraparound porch that surrounded River View Manor and watching the sun rise over the foothills that served as a backdrop to the sprawling senior home. As she often did, she smiled at the inappropriate name of River View Manor, since there was no river anywhere in sight. But Foothill View Manor just didn't have the same ring to it. And at least she could enjoy the near-perfect weather that was so characteristic of Southern California. She particularly relished the sea breezes that so often blew in off the Pacific, reminding her of the many years she and Joe and the children had lived in their beloved two-story home in Carpinteria.

But enough of that, she thought, refusing to allow herself to wander into a melancholy mood. She'd been up since before dawn, having slept only fitfully throughout the night. The few times she'd drifted off, she found herself dancing through flitting images of what she had since decided must have been China, spurred by her unfulfilled wishes to one day return to that vast country and to once again minister to its many people. And yet there was something more. A call to prayer, perhaps? Yes, she imagined that was exactly what it was—God's nudging to pray for the people of China, whether they lived in a thriving, bustling metropolis or on a remote, barren farm outside a backward village. She had been rocking in her chair for nearly an hour now, praying for the Chinese masses—rich, poor, or otherwise—who did not know Christ, and also for those who did, as Julia knew they often paid a price for worshiping the one true God. Each time she interceded for persecuted Christians, particularly in and around Beijing, where she and Joe had spent several joyous though challenging months on their one and only missions trip abroad, Julia found herself awash in a fresh sense of appreciation for her freedom as an American to worship any way she wished.

The unmistakable stirrings of other people getting ready to start their day alerted her to the fact that her time of solitude was nearly over. *That's all right*, she thought. *I'll have more quiet time after lunch. Meanwhile, I think I'll snag Laura at breakfast and see if she can work me into her busy schedule so we can pray together.*

She chuckled at the thought and pushed herself up from the chair. Taking hold of the handles of her walker, she rolled her way to the front door, eager for a cup of coffee and some interaction with her fellow residents.

Darkness was descending.

Chapter 4

Darkness was descending as Zhou Chi steered his rickety bicycle down the rutted road toward home. His back ached from his many hours of labor, but he pedaled a bit faster as he spotted the outline of the little shack in the distance. A slight wisp of smoke spiraled upward from the chimney, reassuring Chi's heart that Zhou Ming was preparing the evening meal—more sticky rice with the last of the bean sprouts and cabbage Chi had brought home the previous day. He was grateful to have earned enough today to purchase extra food for tomorrow. The only thing more difficult than imagining his wife in prison would be to hear his son cry for food and have none to give him.

The wind blew in just the right direction and slightly harder than usual, causing him to shiver as it teased his nostrils with a burning smell from the factories outside Beijing. Though it would take Chi several hours on his bicycle, he knew the trip could be made in under two hours by automobile. In fact, he still remembered making the journey just six years earlier, riding in his neighbor's uncle's car to request Yang Hong's permission to marry his daughter. Hong had refused, declaring that he did not wish his family to be shamed by becoming related to a family of Christians who were also poor laborers and, worst of all, not known as loyal party members.

Chi had worried that Hong's refusal would mean the end to his relationship with Zhen-Li, which itself was a miracle, since they had met by accident nearly a year earlier when she had visited a friend in a nearby village. Unknown to Zhen-Li, the friend was a Christian, who courageously invited Zhen-Li to attend an illegal jiao hui at their neighbor's home. It was there that Chi and Zhen-Li met, and Chi knew from the first moment that he wanted Zhen-Li for his wife. That she was equally smitten nearly stunned him to the point of being unable to speak to her. Eventually he did, however, and the relationship grew until Chi dared to ask her to become his wife. She accepted but insisted that Chi must ask her father's permission, though she doubted he would receive it. She had been right, and upon her father's refusal, Chi worried at the outcome. To his great surprise and joy, Zhen-Li had willingly converted to his faith and married him anyway. Neither Chi nor Zhen-Li had been back to Beijing since, nor had Yang Hong or Yin Xei made the trip to see them, not even when their only grandchild, Zhou Chan, was born.

Yang Zhen-Li had paid a huge price to marry him, Chi knew—even before her arrest. She had given up her family, as well as her respected position in the party and, hence, in the community. She could have had a promising future, a well-to-do marriage, a comfortable lifestyle . . . .

Instead she had chosen to marry Chi, giving up not only her parents but even her second child when it was forcibly aborted. Now she was paying so much more. Would she ultimately pay with her life? The thought seemed more than Chi could bear, though he knew he must. After all, what choice did he have? He prayed daily for a miracle, for Zhen-Li's release and return to them, but the heavens were silent. If Chi could break through the prison walls and free Zhen-Li himself, he would certainly do everything he could to make it happen—even die in the attempt, if necessary. But there was no chance. None. Zhen-Li's fate was sealed until or unless God chose to act. So why didn't He? Why did He procrastinate and leave the little family to suffer, separated from one another and living under the worst possible conditions?

Chi rolled into the patch of dirt in front of his home and eased his two-wheeler to a silent halt. His stomach growled even louder than it had when he left this morning. Despite his desire to make sure little Chan and Zhou Ming had enough to eat, he was glad to know there would be enough for all of them tonight.

✦✦✦

Julia and Laura had spent the better part of an hour in Laura's room praying, forgoing their naps and devoting themselves to interceding for the people of China. Both regularly received mailings and updates on Christians who were persecuted and even martyred for their faith in other countries, so they had specific names to pray for, along with praying for Chinese believers in general and specifically for the few individuals Julia remembered from the trip she and Joe had made there so many years earlier. The two women had also felt impressed to pray for the conversion of the persecutors themselves, including prison guards and members of the government's Public Security Bureau. They had just finished and were about to leave Laura's room when Julia thought of another concern.

"What do you think of the new resident who just came in last week—Margaret, is it? She seems to be a very unhappy woman, don't you think?"

Laura nodded, her once-auburn hair now streaked with white and tightly permed around her head. Peering over her reading glasses at Julia, she said, "I've noticed that, though it's not so unusual when people first come here. I remember when I arrived, I hated it here. And I was so angry at my family for making me come! I just wanted to stay in my own house." She smiled, deepening the creases around her mouth and eyes. "But now I know they were right. I was having a terrible time keeping up with everything—housework, bills, cooking—and I had absolutely no business driving anymore. And now with my heart in such poor shape..." She shook her head before continuing. "The assisted living that River View Manor provides turned out to be an answer to prayer, even though I didn't know it at the time."

She reached out and spanned the space between their chairs, which were drawn up across from one another until their knees nearly touched, and laid an arthritic hand on top of Julia's. Though Laura's hand was cool, Julia appreciated the personal touch. She also appreciated Laura's nonjudgmental response to Julia's observation about Margaret. Julia was well aware of her own tendency toward gossip, often cloaked in the form of a prayer request. She was grateful that God had provided a safeguard in the form of Laura to keep Julia from yielding to such temptation.

"When I was home alone all those years after Marvin died," Laura said, pulling Julia back from her thoughts, "I didn't have a regular prayer partner, someone I could count on to join me in prayer at any time. Now I have you." Her smile widened. "Have I told you lately how much I appreciate you?"

Julia's heart warmed. "You don't have to," she said. "I know, just by your sweet spirit and grateful attitude. Besides, I feel the same about you." She shook her head. "And I know what you mean about it taking a while to get used to things around here. I didn't like it in the beginning either. But I think it may be more than that with Margaret, don't you?"

Laura nodded. "I do, yes. I've even wondered if it might be fear."

Julia raised her eyebrows. Exactly what she'd been thinking! "Well, then, why don't we pray and ask God what we can do to help Margaret with whatever she's dealing with, shall we? Perhaps the Lord brought her here just so we could pray for her and help her in some way."

Laura closed her eyes and began to pray. Julia did the same.

A sharp, quick pain in her ribs jolted Zhen-Li from her sleep. She opened her eyes to see a pair of heavy black boots on the floor just inches from her face. Following the boots upward, she flinched at the sight of the man who was known as the cruelest guard in the prison, Tai Tong. How was it possible that someone so young and otherwise pleasant-looking could have such evil boiling over inside of him and even shining out through his dark eyes?

"Get up," Tong barked. "You are coming with me."

Zhen-Li felt her heart lurch with fear, as she imagined what lay in store for her. Though she'd never been personally interrogated or punished by this guard, she had seen the condition of those who returned after a session with him, and she wondered if she would survive the day.

Not wanting to anger him further, she immediately moved to rise to her feet, but apparently not fast enough, as he kicked her again, this time in the side of her head, sending her sprawling on the cement. She heard a cry from her cell mate, even as she tried to blink away the spots that danced before her eyes. Dizzy from the blow, she nevertheless scrambled to her feet before he had time to assault her again. From the corner of her eye she spotted Mei, cowering in the corner with her blanket wrapped around her.

Qin Ai de Tian Fu, Zhen-Li pleaded silently, *protect Mei…and help me. Be my strength, for I have none.*

With a grip of steel, Tong encircled Zhen-Li's thin arm with his hand and shoved her toward the open door of the cell. "It is time we had a talk," he growled. "And I am quite sure you will agree with my viewpoint before we are through."

Heart pounding against her already sore rib cage, Zhen-Li stumbled forward, continuing to pray as the guard pushed her from behind. An image of Yesu, beaten and bloody, hanging from the Cross while a crowd looked on, some mocking and some weeping, flashed through her mind. Humbly, she placed herself in the hands of the only One who could see her through her coming ordeal.

Margaret was angrier than she'd ever been in her seventy-eight years of life. If there was a way to do it, she would permanently and legally divorce herself from her entire family—all those ungrateful, spoiled brats who had abandoned her to die in this horrible place. Why couldn't they just leave her alone? She was fine living by herself—liked it, as a matter of fact. Sure, she forgot things sometimes, but who didn't? And so the house was a bit messy and cluttered. So what? Where did those nosy, money-grubbing ingrates get off taking over her life?

Money-grubbing. Yes, that was the real reason they had stuck her here; Margaret was sure of it. Her two grown sons and their overfed wives, not to mention the whiny children they'd produced, were only too happy to take over Margaret's care after she wrecked the car and ended up in the hospital with a broken leg. Did they think for one minute that she bought their story of wanting to help her? Ha! Not a chance. They just wanted to get their greedy hands on what little she had left, and they weren't willing to wait until she kicked the bucket to do it.

She hated them all—and all the old coots who lived in this pathetic home for the ancient and demented as well. If they thought she was going to get chummy with any of them or cooperate in any way, shape, or form, they had another think coming—especially those two old biddies who were always going around praying together and talking about Jesus. What a couple of loons! If anything, they just reinforced Margaret's long-ago decision that God was a myth for weak-minded fools who couldn't stand on their own two feet. Well, she'd show them. Every last one of them! Margaret Snowden wasn't about to go down without a fight.

The terror of that thought
overshadowed any sense of relief.

Chapter 5

ZHEN-LI HAD NEVER EXPERIENCED SUCH TORMENT, NOT EVEN when she gave birth to Chan with no one at her side except her beloved Chi, who did his best to comfort her throughout the exhausting incident. But at least then she had known a child would enter the world as a result of her painful efforts. This time there was no bright ending, no hope of new life to sustain her. Yet she clung to Zhu Yesu as if by her fingernails, grateful when the pain became severe enough that she passed out.

At last it was over—at least for now. The monstrous guard named Tong, who quite obviously took great delight and pride in what he termed his "creative and persuasive techniques," had promised her that he would be back to continue their conversation in the very near future. The terror of that thought overshadowed any sense of relief at the brief respite she experienced as she lay on the cold, hard cement floor of her cell, wondering what it was that Tong had expected to get from her. He had never been clear, though he continually mocked her faith and accused her of "surrendering state secrets to foreign devils." Then he blasted her for proselytizing children by way of her treasonous printing and distribution of Bible stories. His accusations had little effect on her, however, as her primary concern had been how much she would have to endure before passing into the presence of her loving Father.

The thought of her ultimate destination sparked a faint surge of hope, and Zhen-Li reminded herself that she had been wrong about there being no promise of new life at the end of the suffering. Of course there would one day be an end to this—though she shuddered to think how long and horrible it might be until then—and she would at last stand triumphant with Zhu Yesu, her Savior, who had already suffered and died on her behalf and gone on ahead of her. She knew at that moment that it was the only truth she had to cling to, the only source of strength to get her through.

The sound of a moan pierced her conscience. Where had it come from? Herself? No. The pitiful noise had come from Mei. With great effort, Zhen-Li turned her head to locate her cell mate. The explosion of fire in her aching neck and shoulders as she moved forced a cry from her cracked lips, even as her eyes fell on Mei, sitting huddled in the corner, shivering and weeping.

"Do not cry," Zhen-Li heard herself whisper, though she was astounded to realize she could speak. "I am all right. Zhu Yesu has sustained me. And He will do the same for you."

As Zhen-Li watched Mei's thin face crumple in a fresh onslaught of tears, she felt herself slipping away into darkness, and she welcomed the escape, knowing it wouldn't be long before the pain pulled her back again.

★★★

Chi sat on the hard ground beside his shack, leaning back against the flimsy wall and enjoying a rare opportunity to watch little Chan at play. It wasn't often he had an entire day free from work, but occasionally his employer told everyone not to come in for a day or two. Chi suspected it was because the man did not have the means to pay them, causing Chi to pray fervently that the funds would materialize and the employees could return to work quickly. But at least today, since he had been home, he had been able to contribute to tending the small garden in front of their house. Though the annual garden seldom produced much, each bite was a help. And with spring at last beginning to announce its arrival, he had been able to plant a few seeds in hope of a meager harvest.

Now, despite his concern over being temporarily out of work, Chi smiled at the sight of his young son, digging in the dirt with a scrap of metal and humming softly to himself. It pleased the humble father that Chan was able to find simple ways to entertain himself and that he seemed oblivious to the poverty that surrounded him. It seemed the only time the child cried was when he thought of his mother. It grieved Chi to realize that those times of crying over his mother grew fewer and fewer with each passing day. If Zhen-Li had to serve her entire sentence, Chi doubted that their son would remember her at all.

I must keep her memory alive in his heart, Chi told himself, his own heart constricting at the implications, *even if it is easier to let it fade so he won't miss her so much. But what if she never—?*

He could not bear to complete the thought, even silently. That his wife, the mother of his only child, might not return alive from her exile, that he might not see her again this side of eternity, was more than he could allow himself to consider.

A cold gust of wind stirred his thoughts, even causing little Chan to look up from his digging. It grieved Chi that he could not provide warmer clothes for his son, but at least summer was coming soon, and he wouldn't have to worry about it again for several months.

Chan's eyes landed on his father, and he grinned, his dark eyes lighting up his pudgy face. Chi blinked back tears and returned the boy's silent greeting. *Help me to be thankful, Zhu Yesu,* he prayed. *Don't let me think of what we don't have or what we've lost, but keep me focused on You, Tian Fu, and on all the blessings You have given us. It is what Zhen-Li would want us to do, what she would do if she were here with us.*

The tears came then, quickly and unbidden, though Chi fought to restrain them as his shoulders shook and his stomach churned. *Oh, Qin Ai de Shen, dear God, I want her here—with us, with her family, where she belongs!* It was all he could do not to cry out the

45

accusations, but he could only plead silently, hoping little Chan would not recognize his father's distress. *Why have You taken her from us? Why don't You bring her back, Yesu? Please!*

Chan laid his piece of metal in the dirt and eased toward Chi, his smile replaced by a questioning frown. "Baba?" he said, stopping just inches away from Chi and then laying a soft hand against the man's cheek. "Baba is sad?"

Tears exploded from Chi's eyes then, pouring down his face in seeming torrents, as he nodded and pulled little Chan into a tight embrace. Within seconds, the child was crying as well, calling for his mother as they sobbed out their pain together. From the corner of his eye, Chi noticed that his sister had come to stand in the open doorway of the house, peering out at the weeping duo. After a moment, she disappeared back inside.

***

Tong was furious. Despite his best efforts, it had been reported that the woman named Yang Zhen-Li continued to speak of her foreign god and her traitorous religion. It was apparent the stubborn young woman would be much more of a challenge than he had anticipated. But perhaps a challenge was just what he needed. Lately he had found himself getting bored quite easily, particularly at home. His wife no longer appealed to him, and even his son got on his nerves. He needed something to spice up his life, to entertain him.

Yang Zhen-Li's face popped back into his mind as he trudged toward home at the end of the day. How had he missed the obvious? He had been working at breaking her down through pain and brute force, but was it possible that she might respond more readily to charm and favor?

Tong smiled. Of course, that was it! She would expect more pain and might even be prepared to resist. But a little unexpected kindness and attention? Surely that would bring a ready response from the woman who could almost be considered appealing—under the right circumstances.

With his new plan forming in his mind, Tong turned onto the street where he lived, his little house coming into view as its residents awaited his return. He doubted he would sleep much tonight, as he planned for the next day, but at least the anticipation would help dispel his growing boredom.

***

Julia had hoped to spend more time with Laura that day, but her friend hadn't felt well and had gone back to bed after breakfast to "sleep it off"—whatever "it" was. So Julia had been on her own for most of the morning. She visited with the other residents and even got involved in a game of Scrabble, but eventually she had retired to her room after lunch and spent the next hour or so praying in between dozing and nodding off. When at last she had emerged from her seclusion, she had been surprised to enter the family room and find it occupied by one wide-awake resident, Margaret Snowden, staring at the large wall-mounted television, which blared some sort of game show.

"Hello, Margaret," Julia had called as she pushed the walker ahead of her in the woman's direction. "Mind if I join you?"

The husky woman with the salt-and-pepper hair, swept up into a bun on top of her head, shrugged her shoulders. "It's a free country," she announced, scarcely looking at Julia.

Not a very warm welcome, Julia observed. *But then, what else did I expect?*

She smiled. "I'll just park my walker next to yours and plunk down in this chair for a bit. We'll look like geriatric twins!" Julia chuckled, but Margaret continued to stare at the television.

"So," Julia said, "how do you like it here at River View?"

"I don't."

The curt answer stopped Julia, but not for long. "You seem to have a nice family. I noticed them when they brought you here. I could tell they really care about you."

"You're wrong," Margaret answered, turning to glare at Julia. "They don't care . . . and neither do I. So can we please not talk about them?"

Julia opened her mouth to answer, but before she could think of a thing to say, Margaret added, "In fact, can we just not talk at all? I'm trying to watch this show."

Julia's mouth slammed shut, even as she felt her eyes open wide. Well! She hadn't been insulted like that in a very long time, and she wasn't about to put up with it now. Blinking back tears, she pulled herself to her feet, gripped her walker tightly, and shuffled out of the room as fast as her old bones and joints would allow.

Dinner was long finished and the television in the family room continued to drone on.

Chapter 6

AS THE DAY DREW TO A CLOSE, THE RESIDENTS OF RIVER VIEW Manor began their nightly rituals in preparation for retiring to their rooms. Dinner was long finished and the television in the family room continued to drone on, though no one paid any attention. The two elderly gentlemen who still sat plunked in their chairs in front of the animated box were asleep and had to be awakened so they could head for their rooms to continue their rest. Julia had checked on Laura, who assured her she was feeling much better and was positive she'd be up and around in the morning. Margaret had sat silently throughout the evening meal and then bolted from the table as soon as the first dishes were cleared away. Julia hadn't seen her since.

Which is just fine with me, she huffed silently, standing before the bookshelf in the library, searching for something to help her fall asleep. She'd already spent nearly two hours reading her Bible earlier in the day, and she'd polished off every other piece of reading material in her room. She made a mental note to sign up to ride the manor's van to town later in the week so she could make a stop at the Christian bookstore at the small shopping center near the grocery and drugstore. Meanwhile, she needed something to make her sleepy. For some reason she felt wide awake tonight.

Probably because that woman made me so mad, she thought. *After all, I was just trying to be friendly. She didn't need to be rude.*

The memory of her conversation with Laura just a couple of days earlier interrupted her silent tirade. They had commiserated about Margaret's anger, remembering how they, too, had been angry when they first arrived at River View. But they had also commented that perhaps Margaret's attitude was fueled by fear. The reminder softened Julia's heart ever so slightly, as she considered what the source of that fear might be.

Is it something as simple as fear of being left here to die, forgotten by family and friends alike? We all go through that, to a point. Or is it something more? She sighed and reached up to a shelf just above eye level and pulled down an old hardbound book of poetry. *Perfect*, she thought. *Just what I need to help me drift off.*

Tucking the book into the colorful carrying pouch that hung from her walker, Julia exited the library and headed for her room. If Laura really was feeling better tomorrow, Julia would make a point of talking and praying with her about what had happened with Margaret earlier in the day. Julia had a nagging feeling that Laura was going to tell her she needed to forgive Margaret and to pray for her. She knew that was true, of course—in theory. But right now she wasn't completely over being miffed at the woman, so she'd just wait until tomorrow after talking with Laura before making her forgiveness of Margaret official.

Zhen-Li's eyes opened wide with terror the moment she heard his voice.

"Get up," he ordered, though the tone was less threatening than Zhen-Li had expected. Remembering the feel of the man's boot in her ribs, she scrambled to her feet, despite the lingering pain from the previous day.

"Come with me," he said.

She obeyed, following him without question or even looking back to see the reaction of her cell mate.

Zhen-Li's heart raced as she hurried to keep up with the tall, broad-shouldered man in front of her. His uniform seemed molded to him, as if he'd been born to it. She couldn't imagine him any other way, though she assumed he must have dressed like any common citizen before joining the military. Still, his personality fit the image of strength and authority that he so obviously enjoyed.

As they approached the doorway through which he had shoved her the previous day, she thought she would faint from fright. The memory was still so fresh of what had happened to her behind that door, and she wondered how she would survive such torture again. But instead of opening the door and dragging her inside, the man named Tong continued walking. She followed, her feet feeling like lead as she wondered how much worse the place would be where he took her today.

And then he stopped in front of another door, unlocked it, and beckoned her inside. Hurrying to comply so he wouldn't grab her already bruised and battered body and toss her through the door, she found herself in a room much less stark than the one from the previous day. Where the first torture chamber had been devoid of any furniture except the one chair where Tong occasionally rested from his efforts, this room contained a couch, a lamp, and a small table with a green thermos and two cups. Afraid to look at her captor, Zhen-Li stood, head down, staring at her feet and praying for strength.

"Ni zen me le?"

How are you feeling? The man who had hurt her nearly beyond endurance yesterday now wanted to know if she was all right. How was she to answer such a question? What did he want her to say? What did he expect? Would she be punished more strenuously if she gave the wrong response? Her terror and confusion growing, she continued to wait and pray in silence.

"Ni zen me le?" the guard repeated. "Are you all right? Do you need anything?"

Slowly Zhen-Li raised her head, scarcely able to force herself to peek from beneath her eyelids at the man she was sure was toying with her, waiting for her to open her mouth so he could slam her to the floor.

Instead she found him gazing down at her with what could only be interpreted as concern. Where his dark eyes had been hard the day before, they now appeared gentle. Then he smiled, and she thought surely she was dreaming. She would awaken any moment, and he would be kicking her, hitting her, hurting her as he had done before.

"Sit down," he ordered, indicating the couch. Terrified to obey but more terrified not to, she hurried to the couch and perched on the edge.

"Relax," he said, sitting down beside her. "Would you like some water?"

Throat dry and tongue swollen, she shook her head no, trembling as she waited.

Tong smiled again. "Perhaps we got off to a bad start yesterday," he said. "I would like to remedy that."

Zhen-Li's heart froze. What did he mean? What was he trying to say? The questions that raced through her mind were more terrifying than the beating she'd received the previous day. What did this man have planned?

Zhen-Li watched his every move as he opened the thermos and poured two cups of warm water, then held one out to her. Everything in her cried out to take it. She could nearly taste the refreshing liquid. But was it a trick? What would happen if she took it? Would he consider her insolent? And if she didn't take it, would he be insulted?

Still trembling, she waited, her eyes fixed on his extended hand and the cup that looked so small inside it.

"Take it," he said again. "I insist."

Scarcely able to respond to her own mental command, she finally managed to retrieve the cup and bring it to her lips. She sensed his eyes following her as she allowed herself to sip the life-giving fluid, her body nearly collapsing in relief as strength flowed through her.

"Slowly," she heard him say, as he lightly touched her hand in an act of caution. Lowering the cup and raising her eyes, she discovered he was smiling at her again, and she wondered if she would be able to keep the precious water in her stomach.

"That's better," he said. "You are not well. You must drink slowly. You must take time to heal."

Take time to heal? Again she questioned his meaning. He was the one who had inflicted her injuries. Why, then, would he be concerned with her need for healing?

Gently, Tong took the cup from her still trembling hand. "When you are ready for more, I will get it for you," he said, replacing the cup on the table. "Meanwhile, if you are hungry, perhaps I can get you a bowl of cabbage or cauliflower. And even a thermos of tea. Would you like that?"

Zhen-Li had not had time to eat the previous day before being taken by Tong for their "conversation," and she'd been in too much pain when she returned to her cell to consume the tiny ration of rice that had been left for her. She had finally offered it to Mei, who had protested only slightly before devouring it. By now, Zhen-Li's stomach growled audibly, and the thought of a bowl of vegetables and a cup of tea nearly made her head spin.

She knew she should refuse the man's offers of kindness, as she had no doubt that he had an ulterior motive. But his gentle treatment and generous offer was such a welcome relief that she could only nod her head and cry. "Yes, please," she whispered. "Please."

Tong's smile widened. He excused himself and opened the door, calling to another guard to bring the requested food and drink. Then he returned to sit beside Zhen-Li on the couch.

Zhou Ming lay in the dark, staring at the unseen ceiling and listening to the silence. She was glad she had not heard her brother or nephew crying again since seeing them weeping in each other's arms the previous afternoon. Chi had gone back to work this morning and had then come home and gone straight to bed after eating a little rice. Thankfully Chan had not spoken of his mother during the day, but the sadness in his eyes broke Ming's heart.

She herself often wept silently, grieving the loss of her husband and feeling ashamed that she was glad they had not had a child before he died. She could not imagine the difficulty of being responsible for a young life, particularly knowing that as nonregistered Christians they nearly always lived on the edge of danger. It was enough that Zhu Yesu had brought her here to help her only brother care for his little Chan now that Yang Zhen-Li had been arrested. As Chi's older sister, Ming had found her place in her brother's household. With their parents already gone to be with Zhu Yesu, Ming, Chi, and Chan must stick together, even as they continued to pray for Zhen-Li's release from prison.

Will it ever come? With a sigh, Ming tried to cling to hope, reminding herself again that Zhu Yesu could do anything. If it was His purpose to bring Zhen-Li back to them, He would certainly do so. Until then, they would struggle on as best they could.

For the first time in so very long, her stomach didn't ache or burn with emptiness.

Chapter 7

B Y THE TIME ZHEN-LI WAS RETURNED TO HER CELL, IT WAS midafternoon and she was more confused than ever. For the first time in so very long, her stomach didn't ache or burn with emptiness, and despite her misgivings, she was grateful. Still, throughout the time she had spent with Tong in the locked room, she had waited for him to turn on her, to reveal his true reason for bringing her there and for treating her in such an unusual manner.

He said he understood that I was from a good family, that I had been misled by my husband and others into accepting false teachings. I know that's not true, but why did he say it? Why did he say he wanted to help me return to the truth of my parents? Surely he isn't being honest about wanting to help me. He can only be trying to trick me, to beguile me with kindness. But why, when he has the power to punish me as he did yesterday? Does he think he cannot convince me that way, that a gentle approach will be more effective?

If so, Zhen-Li was thankful for the reprieve, though she knew it wouldn't last if Tong did not see the desired results. But how could she give them to him without betraying her faith and her God? She couldn't. And so the eventual return to physical punishment was inevitable.

She glanced around the tiny cell. Mei was gone, as she often was during the day. Zhen-Li assumed she had some sort of work assignment, as did Zhen-Li most days. That they hadn't sent Zhen-Li to work yesterday was undoubtedly because Tong had excused her to spend the day having a "reeducation session" with him. Had he excused her from work again today, or would they be coming for her to work for the remaining hours until dark?

Slumping against the wall, she slid to the floor and pulled her knees to her chest. The slight warmth in the air reminded her that winter was nearly over. Though she welcomed the absence of the bitter cold that had tortured her these last months, she also knew the passing of seasons meant she would soon be toiling outside in the sweltering sun. Her labor would be that much more difficult, and she knew that some prisoners did not survive the extended working hours of the long summer days.

She shook her head. She would not consider that now. *Sufficient unto the day is the evil thereof.* The words of the Shengjing reminded her to think only of today, to seek Him this day, this moment, and to trust Him for tomorrow. And so she must, for what other hope did she possibly have?

The employees and residents of River View Manor were in a tizzy—and the sun hadn't even topped the horizon yet. But at four o'clock in the morning Emily Johnson had awakened everyone by pounding her cane on the floor and screaming that she'd been robbed.

It took a while for the two live-in caretakers to settle her down and to confirm that she was indeed missing what little bit of jewelry she owned—a strand of pearls and a gold brooch that had been given to her by her third husband. Though most everyone, including the other residents, suspected she'd simply misplaced them, a thorough search of Emily's room proved otherwise. Because she'd been seen wearing both pieces of jewelry only two days earlier and had not left the manor since, the police had now been called, setting off the most excitement the home's residents had seen since old Harley Walker ran off to marry the fiftyish woman who lived in the house next door.

Julia hung back and watched and listened, as the other residents huddled and offered solutions.

"She probably dropped them down the toilet."

"Don't be ridiculous. The pearls might have flushed, but not the brooch. Have you seen the size of that thing?"

"Maybe her third husband came back from the grave to get it. He's probably mad that she had two more husbands after him."

"Shame on you! How can you say such a thing?"

Julia smiled as she listened, amused to realize she wasn't the only one in the house who was prone to gossip. With that thought as a reminder, she refused to get involved in the speculations. Besides, she had promised Laura to report in as soon as she discovered what was going on. But even as she leaned into her walker to head toward her friend's room, she couldn't help but notice that Margaret was standing away from the others, leaning on her own walker and looking more upset than usual. For a brief moment Julia wondered if she should go and talk with her, but the memory of the woman's sharp rejection the previous day still stung, so she thought better of it and opted to go see Laura instead.

Much more pleasant to spend time with my prayer partner than with a grumpy old woman who would probably just tell me to mind my own business, she reasoned. *Who needs that?*

Ignoring the nudging at the edge of her heart, Julia pushed her walker down the hall toward Laura's room, sensing the entire time that a pair of eyes followed her every move. And she knew exactly whose eyes they were. Well, she wasn't going to let it get to her. She and Laura would pray about the missing jewelry, and maybe even about grouchy Margaret while they were at it. And if they still had time before breakfast, they'd pray for someone in China.

Mei was scared—not in the same way as when the guards took her away for the day, but scared that Tong would use his clever tactics on Zhen-Li, as he had on her. If it worked, Zhen-Li would soon know the truth about her cell mate and would no doubt turn on her in retaliation. If part of that retaliation was to let other prisoners know what Mei had done, her hope of leaving the prison alive would evaporate into thin air.

Lying beside Zhen-Li on the cold floor, wrapped in a blanket and drawing what little warmth there was from the woman's body, Mei scolded herself for being so weak. She had never meant to betray Zhen-Li—or any of the other prisoners, for that matter—but it was the only way she could see to increase her chances of survival. And so she had watched and listened—and reported, sometimes even exaggerating and embellishing the truth just to keep her captors happy. In return, she received extra food rations and little or no physical punishment. She was also spared the hard labor that was a daily part of life for most prisoners, though the "work" she was given in exchange was certainly not easy. The shame of serving the guards as a prostitute and a spy was so great that at times Mei wondered if she wouldn't prefer toiling alongside the other prisoners. In fact, she was nearly sure of it, though she was past the point of being able to choose how she spent her days. She was already labeled by prison officials as their personal sex slave, and they weren't about to release her from that anytime soon.

A tear escaped her eye at the ugly truth, buried deep within, that though she had traded her dignity for a chance at survival, she would undoubtedly never be released from her current demeaning position except through death. And the only thing that terrified Mei more than spending her remaining years enslaved to her perverted overseers was the thought of what lay waiting for her beyond the grave.

Tong lay in bed, staring at the ceiling and grinning into the darkness. His pathetic wife was no doubt confused, but greatly relieved that he had not forced himself on her before she fell asleep, nor had he reprimanded his son for any infractions of behavior. No, he was too preoccupied with the initial success of his plan with Yang Zhen-Li to waste time or energy on his family. He could deal with them anytime. Right now he wanted only to conquer the pitiful creature who had broken allegiance with the party and her parents to join ranks with those who subscribed to a foreign religion. Before he was done with her, she would be cursing the One known as Yesu and praising the party as all good Chinese people should do.

And in the process, Tong would gain another sex slave, further humiliating the woman who no doubt prided herself on her faithfulness to her religion and to her husband.

Tong nearly laughed out loud. By the time he was finished with the prisoner whose name meant "Truth," neither her God nor her husband would want anything more to do with her.

Julia sighed. It had been quite a morning.

Chapter 8

IT WAS OFFICIAL NOW. EVERY INCH OF RIVER VIEW MANOR HAD
been searched, to no avail, and a police report had been filed.
As a result, Emily Johnson had gained a sort of notoriety as the
only resident of River View Manor ever to have been robbed—
though Julia still believed the jewelry would turn up eventually.
After all, who could possibly have taken it? No one had been
there in the last few days except the residents, the caretakers,
and a handful of visitors. And surely there were more lucrative
places to consider when it came to stealing anything worthwhile.
But, if nothing else, it had convinced the owners of River View
to install and use an alarm system.

Julia sighed. It had been quite a morning. Breakfast was
late due to the two policemen who had arrived to question
Emily and the others and to fill out the report. Even after they
left and the residents finally sat down to eat their morning
meal, the main focus of conversation continued to be on the
missing jewelry. Julia imagined it would be the hot topic for
quite some time.

She was glad Laura was feeling better and had come out of her room to rejoin them. Now, as they sat together on the porch swing in front of the sprawling home in the tree-lined neighborhood, breathing in the hint of sea air that floated on the breeze, Julia heard her stomach rumble. She hadn't been hungry by the time the hullabaloo from Emily's alleged robbery had settled down, so she'd skipped breakfast, but she would certainly be able to eat lunch when it was finally served.

"I love it out here, don't you?" Laura asked, interrupting Julia's daydreaming.

Julia smiled and nodded. "I was just thinking the same thing. It reminds me of the way the air smelled when the breeze blew in off the ocean in Carpinteria."

Laura chuckled. "And why shouldn't it? We're less than an hour away, after all."

Julia sighed. "At times it seems so much farther, doesn't it?"

Laura's smile was tinged with sadness. "I know exactly what you mean. It's hard to let go of our old lives, isn't it?"

Julia was surprised at the hint of tears that stung her eyelids, but she quickly blinked them away. "But how wonderful to know that we're not at the end of our lives—just in transition."

Laura laughed. "Exactly. And what a great way to put it! Transition—leaving behind the old and moving on to something so much better." Her pale blue eyes twinkled as she turned them on Julia. "I get homesick sometimes, don't you?"

Julia nodded again. "More than I can say. I often wonder why the good Lord leaves me here instead of taking me home, where I really want to be—where Jesus and so many of my loved ones are waiting for me."

"I've wondered the same thing. I can only conclude that He still has work for us here." She sighed. "Prayer is at the top of that work list, but so is talking to our fellow River View residents about Jesus and helping them see their need to prepare for eternity." She shook her head. "I know that includes Margaret Snowden, but that's no easy assignment, is it?"

Julia's chuckle was tinged with sarcasm, though she tried to hide it. "That's an understatement," she said. "The other day, when I tried to befriend her, she nearly bit my head off. She as much as told me to mind my own business and to leave her alone. And trust me, that's what I would very much like to do."

"As would I," Laura said, nodding thoughtfully. "But all the more reason to pray for her heart to be softened and for God to give us an opportunity to get to know her." She glanced down at her wristwatch, and then back up to Julia. "We still have a few minutes before lunch. Why don't we pray right now?"

Leave it to Laura, Julia thought. *She always suggests exactly what I need to do but don't want to. Forgive me, Lord, and please give me a renewed commitment to reach out to Margaret.*

She smiled and took her friend's hands. "That's a wonderful idea. Will you begin?" And she bowed her head and waited.

✶✶✶

For the second day in a row, Tong took Zhen-Li away from her cell and her work and secluded her with him in the same room as the previous day, where once again they sat on the couch for more than an hour. Tong seemed relaxed, leaning back against the cushions and putting his arm across the back of the sofa, much too close to Zhen-Li as far as she was concerned. But even though she continued to perch on the edge of her seat, as if she could spring up and run away if he touched her, she knew she couldn't escape if he wanted to hurt her in any way. And so she sat, still and stiff, praying silently even as she utilized her chopsticks to scoop the rice and cabbage from the bowl and drank the tea he provided her.

Tong's near monologue continued with talk of Zhen-Li's proper return to the teachings of her parents and the party, offering understanding of how she may have been beguiled by the traitors who had adopted a foreign religion and who regularly "surrendered state secrets to foreign devils." He had used the phrase before, but Zhen-Li couldn't imagine what he meant, as neither she nor Zhou Chi, nor any other member of their little house church, knew any state secrets to pass on to anyone. But for some reason, Tai Tong seemed convinced they did, as he repeated the accusation on a regular basis.

She hated herself for enjoying the food and hot tea Tong gave her, but she nearly cried with joy at the taste of them in her mouth and the strength she felt flowing through her veins as she swallowed. Quite obviously this arrangement could end at any moment and she would be right back to a perpetual state of near-starvation and ongoing fear of pain and punishment. But for today, for right now, she relished the immediate benefits of Tong's attentions, whatever their purpose.

It wasn't until he rose to his feet and reached down to help her to hers that the truth of his intentions broke through her denial. Though he did nothing but let his hand linger on her arm a bit longer than necessary, it was the look in his eyes that betrayed him. He was hungry, and that was a feeling Zhen-Li knew well. She was the prey, and he was stalking her, waiting for the right moment to pounce and devour her. When he did, what would she do? Would she yield to whatever he asked of her in order to save her life, as easily as she'd yielded to the pleasant taste of food in her mouth? If she fought him, would he take whatever he wanted anyway—and then kill her when he was finished?

In that moment she knew her fate was sealed. Her only hope was that he would prolong the inevitable a while longer—or that God would give her a miracle.

Zhen-Li was already in her cell when Mei returned from her workday. Just looking at her cell mate made Mei feel dirtier than usual. She knew Zhen-Li believed in the Christian God and would never approve of what Mei had chosen to do just to stay alive. But how would Zhen-Li react when she discovered that she was going to face the same choice? For by now Mei was certain that was exactly what was going to happen. The fact that Tong took Zhen-Li away with him in the morning and returned her a few hours later without any signs of ill treatment meant he was working at breaking her down. Would Zhen-Li be strong enough to resist the temptation to trade her self-respect for slightly more humane treatment and the hope of living long enough to one day go home to her family?

Zhen-Li raised her head and smiled at Mei. "*Ping an*," Zhen-Li said.

Mei stopped, surprised by the greeting of peace. What a strange thing to say in such a place!

Mei nodded and then sat down against the wall, across from Zhen-Li. "How are you feeling?" she asked.

"I am well, *xiexie*," Zhen-Li responded, thanking her.

It was true that Zhen-Li appeared much better, Mei thought—nearly healed from her beating a couple of days earlier. She looked healthier as well. No doubt Tong was plying her with food. Mei had to admit that the extra provisions were the primary reason she had chosen to shame herself at the guards' hands, hoping it would help her stay alive long enough to fulfill her sentence and be released. And yet, each day, the light of her hope dimmed.

Mei nodded again, accepting Zhen-Li's thanks and expressing her pleasure that Zhen-Li seemed well. Suddenly she remembered her grandfather, who had long been dead, playing his favorite game of chess with the neighbor. Why should this exchange with Zhen-Li remind her of such an event?

"I do not believe I have long to live," Zhen-Li announced suddenly, and Mei straightened up against the wall, feeling her eyes go wide as she stared at her cell mate. What did she mean by that? A couple of days ago, when Zhen-Li had returned to the cell, beaten and bloody, the statement would have made sense. But now?

"I believe they will kill me soon," Zhen-Li said, "and it is important to me that I tell you about Zhu Yesu while there is time."

Mei's heart squeezed. She knew she would have to reveal to the guards everything that Zhen-Li told her, but she also realized how desperately she wished she didn't have to. If only she were brave enough to resist! But, of course, she wasn't. If she didn't tell them—or if she told them only a part of the truth—they would know. And then what little hope Mei had left would be gone. She had no choice. If she was to survive, she would have to betray Zhen-Li...again.

As the one who called herself a Christian began to talk to Mei about a God who loves and forgives all who will come to Him, Mei tried desperately to shut out the words, but the sound penetrated the wall she tried to erect around her heart. The more she attempted to ignore the message, the more it drew her to the memories she had tried so hard to erase. And just for a few moments, Mei hated Zhen-Li for that.

It was all about the profit.

Chapter 9

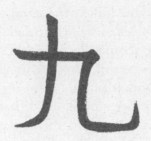

LEO SNICKERED. HE'D BEEN A PAWNSHOP OWNER FOR A LONG time, but his customers never ceased to amaze him. The girl with the cheap nose ring and rhinestone belly-button stud who just left was a perfect example.

Looking down at the strand of pearls and the gold brooch he held in his hand, he nearly laughed aloud at the ridiculous story the girl had given him about where she'd gotten the stuff, not to mention her lie that she was over twenty-one but had forgotten to bring her ID with her.

She wasn't a day over fifteen, Leo mused. *And no way did her aunt die and leave her these things. But who cares? She practically gave them to me. I offered her a measly fifty bucks, and she grabbed it like she'd just won the lottery.* This time he did laugh out loud, and then shook his head. *That money'll go up in smoke before the day's over.*

But what did he care? He'd find someone equally gullible to buy the jewelry at an inflated price, and Leo's Treasures and Pawnshop would be that much more profitable. And wasn't that the reason he was involved in more than one business? It was all about the profit.

Maggie lay sprawled on the floor of her dealer's living room, peering from under hooded lids at the smoky haze that surrounded her. Shapes and voices swirled around her, interrupted by an occasional laugh or shouted curse word. Though the vagueness of the scene still unnerved her occasionally, she was becoming more comfortable with it as time went on.

How long had it been since she'd first dared to stick her toe across the line into this world of smoke and shadows? Three months? Six? She shook her head, but it didn't help. Her thoughts jumbled together like blobs of gelatin, jiggling and bouncing off one another. Nothing seemed clear or sharp anymore, but she told herself that was how she wanted it. Life was easier that way. It worked better—and it hurt less because she didn't have to think about what she was doing to her family.

That was the best part. If it meant she had to steal and lie and cheat—and whatever else might be required to block out her otherwise boring existence—then so be it. She would do whatever was necessary, and cut her losses. If her grandmother turned out to be one of those losses, Maggie would just have to deal with it and move on. After all, it wasn't like they were close or anything.

★★★

The distant hills appeared more barren than usual as Chi labored under the unusually warm spring sun. But he was glad for the warmth, as he knew it would aid his beloved Zhen-Li as she languished in some otherwise cold, ugly prison cell. If only he could be there to hold and comfort her! Better yet, if he could just take her place...

The long hours he spent toiling in the fields in order to feed his family were easier to bear when he allowed his mind to escape to happier times—times when Zhen-Li still waited at home for him at the end of the day. Or even to the times before they married, when the thought of having her as his bride was only a wisp of a dream in his heart.

Today was no different, as he bent over his hoe, chopping at the stubborn weeds that seemed to spring up from the hard ground even without water to encourage them. But no matter. Chi had learned to be grateful for the weeds, as they provided him with work, and work provided for the needs of little Chan and Zhou Ming.

Zhen-Li's beautiful and hauntingly familiar face seemed to float before his eyes, blocking out the tedious work of his hands. How clearly he remembered the day he had first laid eyes on her, and his heart had come to life with a song he had never heard before, but one he knew from that moment he would never forget. It was the first time in many months that Chi had taken the chance to attend a *jia tin jiao hui*, a secret meeting of believers at an unapproved house church in a local village. A female member of the group had invited her friend Yang Zhen-Li to the gathering as well, even though she knew Zhen-Li did not share their faith and she was taking a big chance in exposing them as she did. Though Zhen-Li had seemed a bit confused by the goings-on, to Chi's amazement, she had watched him closely all evening and had later asked her friend who he was and if he was single. The rest seemed to happen quickly, but the memory of how a woman so lovely and pure could enter a room and notice him, to the point that she eventually joined his faith and became a Christian and even gave up her family to be with him, was the most incredible thing Chi could ever imagine.

The vision of Zhen-Li's face kept him going throughout the long day, enabling him to ignore the increasing pain in his back as he continued his work until nearly sunset. Then he climbed on his bicycle and began the lonely ride back home. The only thing he refused to let himself think about was their second child — the baby Zhen-Li had so wanted but the government and her parents had taken from her. Why had she allowed that incident to push her into near-fanaticism? Why couldn't she have been satisfied to continue in secret worship and fellowship with their small house church, rather than reaching out to evangelize every child she met? Why couldn't she have compromised at least that much — as he had done — to preserve what was left of their little family? The answers to those questions were simply too painful to contemplate, and so Chi pushed them away in an attempt to survive what had become of his life.

✳✳✳

Tong knew it was time to move a little closer to Zhen-Li, to tease her with his intentions without clearly revealing them. Let her wonder—maybe even anticipate, but certainly dread—what was to come. For if it increased her fear of him, all the better. It was the power and control that excited him even more than the lust.

As he led his little sheep back to the room that would eventually see her slaughter, he couldn't help but grin at the thought of what lay ahead. This helpless, weak young woman, with no one to protect her, actually thought she could defy him by refusing to stop talking about her foreign god. How insolent! But he would soon show her that he was her god, and then she would finally obey and serve him.

Opening the door to the prepared room, he held it and indicated that she should go in first. Her wide eyes, just before casting them downward, showed her shock at his nearly chivalrous gesture. Good. His plan was working already.

Slowly, the obviously feebleminded woman shuffled through the door and then stopped, standing and waiting for her next order, while he closed and locked the door behind them. Gently taking her arm, he steered her toward the couch and helped her to sit down, firmly pushing her back until she settled against the cushions rather than continuing to perch on the edge as she had done previously. Yet her continued stiffness and discomfort were evident.

Tong took a seat beside her, closer than he'd sat the last two days. Then, immediately, he poured a cup of steaming tea from the waiting thermos and held it out to her. Without raising her eyes to his, she accepted it and drank slowly. When she was finished, Tong took the cup and placed it back on the table.

As she continued to wait in silence, he removed the lid to a large dish, releasing the aroma of rice and fish and garnering the result he'd hoped for as Zhen-Li's head jerked upward and her eyes widened at the feast that sat before her. Tong could only imagine how long it had been since she had regularly seen such an offering, let alone been allowed to eat it. No doubt it was long before she was arrested, as her peon husband certainly couldn't provide her with such an elegant repast.

Did he detect a trembling in her hands? Yes, he was sure of it, and the realization sent a thrill up his spine. This was going to be even more fun than he had expected.

Masking a sneer, he smiled instead and spoke in his most persuasive voice. "Let me prepare a bowl of food for you, Yang Zhen-Li. I am sure you are hungry, since I doubt you have eaten since our little visit yesterday."

He scooped a generous serving into one of the two bowls on the table, and then held it out to her, along with a set of chopsticks. For a moment she didn't respond except to raise her eyes to his and then drop them back to the bowl in front of her. When he moved the food closer, she finally extended her hands and took it from him, though he continued to help her balance it in her shaky grasp.

At last the meal rested on her lap, the delicious aroma drifting upward to tantalize the famished woman. Tong watched with satisfaction as she lifted the bowl and hesitantly snagged a piece of fish with her chopsticks before slowly scooping it into her mouth. With his eyes on her lips as they opened to receive the delicious nourishment, it was all Tong could do to hold himself back from throwing the bowl to the ground and forcing himself on her right then and there. But no, that would take away from the pleasure of anticipation and the thrill of conquest that he so needed. A few more days, and then he would have his reward. For now, he would limit his delight to watching his prey being drawn in by inches.

It was almost too easy to be true.

Apparently there was to be more
upheaval at River View Manor.

Chapter 10

THE RACKET INCREASED UNTIL JULIA COULD NO LONGER ignore it. Just when she'd thought she could finally spend her nap time getting a little rest, and now this! Whatever was going on this time? Hadn't the early morning wake-up call of the previous day provided enough excitement to last them what was left of their abbreviated lifetimes?

She sighed, then hoisted herself from her bed and onto her walker. Apparently there was to be more upheaval at River View Manor, whether they wanted it or not. Julia could hear Emily Johnson's voice rising above the rest of the uproar, and she wondered if the woman had found something else missing.

When she cracked her door and peered out into the hallway, Julia was surprised to see Margaret Snowden, leaning on her walker at her open bedroom door and glaring out at Emily, who in turn stood in the hallway at Margaret's door, staring back and leaning on her cane. It appeared to be a standoff of sorts, with each of the elderly women looking as if smoke might begin erupting from their ears at any moment. As the confusing accusations and arguments flew back and forth between them, a staff member known as Rocky—at least partially due to his muscular build, Julia was sure—stepped between the two ladies and began trying to calm them down.

"Now, Margaret," he said, turning from one to the other, "and Emily, you both know this is no way to settle a disagreement. We can't have this sort of thing going on here at River View, disrupting all the other residents. Why don't the three of us go into the library and sit down and see if we can discuss this like—"

Before he could say another word, Emily pounded her cane on the floor, missing Rocky's foot by inches. "I will not sit down anywhere with this thief," she insisted. "I want her arrested, do you hear me? Arrested!"

Julia raised her eyebrows. Thief? Margaret might be a lot of things—grumpy, unfriendly, rude—but a thief? She found that more than a bit difficult to believe.

Margaret leaned forward menacingly on her walker, causing even Rocky to back away a bit. "I am not a thief," she bellowed. "And you'd better take that back right now, you old biddy!"

Julia imagined Emily's eyes popping out of her head at the word *biddy*, but before the cane-wielding woman could respond, a second staff member, whose name was Gina and who was much smaller than Rocky but no less firm when she needed to be, intervened.

"All right, that's it," she announced, stepping up to the simmering trio and directing her words to the onlookers. "All of you, back into your rooms until we can get this cleared up. Go on now. We'll have this settled in no time, won't we?"

Rocky nodded in agreement, while the two geriatric gladiators continued to glare at one another, and the manor's residents—including Julia—reluctantly stepped back inside their rooms and closed the doors.

Julia wished she and Laura were together so they could discuss the situation and pray for a peaceful resolution of whatever was going on between Emily and Margaret. But since they weren't—and since they'd been banished to their rooms like naughty schoolchildren—she would simply go to prayer by herself, trusting that Laura was doing the same.

★★★

Maggie knew she shouldn't have gone back so soon, but when she came out of her stupor, she couldn't help but wonder if the old woman who lived in the same place as Maggie's grandmother had noticed her stuff was missing. If not, Maggie might be able to scope out some of the other residents and see if they had anything worth stealing. She knew her grandmother didn't, since Maggie had taken the few pieces of jewelry Margaret had before she'd even moved into that place for the near-dead.

Maggie shivered as she hurried back to her dealer's pad and the comfort of another fix. Why had she returned to that creepy house? The only thing she'd accomplished was to discover the old lady knew her stuff was missing and that Maggie's grandmother thought Maggie had taken it. Big deal. It was her word against theirs, wasn't it? But she shouldn't have gone; she knew that now.

All those ancient people roaming around, just waiting to breathe their last and get thrown into the ground. She shook her head. There wasn't enough money in the world to get her to work in a place like that. Just going there was awful enough. Maggie's grandmother had looked genuinely surprised when Maggie walked in, though not necessarily pleased. "I just came by to say hello and to check on you," Maggie had told her, using her most innocent, little-girl voice.

The old woman hadn't bought it. She had squinted her eyes as she sat in her chair beside her bed and hissed, "Is that so? Well, I don't believe you. I think you came here to see what else you could steal."

Maggie had nearly fainted at the words. How had she known? Maggie hadn't said a word to anyone! Sure, she'd been there a couple of days earlier when the old bag down the hall was wearing her ratty jewelry like she was some kind of queen or something. And yes, Maggie had made a point to talk to her and to watch which room she'd gone into, but...

She took a deep breath. This was no time to lose her cool. Besides, they couldn't prove anything, could they?

"I don't know what you're talking about, Grandma," she'd said, hoping her voice didn't sound as shaky as she felt. "Why would I come here to steal anything?"

"For drugs," Margaret had declared, her voice rising as Maggie looked over her shoulder and wished she'd closed the door when she came into her grandmother's room. "Just like you stole things from me for the same reason, before I moved here," Margaret continued. "You're a no-good thief. A druggie and a thief! My own grandchild, stealing from people who are too old to defend themselves. How did you get your hands on Emily's pearls and brooch? Did you climb in her window at night, the way you did at my house?"

Maggie had felt her mouth go dry, just as she'd heard a noise behind her. Turning, she gasped at the sight of the old woman named Emily, standing in the doorway and leaning on her cane.

"You!" Emily exclaimed. "So you're the one who took my jewelry!"

Suddenly afraid she would vomit if she didn't get outside into the air, Maggie had pushed past the old woman, nearly knocking her to the floor as she raced for the front door. She should never have gone back, should have paid attention to the warning bells in her head. What would happen to her now?

Thank goodness she got out of there when she did! If only she could count on her grandmother to cover for her. They might not be close, but they were family, and Grandma Margaret had always said families should stick together—even though Maggie hadn't seen much of that happening in their clan over the years.

And the old woman with the cane? No doubt she'd go screaming to the police about what she'd heard, but why would they believe her? It was her word against Maggie's—and her grandmother's, if she stood by her. Maggie knew her freedom might just depend on whether or not that happened, and that didn't make her feel very secure.

★★★

Zhen-Li hadn't slept much the previous night, and she actually found herself hoping she'd be sent outside to her usual day of hard labor, rather than having to spend another moment locked in that room with Tai Tong. As much as she desperately longed for more of the food he gave her while she was there, the fear of what he would eventually do to her had stolen what little joy she found in easing the burning hunger in her stomach. It was almost easier when he had beaten her. At least then she hadn't felt as if she were betraying everything she believed.

They had already come for Mei, but before they did, Zhen-Li had talked to her as much as possible about Zhu Yesu, sharing Scripture verses with her and even offering to pray with her. But Mei had refused to listen or respond, and that hurt Zhen-Li deeply. She felt as if she were failing her cell mate—failing her God, for that matter—as she was sure her time on earth was limited and she truly wanted to be able to lead Mei to Yesu before it was too late.

When Tong finally showed up at the cell door, Zhen-Li felt her heart drop to her feet. Just when she had begun to hope he wouldn't come, now he was here, smiling at her like a poisonous snake, coiled and ready to strike when she least expected it.

Zhen-Li knew it was coming, of course. The only question was when—and how she would respond when it did.

Be with me, Zhu Yesu, she prayed silently, rising to her feet to follow her tormentor. *I have no strength, my Lord—only Yours. Do not let me dishonor You, Tian Fu, in my time of testing.*

"The girl took it."

Chapter 11

Julia couldn't sleep that night. The altercation between Margaret and Emily had disturbed her, even more so when she learned it had begun when Emily claimed to have overheard Margaret and her granddaughter discussing the theft of Emily's jewelry.

"The girl took it," Emily had announced, loudly enough that the other residents couldn't help but hear, even as they waited in their rooms while the police officer added notes to the previous report. "The one who looks like a hippie, with tattoos and rainbow-colored hair and a ring in her nose. I don't know what's wrong with young people these days—or their parents, for that matter. I never allowed my kids to look like that. And they didn't go around stealing things from people either. Drugs, indeed! No wonder she took my jewelry!"

Even after the police officer left, Emily continued to lament the sad state of a world that allowed old people to be robbed and young people to walk the streets, looking like "crazed clowns" and taking drugs that turned them into criminals.

Margaret had remained in her room throughout the entire episode, refusing even to come out for dinner. When Laura and Julia had gotten together for prayer before retiring to their rooms for the night, Laura had ventured the guess that perhaps Margaret was embarrassed, as well as concerned about her granddaughter. Julia wasn't sure the snippy old woman could be either, but she forced herself to move past her personal opinions and pray for Margaret. After all, if what Emily said was true, Margaret had cause to be concerned.

"I'm so grateful that my children and grandchildren have never been in trouble, Lord," Julia whispered. "Thank You for keeping them safe and for bringing them to You at such an early age. I can't even imagine how difficult it would be to have my loved ones involved in drugs and other such lifestyles. Please give me a heart to pray for Margaret's granddaughter—whether she took Emily's jewelry or not—and give me a heart to see past Margaret's grumpy exterior. Underneath is a heart that desperately needs You, Father. Never let me forget that!"

With that she closed her eyes, thinking she would soon drift off to sleep. Only moments later, however, she was jolted back into prayer mode, at the thought that someone in China was in danger.

"Joe and I never got to go back to China the way we'd planned, Father," she spoke into the darkness, "but You sure have been calling me to pray for someone over there lately—a woman, I think. Perhaps someone near the little farming communities we visited when we were in Beijing? Maybe even one of the believers in the area house churches, like the one we attended once and delivered some Bibles to. It doesn't matter, does it, Lord? Whoever she is, You know. Thank You for the privilege of interceding for her."

And with renewed alertness, Julia went to work.

"Eat," Tong commanded, his voice tinged with concern but over-ridden with authority. "You must keep your strength up."

His dark eyes followed her every movement as she hesitantly obeyed, using her chopsticks to scoop food from her bowl into her mouth. Just the aroma of the meal made her mouth water, and it was all she could do to show restraint as she chewed. Until the past couple of days, she had nearly forgotten how delicious food could be!

And yet she felt as if she were being poisoned—slowly, one bite at a time—and she chastised herself for enjoying it so. She'd never realized how weak she was until she'd faced this particular temptation. The beatings had been difficult, but she'd expected them. Never in her wildest dreams had she imagined she'd be plied with food.

Tong smiled, but Zhen-Li couldn't help but notice that the gesture didn't extend to his eyes. Even when the man tried to show kindness, she sensed a coldness, an emptiness showing through his gaze that mirrored the condition of his heart. And that frightened Zhen-Li more than she wished to consider.

"With a few more meals, you might begin to once again take on the shape of a desirable woman," Tong said, his words sending what felt like an electric shock through Zhen-Li's body. So this was it. Here it came, sooner than she'd expected. What was she to do now?

Qin Ai de Tian Fu, help me, she pleaded silently, slowly swallowing the food in her mouth and dropping her eyes from the predatory gaze of Tai Tong. *I wish only to return to my family, Father. But if that is not to be, may I die quickly and with honor. I am too great a coward to remain brave if my death is slow and painful.*

Even with her eyes downcast, she saw his hand come into view, as he gently laid his fingers on her arm. She tensed as he began to stroke her skin.

"With the right food and treatment, you could be quite beautiful," he crooned. "I could ensure that you receive such food and treatment ... under the right circumstances." He paused, and even his hand stopped moving as he waited. When she didn't answer or raise her eyes to his, he asked, "Do you understand what I am saying, Yang Zhen-Li?"

Though there was no more food left in her mouth, Zhen-Li swallowed again. *"Ming bai le,"* she said, her voice scarcely audible. "I understand."

Tong's hand lifted from her arm and came to her chin, and he tilted her head upward, though she kept her eyes turned down.

"Look at me," he said, a hint of coldness returning to his voice.

Her heart racing to the point she thought she might faint, she slowly obeyed. The look in his eyes was more evil than she had imagined.

"You are mine," he said. "I can do with you as I wish. You know that, do you not? So why not cooperate with me and make our task more pleasant?"

Zhen-Li opened her mouth, but no words made it past the lump in her throat. How was she to answer him? How could she possibly respond to this vile creature?

This time Tong's smile was cold and hard. "I will have you whether you cooperate or not," he said. "Do not think your God will help you. I am stronger than any *shen*, any god, real or imagined, because I represent the Chinese government. There is nothing you can do to change that. So think about that until I come for you again. For when I do, I want your answer. Do I take you with or without your cooperation? It makes no difference to me, but I would imagine it would make all the difference to you."

Despite her silent pleas to Zhu Yesu, Zhen-Li began to tremble, and she knew Tong could see it. She had so wanted to hide her fear, but she felt powerless to stop it. She was terrified of what lay ahead for her with this man, and he knew it. In fact, she was sure he took great delight in knowing it and would do whatever he could to increase that fear.

As she tried in vain to block the tears that pooled in her eyes, Tong spoke again. "If you have trouble making the right decision, why not talk to your little friend Mei? Have you never wondered how she has survived so long in this place? Perhaps she can help you see the wisdom in cooperating with the inevitable."

He smiled again and reached toward her to wipe away a tear that had escaped and now slipped slowly down her cheek. At his touch, her stomach churned with revulsion. "There is no need to cry, Zhen-Li. I am making you a generous offer, one that will enable you to better endure your sentence of reeducation, even as Mei has done. Not every prisoner gets such an opportunity, so you must think carefully about your response." He withdrew his hand and shrugged.

"If you refuse me, I will do what I wish anyway, but you will not get the special care or treatment that I will give you if you cooperate. Does it not make sense to work with me, rather than against me? After all, that seems to have been your problem even before you came here. Instead of working with the state, which wants only the best for you, you fought us at every turn. And look where it got you! Do you want to see your husband and child again? I know you do. So why not do the wise thing and respond to me with a positive attitude?" His smile returned. "If you do, you just might find the remainder of your stay here a lot more pleasant. If not..."

Zhen-Li's head felt as if it were spinning, as Tong's words began to fade into darkness. Just before slipping away, the anguished young woman cried out, "Yesu!" and collapsed into her captor's waiting arms.

Maggie felt sick. She knew much of it was chemically driven, as it had been a while since she'd fed her addiction. But she also realized that fear was fueling her nausea and headache, not to mention her aching muscles. It had been at least two days since she'd slept soundly, and her parents didn't even know. How was that possible? She wondered about that often. After all, they lived in the same house—most of the time, anyway. But when she slipped out her bedroom window and stayed out all night, they never even noticed. She had long since convinced them she needed a lock on her door and did not want to be disturbed when she was in her room. They had complied and left her alone when her door was closed and locked—which was nearly all the time, even as it was right now as she lay on her bed, staring through the darkness at the familiar silhouettes of her former life. So far Maggie had been able to waylay the two letters that had come from school, warning of her failing grades, but it was just a matter of time until it all caught up with her.

Then what? Maggie had no idea. She'd cry and scream, bargain and threaten, and eventually promise to do better. It had worked before, and she hoped it would again, despite her father's warnings that they weren't going to tolerate her behavior much longer.

What did that mean? Were they going to shoot her? Ship her off to a desert island somewhere? Sell her to pirates? What could they really do to her? If they ever got physical and punished her, she'd simply call the authorities and report them. So what was the big deal?

And yet there was something—something that nagged at her with a homesickness she couldn't identify. She was missing out, and a part of her felt cheated. But not enough to do anything about it. Maggie was not about to give up her drugs or her friends. Partying was what she did. Period. So her parents, her grandmother, and even the cops were just going to have to get used to it.

And besides, her dealer, Jake, had been a lot nicer to her lately. In fact, she was beginning to wonder if he was interested in her as a woman. She hoped so, because he was very good-looking and mature. The thought of giving herself to him was sounding more appealing all the time.

With that thought, she closed her eyes, hoping that sleep would finally come.

How had Mei managed to maintain
her sanity?

Chapter 12

TWO DAYS HAD PASSED SINCE TONG HAD WARNED ZHEN-LI what to expect the next time he took her away with him to their little "room of delights," as he had begun to call it. Zhen-Li cringed each time she heard a step outside the cell door, but so far Tong had not shown his face. Not only had he not come to take her to meet her fate, but no one had come to take her to work either.

Mei, however, continued to be escorted from the cell daily, only to return late in the afternoon, looking weary and disheveled. Zhen-Li found herself watching her cell mate through new eyes, now that the evil Tong had hinted at what it was Mei did during the hours she spent outside her cell. Even now, as the fragile woman leaned against the wall opposite Zhen-Li, her head bowed and resting on her drawn-up knees, Zhen-Li wondered what thoughts slogged through her mind.

Zhen-Li shuddered at the realization that it wouldn't be long until she herself wrestled with the same torturous thoughts and memories. How had Mei managed to maintain her sanity in the midst of such degrading, ongoing treatment? Would Zhen-Li fare as well? Did she dare even consider choosing to cooperate with Tong, rather than fighting him? After all, he had promised he would have his way with her, regardless of her response. The only difference was how she would be treated as far as food and physical punishment. She couldn't even begin to imagine the pain that would be inflicted upon her if she refused his advances and he forced himself upon her.

And there was no doubt in her mind that he would. Just looking at Mei and the defeated hunch of her shoulders confirmed her suspicions. How desperately she wanted to talk to her friend, to ask how it had happened to her and what to expect, how to behave . . . how bad it would really be.

But then she thought better of it. Not only would Mei no doubt resist discussing such a thing, but there were some things in life so terrible they were best not known ahead of time. There was no way to prepare for such atrocities, except to pray for mercy and strength and protection. For Zhen-Li knew she would never stand strong on her own. Only Zhu Yesu could give her the strength to survive what lay ahead.

In the meantime, though she had already decided not to mention any of this to Mei, she refocused what little strength she had left on talking to the girl about her need for Yesu. Who knew if this would be their last opportunity to talk of such things — of anything, for that matter? Their lives hung by the slimmest of threads, at the mercy of those who had no mercy. To appeal to the One who was the source of all mercy was the only hope they had.

And so she spoke Mei's name, waited for the young woman to raise her head and gaze at her from sad eyes, and then began once again to tell her of the only thing that truly mattered.

✯✯✯

Why does she speak to me so? Mei listened to the woman's tone more than to her words, wondering as she so often did how it was that Zhen-Li had not yet figured out who had betrayed her. *Especially now*, Mei thought, remembering how Tong had taunted her this very day with the news that he had told Zhen-Li how Mei regularly compromised herself in an effort to survive her sentence. If Zhen-Li knew that, wouldn't she also figure out very soon that Mei was the one who reported Zhen-Li's every word to the guards?

How Mei longed to tell Zhen-Li to resist, to be strong, to pray to her God to help her! *They will promise you better treatment,* she spoke silently to herself, willing Zhen-Li to hear. *But it means nothing. They will give you just enough food to keep you going, and though they will not beat you in such a way as to break bones or leave scars, they still know how to inflict pain and demand obedience, even as they strip you of any honor and dignity you might once have had.*

It is not worth it, Zhen-Li. Do not do it! Fight them. Resist them. Be stronger than I!

All these things Mei thought, and yet she said nothing, even as Zhen-Li continued to speak to her of Zhu Yesu and words from the Shengjing. Mei had owned one of those holy books once, many years earlier, before her parents were imprisoned for spreading their faith to children, even as Zhen-Li had done. How many times had Mei's mother told her daughter of the foreign missionaries, Joe and Julia Crockett, who had come to visit them and left them a Shengjing of their very own. But Mei was convinced the foreigners had done her parents a great disservice, for soon the persecution began.

Mei would never forget it. First they came and posted signs on their door: LOVER OF FOREIGNERS and POISONOUS SNAKES. Mei had been so ashamed! She had begged her parents to stop holding the jiao hui in their home, to stop preaching about Zhu Yesu and reading from their Shengjing, but they refused. And look what had happened. The PSB had dragged them away in the middle of the night, while she lay, huddled and shivering, under the bed, praying they would not take her too.

They hadn't. She had stayed there, alone and terrified, for nearly two days until one of her aunts had come to check the house and found her. Mei had gone home to live with her aunt, where she was beaten regularly by her uncle and never had enough to eat. Perhaps that was why her current life seemed almost normal to her, though she still cried regularly over the memory of the few years she had spent as a wife and mother. She had been poor then also, but it was the happiest time of her life. It was only when the authorities in her village discovered whose daughter she was and her uncle falsely accused her of stealing from him while she lived in their home that she was eventually arrested and thrown into this terrible place, away from her husband and child, whom she had not seen or heard from in four years.

Would she ever leave here alive? For a brief time, Mei had dared to hope that might happen, though the cost to her self-respect was beyond recovery. But now, with each passing day, her hope dimmed, and she had come to believe she would die here—used up and thrown away like so much trash.

Now she silently prayed to a God she didn't even know that this woman who sat across from her, speaking of Yesu, would not end up the same way.

✳✳✳

It was the first time Julia had been on an outing in the manor's van in a while. She often hesitated to go, as getting around on her walker was a bit tricky at times. But Laura had insisted.

"You haven't been out in ages," she'd declared. "It's high time the two of us got a little shopping time together. My goodness, Julia, we can't spend all our time in prayer! The good Lord knows we need a little recreation once in a while too. And at our age, a trip to the strip mall in the van with others in wheelchairs and walkers is about the best we can hope for!"

Julia had laughed, conceding that her friend was right. Even their church services were held there at the manor, with a visiting pastor and pianist coming in each Sunday afternoon to gather together whichever residents were willing and interested for an hour of worship. Of course, Julia's family came to visit and took her out to eat on occasion, but it wasn't the same. Laura was right that they needed some "girlfriend time."

"So, where to first?" Julia asked as she and Laura parted company with the other four residents who had come along, all of them promising to return to the van at a specified time.

"Let's do the grocery store last," Laura suggested. "We'll hit the Bible bookstore to look for something new to read, and then the drugstore to see what's on sale in the cosmetic department." She chuckled. "Not that it's going to do any good at my age, but I always figure a little extra color on my cheeks can't hurt."

Julia laughed. "You're right about that. We need all the help we can get, don't we?"

With Laura matching Julia's slow pace on the walker, the two of them meandered toward the drugstore, only to be waylaid at the ice cream parlor.

"I haven't had an ice cream cone since the last time we came to town together," Julia observed. "What do you think? Should we stop here before we do anything else?"

"I think we're overdue," Laura announced. "Let's get a double-decker and sit here by the sidewalk and watch the people walk by."

In minutes they were sitting at a wrought-iron table, their purses firmly planted in their laps, trying to keep the warm afternoon sun from melting their treat before they finished it. Laughing like schoolgirls, they were nearly done and ready to resume their trek to the drugstore when Laura's eyes opened wide and she nodded in the direction of the incense and wind chime store across the way.

"Isn't that Margaret's granddaughter coming out of there?"

Julia followed Laura's direction and spotted the girl exiting the shop with a man who looked to be in his mid- to late-twenties. She nodded. "Yes, I'm afraid it is. Though I can't say much for the company she keeps."

"He looks quite a bit older, doesn't he?"

Julia nodded again. "He certainly does. And why do I think he doesn't have her best interests at heart?"

Laura laid her hand on Julia's. "Something else to pray about, wouldn't you say?"

"It certainly seems that way," Julia agreed. "In fact, it seems we just can't get away from our need to pray for Margaret Snowden, and everything connected with her life. I would say it's a safe assumption that God has placed that woman and her family in our path for a purpose, wouldn't you?"

Julia watched with a growing sadness as the young girl named Maggie sauntered away with her companion. Though

Julia knew they would also pray for that companion, she sensed it was Maggie who would become the primary focus of their prayers when they returned to River View that evening—her and the ever-present call to pray for someone in China.

Julia sighed. She had no idea who that someone in China might be, but her sense of urgency to pray seemed to grow daily.

Oh, if only the headstrong girl
hadn't met that peon Zhou Chi!

Chapter 13

Y IN XEI WAS PLAGUED BY DREAMS OF A LITTLE GIRL, A FACELESS child with a loving spirit who cried out to her with outstretched arms. Xei awoke from these dreams drenched in sweat and fighting tears, knowing full well the identity of the little girl with no face but refusing to admit it.

And always her husband, Yang Hong, snored with irritating regularity beside her, seeming never to miss a beat in his carefree slumber. How was he able to do it? Xei told herself that he, too, had loved Yang Zhen-Li, that his hopes and dreams had rested on the child as they watched her grow into an intelligent, sensitive, and beautiful young woman. But at times she found it hard to believe. Oh, if only the headstrong girl hadn't met that peon Zhou Chi and insisted on marrying him instead of Han Bai! How different her life could have been. And how different the lives of her parents! Instead of living as if they had no child, scarcely mentioning the name of their once-beloved daughter, they would be bouncing their grandson on their knee, enjoying the fruits of their faithful labor.

Their grandson. As always, the thought of the little boy named Zhou Chan, the child they had never even met, tugged at Yin Xei's heartstrings. The one who should bring her such joy instead added to her already far-too-heavy grief. Was there no solution to this situation, no end to the pain? Dare she hope that Yang Zhen-Li would survive her sentence and one day return to them, a repentant and faithful daughter once again? But even if she did, by then the boy, Zhou Chan, would be nearly grown, and Xei and her husband would have missed out on the formative years of his life, leaving little hope of ever establishing a close relationship.

Why did things have to be this way? Xei nearly cried out in the darkness at the unfairness of it all. She had done all the right things—worked hard at her teaching position, been faithful to her husband, despite the coldness in her heart toward him, and taught her daughter the ways of the state. But what had it gotten her? A lonely, empty spot in bed beside her obnoxious, snoring husband, and a future with no hope. Is that all there was in life? If so, Xei wondered why she bothered to continue living.

Julia's arthritis was acting up today, especially in her right hip, which had been replaced but still seemed to ache more than any other part of her aging body. Some days were worse than others, of course, and the dampness from today's late spring fog certainly didn't help. Still, she knew she was in better shape than some of River View's other residents, and she wasn't about to complain or allow a few aches and pains to keep her down.

Pushing her walker ahead of her, she made her way out of her room and down the hall toward the main part of the house. She could smell breakfast cooking in the large kitchen, and though she wasn't normally a big eater in the morning, her mouth watered at the tantalizing aroma of sausages simmering in a pan.

Laura hadn't come out of her room yet, but that wasn't unusual. She was nearly always one of the last to emerge from hibernation each morning, so Julia hadn't expected to see her waiting at the table. In fact, only two residents were there ahead of her, and they were already ensconced in conversation about their similar health conditions. Since Julia had nothing to contribute to the topic, she sat down at the opposite end of the table and decided she would pray silently while she waited.

She'd scarcely bowed her head and closed her eyes when she heard another walker rolling toward her. Looking up, she found herself staring straight into the bespectacled eyes of Margaret Snowden. As always, Margaret's once-dark hair was fastidiously swept up in a bun and held in place with several pins. Though stocky, the woman appeared strong and steady, despite the walker she had apparently used since the accident that broke her leg. Julia could understand the woman's dependence on the device. Though Julia herself had been told she could probably do without hers—and occasionally she did in the secluded safety of her own room—she still felt more secure with it in front of her. No doubt Margaret shared her insecurities.

It's probably the only thing we do share, Julia thought, then quickly scolded herself. *That is hardly a Christlike attitude, Julia Crockett. For goodness' sake, stop being so judgmental and cranky.*

She forced a smile. "Good morning, Margaret."

Margaret nodded in response but said nothing as she pushed past Julia and went on to take a seat on the opposite side of the table.

Julia's smile was beginning to feel more than slightly wooden. "So how are you today? Did you sleep well?"

Margaret looked at Julia and blinked, as if surprised by the question. She raised her eyebrows, then lowered them again before answering. "Yes. Thank you."

That's it? No, "And how about you?" Julia sighed. Well, she'd tried, hadn't she? What else could she do? The woman quite obviously did not want to be friends, and so Julia would honor her wishes. Turning her attention back to prayer, she ended the one-way conversation by once again dropping her head and closing her eyes. But instead of being able to pray for anyone else, she found herself asking God to forgive her bad attitude and to change her heart. *I don't even like the woman, Lord*, she prayed, *but I know You love her so much You died for her. Please give me Your love for her, Father.*

Before she could go any further, the other residents began rolling and rattling into the room, and soon the chatter level rose to its usual intensity as the elderly diners compared illnesses and ailments, procedures and medications, and pondered whether or not their relatives would come to visit them any time soon. When Laura took the empty seat to Julia's left, they smiled at one another in welcome. Another day had officially begun.

✦✦✦

Margaret fumed. *The silly old biddy! Does she really think I want to get chummy with the likes of her? Or that I buy her friendship act in the first place? She doesn't care about me one bit. She just wants to find out what's going on with Maggie and the jewelry. An inside track for some juicy gossip, no doubt so she and that other religious nut she hangs around with can go around "praying" about my problems and feeling superior.*

Though she tried to be discreet, she couldn't help sneaking a peek across the table as the woman named Laura joined Julia. The two were as thick as thieves, always huddling together and whispering about everyone else. As far as Margaret was concerned, it was the most immoral display she had ever witnessed, and she wouldn't want to be a part of it even if they begged her.

Fat chance of that happening, she thought. *Those two wouldn't want to lower themselves to associate with the likes of me. In their eyes I'm probably just a sinner. Well, as far as I'm concerned, they're the sinners, with their gossip and judgmental attitudes. Who needs them?*

The arrival of bowls and plates of steaming food interrupted her thoughts, and despite her irritation, she heard her stomach rumble. She'd make a point to eat quickly and then return to her room for a little privacy, something that was sadly lacking around this place. At least before her so-called loved ones had relegated her to this trash heap of ancient relics she had been able to eat her meals in peace and quiet, to come and go as she pleased, and to avoid other people for days on end if she so desired. Now she was stuck living in the same house as these babbling old fools, but it didn't mean she had to join them in their senseless chatter or pointless activities. She would maintain her distance, regardless of how long she had to stay in this place, and she wouldn't so much as give any of them the satisfaction of a conversation or a smile. Let them find someone else to share their last days on this miserable planet. As for her, she'd go out on her own terms—alone and without any help from anyone.

It had been three full days since Zhen-Li had laid eyes on Tong, and though she dared to hope he might have chosen to leave her alone after all, she knew better. He was toying with her, teasing her with his absence, but surely he would reappear very soon, and then Zhen-Li's time of choosing would be upon her at last.

If only they would come and reassign her to her outside labor! As difficult as it was, it was better than waiting in the cell alone during the daylight hours when Mei was off at her own work assignment. Now that Zhen-Li realized what sort of work it was that Mei did when she was gone, her heart ached even more for the sad young woman who still cried for her husband and child. So far Zhen-Li had seen no reaction from her cell mate during their one-sided conversations about Zhu Yesu and the words of the Shengjing. But she continued to try, every chance she got, each time the two of them were alone, particularly at night as they huddled together under their filthy covers.

Oh, Zhu Yesu, Zhen-Li prayed, as once again the daylight hours passed in solitude, *please make my words effective in touching Mei's heart. Show her Your great love, my Father. Help her to see her need of You. Use me, Yesu.*

And then she heard the familiar step behind her, the hideous sound of Tong's boots as he arrived at her cell door. Without turning to look, Zhen-Li knew her time had come, and with no hope of her own, she placed herself in the nail-scarred hands of her Savior.

Tai Tong was a miserable man, a
man without hope or peace.

Chapter 14

WHY NOW? ZHEN-LI WONDERED. *WHY, WHEN I AM ON MY WAY TO what will no doubt be a violent end to my life here on earth, would I think of my baby—the one they stole from me?*

And then it came to her, even as she trudged with legs of lead after her tormentor, who apparently delighted in what lay ahead. The only joy this poor man had was in stealing it from others, while she had the joy of the Lord continually strengthening and protecting her. Why hadn't she realized that before? Tai Tong was a miserable man, a man without hope or peace, a wretched man whose only future was eternal separation from God. Zhen-Li, on the other hand, though she might suffer temporarily in this world, knew exactly where she would be the moment she breathed her last. That thought put everything else in perspective, even answering her question about why she would now think of the baby she had lost.

He waits for me there, she realized. Her tiny son, who never saw the light of day in this life, instead basked in the light of the Father, free of all pain and sorrow and fear. *And now I shall join him! In a few hours—possibly even a few moments—I will step away from this place of torment and stand in the presence of Zhu Yesu! No more tears, no more fear or sadness.*

But tempering the anticipation was the thought that she would not see her beloved Chi or Chan until they joined her around the heavenly throne. *Will they suffer before they come?* she wondered. *Will they, too, be arrested and tortured for their faith?* The thought squeezed her heart, and yet she knew she would choose that for them over a life of ease that had no room for Zhu Yesu Jidu.

Oh, cover and protect them, Qin Ai de Tian Fu! Keep my family safe—my husband and child, and yes, my parents too. Please bring them to You while there is time.

And then they stood at the door. Tong, key in hand, turned to look down at her, his dark eyes gleaming. "Today you will choose," he said. "Will you cooperate, or must I force you to do my bidding? Either way, you are mine."

The fear of his words had scarcely penetrated her heart when they were displaced by what felt like a soothing flow of sweetness, which reminded Zhen-Li of the few times she had tasted honey, many years ago when she still lived at home with her parents. And suddenly Tong's words and his menacing looks didn't seem to matter as much. Keeping her eyes locked on his, she smiled. "I am not yours," she said. "I belong to Zhu Yesu."

Almost immediately his look turned from triumph to fury. Grabbing her arm, he threw her into the room, where she stumbled and landed facedown on the cement floor. Before she could attempt to rise, he was standing over her, kicking her in the ribs and shouting.

"Get up," he demanded. "Get up and stand before me, you ungrateful coward! How dare you defy me, after all I have done to help you? I will show you whose you are, and when I am through, you will beg to belong to me!"

Slowly, coughing and trying not to retch, Zhen-Li gathered her arms and legs beneath her and pushed herself to a standing position, though she swayed with the effort. The angry, reddened face of her captor swam before her eyes, as he continued to scream at her with a vehemence she could scarcely fathom.

She knew she had angered him, but his reaction was beyond anything she would have expected.

"What have you to say for yourself?" Tong demanded, his face just inches from hers now. "Explain yourself. Offer a defense, if you have one."

Zhen-Li blinked away tears, praying silently for wisdom as she opened her mouth to speak. "I...have none," she said. "Even as my Savior offered no defense to His tormentors, so I offer none. I trust only in His care for me."

Tong's eyes opened wide, and he lunged backward, as if someone had slapped him. Then a laugh erupted from his lips, launching spittle onto Zhen-Li's face.

"His care for you?" The sneer on Tong's face bothered Zhen-Li more than the slime that dripped down her cheek. "Even now, do you still believe this foreign shen cares for you?" He laughed again. "Before this day is over, we shall see just how much He cares. And when we are through and what is left of you is dragged back to your cell this night, you will know what I already know at this moment—that if such a God even exists, He does not care for the likes of you one bit. Not one bit!" He leaned close, and Zhen-Li could feel the heat of his foul breath. "Perhaps He will even laugh at your torment. We will listen and see if we can hear Him cheering me on!"

Despite the assurance of God's presence that she had felt just moments earlier, Zhen-Li thought she would faint from fear. There was scarcely enough strength in her legs to keep her from falling to the floor then and there, but she cried aloud, "Strength, Zhu Yesu! Give me Your strength!"

And even as Tong's laughter intensified, she felt an invisible arm slip around her waist, and she leaned into it with joy.

✷✷✷

Julia awoke with a start, her eyes wide open and staring into the dark. What was it? What had awakened her from so sound a sleep? Had she heard a noise? Had someone called her name?

Straining, she listened, knowing her hearing wasn't what it used to be but that it was still good enough for her to get by without hearing aids. But as hard as she tried, she heard nothing but the usual River View Manor sounds—an occasional snort or mumble from a nearby room, a distant dog barking at an imagined intruder, an occasional car passing by. Nothing out of the ordinary.

Was it You, Lord? Her thoughts turned immediately to the need for prayer. *Is someone in trouble? Is it Margaret's granddaughter, Maggie?*

No response. She waited some more.

China. Of course! The one in China whom Julia had sensed needed prayer for some time now, the one Julia had come to believe was a young woman in some sort of serious trouble. *Is that it, Lord? Do You want me to pray for her?*

The assurance was so clear that Julia's questioning died away immediately. She wished she knew more details about the woman's situation, but it didn't really matter, did it? After all, God knew. He knew every detail, and He had called Julia to intervene. With a heart crying out for mercy and protection, Julia responded, knowing it would be a long and sleepless night, but knowing, too, that someone on the other side of the world was struggling through the daylight hours and desperately needed her prayer support.

✶✶✶

Zhou Chi labored in the fields as he did nearly every day of his life. The weather wasn't unusual for late spring, and nothing different or alarming had happened before he left home that morning. And yet he sensed danger. For himself? He couldn't be sure, though he suspected it was more for Zhen-Li—and that was worse.

Why her, Yesu? Why not me? Why must she suffer so? She is so much more faithful than I, even though I have known You since I was a child. I wish I were as strong as she, but You know I am not. Still, I would gladly take her place—

I already took her place. The words pierced his heart like fire, nearly doubling him over with the pain. Chi knew where the words had come from, and he knew what they meant. But he hadn't expected to hear them so clearly, despite the fact that they had seemed to float to him on the wind.

And yet there was no wind that day.

"Zhu Yesu," Chi whispered, gasping for air and unable to say anything more. "Zhu Yesu!"

When at last his breathing returned to normal, Chi continued his work, though he stopped on occasion to wipe the stream of tears that trickled from his eyes. *Protect her*, he pleaded silently, over and over again. *Protect my beloved Zhen-Li!* For no longer did he doubt that his sense of danger and need to pray were centered on his wife. Yang Zhen-Li was in trouble, he was sure of it. And there was nothing he could do but pray. In fact, it was the only thing God would allow him to do.

And so he prayed, with an intensity that built within him as he continued to work at his mindless task.

***

How much time had passed since Tong had brought her here? Zhen-Li could no longer be sure, as she drifted in and out of consciousness, the pain not allowing her to slip away for long. But at least he hadn't yet humiliated or disgraced her, though he continued to taunt her with threats and promises of what was to come before the day was over.

Every muscle in her body screamed with protest each time he yanked her from one spot to another, which he seemed to take delight in doing. One moment he wanted her to stand before him, the next to kneel at his feet. When she whispered that she could kneel only at the feet of Zhu Yesu, he forced her to her knees, holding her there by sheer force until she wept with shame.

She knew he delighted in her fear and suffering, but mostly in her shame, her xiu chi, which was undoubtedly why he was prolonging the worst for last. Once he had finally used her, would he then kill her and put her out of her misery, sending her on to her heavenly home, where she so longed to be? She hoped so—and she hoped it wouldn't be much longer.

Just get it over with, she begged silently, wishing the evil man would stop threatening and just finish her once and for all. Her life was worthless here anyway. Once he had used her, how could she ever return to her beloved Chi, even if she lived long enough to do so? No, death would be preferable, though she dared not voice that thought for fear Tong would only prolong her waiting.

Then, suddenly, he pulled her to her feet and lifted her into his arms, carrying her to the couch. She shut her eyes tightly, knowing what was coming and willing it to end quickly. But the man who delighted in hurting her now laid her gently on the cushions and sat down on the edge of the sofa beside her, stroking her hair back from her face and whispering her name.

"You are even lovelier when you weep with pain, dear Zhen-Li," he whispered, the lust in his voice drowning out what she imagined he meant to sound like concern. "So much lovelier than your friend Mei—and stronger too. She was much too easy, scarcely a challenge. Her terror was so great that she didn't resist me even for a moment."

He leaned down and breathed against her neck as he spoke into her ear. "You are just the challenge I've been looking for, a woman with enough mixture of fight and fear to make the victory so much sweeter. And when I have taken you, I will not miss Mei at all. I want no more of that worthless coward. I want you, Zhen-Li. You will belong to me and no one else. You won't even have to worry anymore when you speak to Mei of your foreign shen, for she will no longer report to me of your activities. I will beat that confession from you myself, and then heal your wounds with our physical union."

Zhen-Li felt her eyes open wide, despite her resolve to keep them closed. *Mei, reporting to Tong?* Oh, what a fool she had been to trust her cell mate, even after learning what the young woman did in an effort to survive! Mei was a traitor, a spy, and Zhen-Li had played right into her hands.

Tong had lifted his head and was looking down at her now, a sneer of contempt on his lips. "You did not know about your friend, that she was the one reporting to me of your illegal conversations?" He shook his head. "Ah, my poor little Zhen-Li. How easy you are to fool! If your shen cares so much for you, why didn't He warn you?" Tong's eyebrows raised questioningly. "Is it because He does not exist and therefore cannot speak to you?" He leaned closer, their noses nearly touching. "Or is it that He doesn't care enough to bother? Which is it, dear Zhen-Li?"

When she didn't answer, he grabbed her shoulders and shook her, pressing her into the couch and intensifying her pain. "Which is it, Zhen-Li? Does He not exist, or does He just not care?"

She opened her mouth to answer but could think of nothing to say, as he rose from the couch and began to unbutton his shirt. "Enough of this foolish talking and waiting," he smirked. "I have worked hard for my reward, and I am not going to put it off a moment longer."

Zhen-Li heard herself gasp, and she fought to breathe deeply and evenly, though she wondered if it would be better if she allowed herself to lose consciousness. How much better to awaken when it was over—either here or in heaven—than to be aware of the entire ugly process of her final degradation.

Once again she closed her eyes, blocking out the sight of the now-shirtless man who had begun to loosen his pants. She steeled herself for what she was sure would be the ripping off of the rags that served as her clothes...but even as she felt his hands grasping at her shirt, an explosion rocked the room, knocking her to the floor and rolling her over until Tong was back on top of her. The rattling and swaying continued, as the floor rolled beneath them and walls and ceilings creaked and swayed. Another jolt knocked Tong off her just as a huge slab of the ceiling fell from above and landed directly upon him. She heard him cry out, and she instinctively curled up into a ball, head down and covered by her arms until the movement stopped. When she finally dared to lift her head and peek out from her self-styled covering, she saw Tong lying beside her, eyes open, blood covering his face, one hand reaching toward her, his fingers just inches from her leg.

Terrified, she shrunk back, not believing that the man could be dead and no longer a threat to her. But even if he were, what was she to do about it? For though she had come to realize that they'd been hit by a terrible earthquake, she had no idea what she should do next. Was it possible she could escape? If so, she would have to hurry. But would her legs carry her to safety, even if the prison walls themselves had been knocked down and all the guards killed?

Before she could estimate her chances or gather her wits enough to come up with a rudimentary plan, she felt a hand on her leg, squeezing, clutching, even as a tortured voice cried out, "Help me! Do not leave me here to die. Help me, Zhen-Li..."

Swallowing her scream, Zhen-Li stared down at the man who had caused her so much pain and had been at the point of raping and possibly even killing her, who now looked up at her with pain-filled eyes, begging her to help him.

No, she thought. *No, Zhu Yesu, this is too much to ask! If I go now, I might have a chance to escape. But if I stay, if I try to help this man — this horrible man who has tormented me so — I will have no chance at all!*

And then she heard it: *Do it for Me.*

The voice echoed in her heart, as the tears burst from her eyes. "No," she cried. "No, Tian Fu, please do not ask me to do this!"

But the echo continued: *Do it for Me.*

God knew, and that was enough, wasn't it?

Chapter 15

J ULIA'S EYES SEEMED TO HAVE A MIND OF THEIR OWN. THEY SIMPLY would not stay open. She sat alone in a rocker on the front porch, her head leaning back against the chair. Laura hadn't felt well again and had eaten breakfast in her room, and each of the other residents seemed preoccupied with their morning routines, so Julia had the porch to herself, though the dampness of the morning fog was quickly robbing her of the joy of solitude.

It had been a long and nearly sleepless night, as she lay awake interceding for the person in China whom she'd firmly come to believe was a young woman in great danger. If only Julia knew her name! But then, God knew, and that was enough, wasn't it? He also knew the circumstances and cared so deeply for the Chinese woman that He had called an old prayer warrior from the other side of the world to pray for her. God's faithfulness and mercy never ceased to amaze the elderly saint.

Now, however, having nearly slept through breakfast, Julia wondered if she'd be able to hold up until after lunch before giving in to her need for a nap. She had just about decided to yield to the wooing and warmth of her bed when she heard the unmistakable sound of a walker rolling out onto the porch.

Julia looked up, apparently having become aware of the resident's arrival at the precise moment Margaret realized she wasn't going to have the porch to herself. Margaret Snowden, her long salt-and-pepper hair perched on top of her head as usual but slightly askew, stood leaning on her walker, staring down at Julia with glasses that couldn't hide her surprise, and lines in her face that appeared to have deepened in the last few days.

For a moment, neither of them spoke. Then, when it seemed Margaret was about to turn and go back into the house, Julia said, "Good morning, Margaret. Please, come and join me, will you? It's much too lonely out here by myself."

Even as the words came out, Julia wondered why she spoke them. The last thing in the world she felt like doing that particular morning (or most any morning, for that matter) was trying to have a conversation with a woman who obviously did not like her or want anything to do with her. So what was the point?

But it was too late. To her astonishment, Margaret maneuvered her walker in front of the companion rocker next to Julia's and plunked herself down.

"Don't really feel much like talking," she announced before she'd quite settled in, "but at least there's only one of you out here. That's better than that whole gaggle of silly geese in there, I suppose."

Julia felt her eyebrows shoot up. No one would ever accuse Margaret Snowden of being a diplomat, that was for sure! Julia harrumphed silently to herself and wondered why Margaret didn't just go to her room if she disliked other people so much, but then she reminded herself that she could go to her room too—which she just might if their conversation continued along such an antisocial line.

And then she sensed God's nudging to make another effort. She sighed. *All right, Lord. One more time...*

"So," Julia said, forcing a note of cheerfulness into her voice, "how is your granddaughter doing? Maggie, is it? She must be named after you."

Margaret, who had been staring straight ahead, turned toward Julia, a frown creasing her forehead. "Yes, I suppose she is—though it wasn't my idea. And she's certainly nothing like me. Why do you ask?"

Why do I ask, indeed? I knew I should have just kept my mouth shut and gone to my room, Julia fumed to herself. But at God's silent reminder, she smiled. "I have grandchildren too. Seven of them. They're all so different...and so special. Don't you agree?"

Margaret blinked before answering. "Not really," she said, her tone cool and firm. "They're all nearly the same, so far as I'm concerned. Like their parents—ungrateful, money-grubbing brats. It wouldn't bother me one bit if none of them ever came to see me again."

Julia couldn't restrain the gasp that she was sure Margaret heard. But no matter. Why shouldn't the crabby old woman hear Julia's shock? What sort of person spoke that way about her own family?

"Excuse me," Julia said, as soon as she was able to get the words out. "It's getting a bit chilly out here. I believe I'll go to my room for a while."

Tong's body ached from head to toe, but particularly his head and chest, where he had taken the brunt of the hit. Overall, however, he knew he had escaped death by a thread—and that thread's name was Zhen-Li.

Why hadn't she just left him there—run while she had a chance and possibly escaped? Some of the other prisoners had, and though most had been caught, a few had gotten away.

Now, as Tong rested in his hospital bed, he thought of the two guards who hadn't been as fortunate as he. They were dead now—gone. Crushed under rubble and awaiting cremation, while he needed only a little time to heal before returning to his duties at the prison. Would Zhen-Li be pleased to see him? He doubted it. He doubted, too, that she realized how her foolishness in calling for help rather than trying to escape had just doubled his determination to humiliate and break her. Weakness was something for which he had no tolerance, and her choice to help the one who tormented and persecuted her could be interpreted as nothing but weakness of the worst kind.

Yes, it would be a while until his strength was sufficient to pick up where he had left off in his conquering of the foolish young woman named Zhen-Li, but as soon as he was able, he would return to work and let her know of his intentions. That would give her something to think about, as she lay in her dark cell at night, cursing herself for not trying to escape while she had the chance.

Would these Christians never learn? He shook his head slightly, though the effort fired a sharp pain down his spine. He nearly growled in reaction. *They will if I have anything to say about it,* he promised himself.

Zhen-Li and Mei had been moved to another cell, as theirs had been nearly destroyed in the quake. Beyond a few bruises and cuts, neither had been injured seriously. Though Zhen-Li still second-guessed herself about whether or not she'd done the right thing in calling for help for Tai Tong instead of trying to escape, deep down she knew she'd been obedient to God's voice. And that, after all, was the only thing that mattered.

What mattered to her now, however—and surprised her as well—was the fact that she was pleased to find that she and Mei were still together. A part of Zhen-Li felt betrayed by the frail young woman whose almond eyes seemed far too large for her face, yet she also found comfort in Mei's familiar presence.

Should she tell Mei what she knew, what Tong had told her about her cell mate's spying activities, not to mention the other activities she had become involved in to try to stay alive? She was sorely tempted. After all, hadn't Zhen-Li also been offered the same opportunities for somewhat better treatment if she had been willing to compromise her own faith and honor? And hadn't she resisted, choosing to suffer the consequences rather than yield to her captor's advances?

Zhen-Li was nearly at the point of opening her mouth and unleashing her accusations against the traitorous and cowardly Mei when the fragile girl fixed her eyes on Zhen-Li in silent pleading, and Zhen-Li felt the hardness in her heart melt away.

Mei already knew. Whether Tai Tong had informed her that he had told Zhen-Li about her cell mate's betrayal, or whether she simply sensed it, the young woman knew. What she did not need was a tongue-lashing from Zhen-Li. In fact, Zhen-Li realized, if ever the guilt-ridden woman needed to hear of the unconditional and unfailing love and mercy of Zhu Yesu Jidu, it was now, when her condemnation seemed ready to overwhelm her.

Without another moment's hesitancy, Zhen-Li scooted across the few feet of cement that separated the two women and took Mei in her arms. Then, as warm tears flowed from Mei's eyes onto Zhen-Li's shoulder, Zhen-Li sang to her the first song that came to her mind, one she had learned only a few years earlier and had sung to her precious Zhou Chan many times — a story about one silent, holy night, when the baby Yesu was born in a faraway town called Bethlehem. Though the Christian holiday known as Christmas was many months away, it somehow seemed the appropriate focus that lonely evening as they huddled together in their barren prison cell.

Ping' an ye, sheng shan ye . . .

The night was indeed silent, but for an occasional groan or moan from a distant cell. Now that Zhen-Li had begun to sing, she sensed the presence of Zhu Yesu, and she knew the night was holy as well.

Mei couldn't decide if she loved
Zhen-Li or hated her.

Chapter 16

DESPISING HERSELF FOR HER TEARS, MEI STRUGGLED WITH THE war of emotions that battled within as she listened to the words of the vaguely familiar Christmas song. How many years had she consciously suppressed the memories of her parents and their Christian faith, only to have them dug up by her soft-spoken, hymn-singing cell mate? Mei couldn't decide if she loved Zhen-Li or hated her.

One thing was certain: She did not understand her. Mei had been alone with one of the guards, locked away in a room with him as she so often was during the day, when the earthquake hit. The room they occupied hadn't been severely damaged, and Mei had immediately been confined to the nearest available cell while the guard who had been her companion for a few hours rushed to join the others in assessing the damage and trying to prevent any prisoners from escaping. Mei had experienced no such opportunity, though she told herself she would have taken it if she had. Zhen-Li, on the other hand, had since told Mei of her own situation at the time the quake hit, and it seemed to Mei that her cell mate could at least have made an effort to run. Instead she had called for help and stayed with her tormentor until that help arrived. What a fool the woman must be! Mei had suspected as much, but Zhen-Li's most recent behavior confirmed Mei's suspicions.

And now the woman was singing about Zhu Yesu when He came as a baby. Did she never tire of talking and singing about this One long dead, the One whom Zhen-Li and others like her claimed was the Son of God and had risen from the grave?

It was so much nonsense, Mei was certain of it. And yet, the passion and commitment with which these Christian believers held to their devotion to their Savior and allegiance to their faith was more than slightly disconcerting.

If only she would stop singing that song about that silent, holy night so long ago! Mei could scarcely block out the memories of her mother, singing that very same song to her when she was just a little child.

Zhou Chi was nearly frantic. Though their own fragile shack had withstood the shaking, rumors were beginning to reach his ears that the situation in and around much of Beijing was worse. A traveler passing by Chi's place of employment had even now stopped under the midmorning sun to talk with the owner. Chi was working in the fields nearby and was able to overhear most of the conversation, as the man reported that many buildings had been destroyed and lives lost. The death toll was bound to climb as more bodies were dug out of the rubble, he said.

Chi's heart nearly failed him as he listened, forcing himself to continue working and to restrain himself from crying out to ask about the condition of the prisons in the area. Had they been destroyed? Were many prisoners lost? Had any managed to escape in the chaos that must have followed?

But he knew he dare not say a word. Though everything in him cried out to throw down his hoe, jump on his bike, and pedal toward Beijing as fast as he could, he knew he had to continue working so he would have enough money to feed Zhou Chan and Zhou Ming at the end of the day. Besides, even if he left everything behind to go to Beijing and search for Yang Zhen-Li, where would he start? He had never been to the prison to visit her; he knew the name of the facility only because Zhen-Li's mother had shown him that one small kindness in writing him a letter soon after the arrest and letting Chi know where his wife was being held. But Beijing was huge, and the prison could be anywhere—no doubt somewhere just outside the city. If it took Chi too long to locate it, his boss might not hold his job for him, and then what would he do? And even if he found the prison, then what? He would no doubt be denied access to his wife, and the trip would be for naught.

Oh, Zhu Yesu, why? Why must my wife be kept in that awful place, away from me, from her family? We need her here with us! Chi's tears dripped down his face as he worked, his head bowed under the silent heavens. *Can You not at least send us word that she is all right? Please, Father...*

A puff of breeze brushed his cheek. Chi lifted his head, nearly certain he would see someone standing beside him. There was no one, only the owner and the traveler, standing together on the edge of the field, continuing their discussion of the earthquake. But in that moment Chi knew he was not alone. The puff of air had seemed to him a kiss of hope from One whose care for His children stretched beyond time or place.

Using his sleeve to wipe the tears from his face, Chi felt himself smile for the first time in what seemed months, or even years. Zhu Yesu had given him a promise, and Chi would wait for the fulfillment. Somehow, some way, Chi would soon receive word about his beloved Zhen-Li. Until then, he would work hard and wait patiently, for surely the news would be good.

The first word of an earthquake in China reached Julia's ears as she sat in the family room with Laura and two of the other residents, watching a game show while they waited for dinner to be served. When the game show was interrupted by a news update on the quake, she wondered why she hadn't paid more attention and caught this when it first happened. Nearly twenty-four hours had passed now, and she should have been praying—for the entire country, but also for the area outside Beijing that was so dear to her. And, of course, she should be praying for the young woman God had recently laid on her heart. Was she all right? Was the earthquake the reason God had called Julia to pray for this particular woman? Somehow Julia didn't think so, though she imagined that might be part of it. Still, she was sure there was more...much more.

Julia glanced at Laura and found that her friend was watching her. The moment their eyes met, Laura's brows rose questioningly, and Julia knew what she was asking.

Yes, she answered silently with a nod. *Let's go off by ourselves and pray.*

Without another word, the two friends gathered themselves together and left the other residents behind, as they made their way down the hall toward Julia's room for a time of prayer and intercession. Living in California, both women were well aware of the dangers of earthquakes, but they also knew that God was greater than anything the world might throw at them— earthquakes included. So they would take the people of China to the Lord in prayer and ask for mercy and protection. They would also ask that God would use this natural disaster to turn many hearts to Him.

✯✯✯

Leo swallowed a smirk. The girl with the tattoos and multi-colored hair was back. Of course, that could describe a lot of his customers, but this one was especially pathetic. She always came in reeking of alcohol and marijuana, and insisting she was over eighteen—sometimes she even said twenty-one—though Leo knew she wasn't even close. Still, business was business, and if the girl had something worth selling, he was ready to buy—at an undercut price, of course—regardless of her age.

Her eyes were glazed, and it seemed she was having problems focusing as she looked at him. Enjoying her discomfort, he waited, making no move to ease her obvious confusion. Finally she took a deep breath and opened her mouth to speak, though she still appeared to be having trouble formulating the words.

"I...have something to sell," she said, her eyes drifting only slightly in the process. Then she frowned, as if trying to remember something. At last Leo saw a glint of clarity light her face as she reached into her ragged purse and pulled out an elaborate pocketknife with a carved ivory handle. Looking down at it as it rested in the palm of her hand, she hesitated only briefly before laying it on the counter between them.

"It's worth a lot of money," she said, still staring at her offering.

Leo could no longer restrain his smirk, though the girl's eyes were still downcast so she didn't see it. "Looks like any old pocketknife to me," he said. "What's so special about it?"

The girl jerked her head up, surprise registering on her face. "It's got an ivory handle. Hand carved."

Leo shrugged. "Big deal. I've seen hundreds just like it. What do I need with another one?"

Her expression turned from surprised to panic at that point, and Leo wondered if she might cry.

"I...need the money," she said. "Please..."

Leo nearly laughed, but he pressed his lips together and held the knife up to examine it before answering. "Twenty bucks," he said. "That's the best I can do."

Her eyes went wide, and her mouth opened in silent protest. She swallowed then and said, "But it's worth so much more."

Leo shrugged again. "To you maybe. Not to me. Twenty bucks. Take it or leave it."

The wrestling that went on behind her tortured eyes was brief. Finally she sighed. "Fine. Twenty bucks. I'll take it."

Leo reached in the cash drawer and pulled out the required payment, transferring it to her shaking hand. "Don't spend it all in one place," he cautioned. But his sarcasm was wasted on the girl who had already stuffed the twenty in her pocket and was heading for the door.

Pitiful, Leo thought, shaking his head. *She was probably a pretty little girl once. But now? Where in the world are her parents anyway? You'd think somebody would be watching out for her.* He shook his head again and shoved the cash drawer closed, then held the knife up to the light and smiled as he examined it more carefully.

Just as well that they're not, he thought. *Someone's going to love this—and they aren't going to get it cheap.* He looked up at the door where his customer had disappeared back into the street. *Too bad about the girl, though.*

The thought that they had been young and maybe even beautiful once caused her to frown.

Chapter 17

MAGGIE TOLD HERSELF SHE'D BEEN IN WORSE PLACES BEFORE. After all, she had twenty dollars in her pocket—better than nothing. But how long would it last?

She shook her head as she continued down the sidewalk, away from the pawnshop. *No. Can't think about that. Gotta stay focused. Buy the stuff from Jake and crash at his place till it wears off. Besides, I love going there. Lately he's been really glad to see me. And just yesterday he kissed me and told me I was beautiful.*

A picture of her grandmother and the old woman with the cane flashed through her mind, nearly stopping her in her tracks. The thought that they had been young and maybe even beautiful once caused her to frown, though she blamed it on the bright noonday sun. What had she done with those supercool shades her parents had given her for her birthday? Those sunglasses were one of the few decent presents they'd given her lately and she really needed them, but she had no idea where she'd left them.

She shrugged. What difference did it make? If she whined enough about losing them, they'd break down and get her another pair. That's just the way they were—easy to read, even easier to manipulate. And Maggie had learned how to do that at a very early age.

As she turned the corner she felt a smile tug at her lips. Jake's house was in sight, the place where she was able to have her need for drugs and maybe even love met at the same time. Things were looking up. Despite the vague loneliness that seemed to follow her everywhere she went lately, she sensed this was going to be a good day after all.

✯✯✯

Julia dozed in the rocker on the porch, the warm afternoon sun wooing her to drift away. But an even stronger force seemed to pull her back each time she nearly slipped from consciousness.

"What is it, Lord?" she whispered. "Is it the lady in China again? Do I need to pray for her?"

The only sound she heard was the distant cawing of a crow, drifting lazily on an updraft just above the treetops.

Julia waited. If she had learned anything in her many years on this earth, it was to wait on God. He would speak in His time, if she would just be patient and listen.

Voices drifted out to her through the screen door, and she recognized them as belonging to Margaret Snowden and Emily Johnson. Though Julia couldn't understand every word, she heard enough in their tone and the few words she was able to catch to know that they were once again arguing about Margaret's granddaughter Maggie and Emily's stolen jewelry. It seemed Margaret and Emily couldn't be in the same room without exchanging bitter and accusatory words on the subject, and today was obviously no exception.

Maggie.

The girl's name seemed to float on the same updraft as the ebony bird whose feathers shone in the afternoon sunlight.

That's it, isn't it, Lord? Julia thought. *I'm to pray for Margaret's granddaughter.*

The crow cawed again, and Julia had her answer.

Yin Xei was awake once again, lying in the same bed and staring at the same ceiling, even as she listened to her husband's usual snoring.

Does nothing ever change? From first breath to last, is there any hope, any reason to continue living? Xei's breathing hiccupped with a suppressed sob, as she refused to give in to the grief that seemed to increase in intensity, even as it threatened to envelop her with no chance of escape.

Memories of her beloved Zhen-Li tortured her, and yet she couldn't dismiss them. They were all she had left of the years they shared together, when Zhen-Li had been such a joy to her parents, growing up healthy and strong, bright and promising—only to trade it all for marriage to a Christian peasant. Though Xei tried to hold out hope that her daughter would see the error of her ways and not only recant her faith but reestablish her loyalty to the government of China so that she could be released from prison, the brokenhearted mother doubted it would ever happen. She knew Zhen-Li too well. The girl was stubborn and strong-willed, admirable traits if properly directed. But Xei knew it was unlikely the wife and mother would turn her back on her family, which meant Xei might very well never see her again.

And the child, Zhou Chan? He was four years old now, and yet Yin Xei had never held him on her lap, kissed the softness of his head, or even seen his face. Should any grandmother have to endure such shame and sorrow? With each passing day, Yin Xei wondered how much longer she could bear the pain.

And through it all, Yang Hong continued to sleep. How was it possible to remain so detached—and so hardened to his wife's pleas to relent concerning their grandson?

Zhen-Li had heard rumors among the prisoners that Tai Tong would soon recover and return to work. What did that mean to her? She tried not to think of it in those terms, to limit herself to praying for his healing and, of course, that his heart would be softened toward Zhu Yesu. But she was not so foolish as to think there would be no repercussions. Though she dared to hope that Tong might be grateful for her help, the memory of the evil glinting from his dark eyes and the joy he so obviously experienced from inflicting pain on others continued to stir up the fear that seemed to have taken up permanent residence in the pit of her stomach.

Today, however, she and even Mei had been rousted early to work with the other prisoners in clearing away the rubble in an attempt to restore order to the prison. Though the work was strenuous and difficult, Zhen-Li much preferred it to what she anticipated lay in store for her when Tong returned.

Glancing at Mei, who worked beside her, she wondered if the guilt-ridden woman felt the same. Zhen-Li was convinced that Mei was tortured by guilt, though it appeared she had willingly agreed to serve as a "companion" to the guards in order to ease the otherwise harsh living conditions inherent in prison life. Did Mei regret the decision, wishing she could go back to the physical labor the other prisoners endured, rather than compromising and demeaning herself as she had done daily for so long now?

But of course it was too late to change her mind. It wasn't even an option. Had it been at one time? Could Mei have refused to cooperate in her final yet ongoing demoralization and degradation? And if she had, would she still be alive today?

Zhen-Li imagined she would not. And if that was true for Mei, then it was true for her as well. Her own life-and-death choice had not been overridden by the earthquake, only postponed. The realization brought tears to Zhen-Li's eyes, even as she struggled to continue lifting the heavy stones and pieces of concrete from the floor and carry them to the waiting wheelbarrows as they'd been instructed. Though death didn't frighten her, the thought of not seeing Zhou Chi or Zhou Chan again on this earth was nearly too painful to contemplate. And yet, what else could she do? If Tai Tong returned and put her back in the situation she'd been in just before the earthquake hit, she would gladly choose death over the shame of what the guard required of her.

If only she could be certain he would kill her quickly—before she lost her dignity, or her nerve.

Tai Tong wanted nothing more than to get out of his hospital bed and return to work, but he knew he first had to regain his strength. It was bad enough that the woman named Zhen-Li, who dared to defy him and even spit in the face of his kindness, had seen him in his weakness, but now she no doubt assumed he owed her for saving his life.

Nearly growling with contempt, he shut his eyes and focused on the helpless, terrified expression on her face as she lay on the couch, completely at his mercy. He had been ready to claim her once and for all, to show her that he, not her imaginary foreign God, was in charge of her life—and then the earthquake had come and changed everything. Cursing fate, he allowed himself to escape in his mind to the time in the very near future when he would return to the prison and once again single out Zhen-Li for his own pleasure and amusement.

But it was so much more than that, he reminded himself. How dare she think that she could stand up to his strength and power? He had attempted to break her down with favors and special treatment, but she had shown him that would not work. Therefore there would be no more favor for her when he got her alone again. He would use her, roughly and painfully, and when he was through, he would crush her until she was unrecognizable—until even the memory of her face disappeared from his sight.

Strange sensations indeed, but worth every penny of her twenty dollars.

Chapter 18

MAGGIE SAT ON THE FLOOR, HER BACK AGAINST THE WALL, AS THE room seemed to take on a personality of its own. She liked this feeling of being detached, the sense of power that surged through her, whispering to her heart that she could do anything, though in reality she often questioned her ability to carry out the simplest of tasks. Strange sensations indeed, but worth every penny of her twenty dollars. And if her dad missed his ivory-handled knife and accused her of taking it, she'd look him in the eye and deny it with such vehemence and indignation that he would finally believe her...or at least give up trying to coax the truth from her.

She smiled. She had her parents right where she wanted them, and it had all been so easy. And though she occasionally missed the closeness they once shared, it wasn't enough to call her back from this exciting new life she had discovered.

Jake appeared in the doorway that led to the kitchen, and Maggie felt her stomach churn with excitement, for wasn't he the one who had introduced her to her new life? That someone so handsome and mature was attracted to her was more than she could ever have imagined. But it was true. He had told her so just a few moments ago, and didn't he always give her huge discounts on her drugs? Sometimes he even gave them to her for free. Why would he do that if he wasn't serious about her?

The tall, slim blond smiled down at her, his piercing blue eyes and disheveled hair adding fuel to the fire that already smoldered in Maggie's gut. Immediately she returned his smile, confident he would accept the silent invitation without hesitation.

The shirtless man in ragged jeans, nearly twice Maggie's age, quickly took her up on her offer and crossed the room to drop down beside her on the floor. Pulling her toward himself, he cradled her head against his bare chest where she could hear his heart pounding out his passion. "Have I told you how beautiful you are?" he whispered, nuzzling her hair as he spoke.

"Not today," she answered, her heart rate now surpassing his.

He placed his hand beneath her chin and tipped her head upward until their eyes met. Maggie's thoughts swirled with the emotions she saw reflected in his gaze, and she wondered if it was possible to love someone any more than she loved Jake at that very moment.

"You're beautiful," he said, his voice husky. "You're beautiful today, and tomorrow, and every day." He bent his head and kissed her, gently and slowly, then pulled back. "You know you belong to me, don't you?"

Maggie's heart felt as if it would leap from her chest. "Yes," she said, nodding at the joy she sensed in the thought of belonging to someone. "I do. I know that. And I'm glad."

Smiling down at her, Jake leaned her back until she was lying on the floor, staring up at him. "Don't ever forget it," he said, as he kissed her between words. "That means...you do whatever...I tell you...no questions asked."

"Yes," she answered, scarcely able to speak as she pulled him tighter against herself. "Oh, yes, anything! So long as I know I belong to you, that's all that matters."

In the heat that followed, she did whatever she could to seal that truth between them.

***

For nearly two days now, Julia had been unable to shake the image of young Maggie from her mind. It seemed God was calling her to pray for the girl even more often and more urgently than for the woman in China. Julia had enlisted Laura's help, and the two of them prayed together as well as separately for both Maggie and the nameless one on another continent. They even asked their believing relatives to join them in intercession for the two, which they seldom did unless they felt the prayer needs were serious. Quite obviously they were in both cases, or God wouldn't continue to stir up the two senior saints with such an ongoing urgency to intercede.

"We know what Maggie looks like," Laura said that afternoon as they sat in Julia's room, having just finished a time of prayer. "But have you ever wondered about the woman in China? Especially now that we're so sure it is indeed a specific woman we're praying for over there?"

Julia nodded. "I have. Many times. I wonder what her life is like—her family, her living conditions. I wonder, too, if she lives anywhere near or has any connection to the area and people that Joe and I visited on our trip there so many years ago. Above all, I wonder what she might be enduring that warrants such a continual call to prayer." She sighed. "But we have no way of knowing, do we?"

Laura shook her head. "I suppose not. But I like to think she's a young wife and mother, much like you and I used to be in the not-so-distant past. Thinking of her that way makes it easier for me to personalize my prayers, to imagine what must be on her heart, even if I don't know her situation or circumstances. I don't imagine I can even begin to picture what her life must be like or what she goes through, but I can certainly imagine how a wife and mother would feel about her family."

Julia smiled. "What a lovely way to put it! You are absolutely right, my dear friend. Whatever else we don't know about her—which is most everything—we know that if she has a family, she loves them and is deeply concerned for their welfare."

"Exactly. I consider how I would have wanted someone to pray for me when I was raising my family, and that helps me know how to pray for the woman in China. We may be separated by cultures and oceans and even generations, but we are connected in our common desires and longings."

Julia, who sat next to Laura on the edge of the bed, laid her hand on her friend's knee. "Yes. We do have certain things in common with others, even though our lives are so vastly different. And somehow I sense she's a Christian, don't you?"

Laura nodded. "I'm certain of it. I don't know why, but I am. That's why I pray for her to stand strong in her faith... because I'm sure she has it."

"It's an amazing thing, isn't it?" Julia asked. "That God can knit us together in the same family with people thousands of miles away, people we will probably never meet this side of heaven."

"It certainly is," Laura agreed. "And oh, what a wonderful Father we all have!" She hesitated before continuing. "Maggie, on the other hand..."

Julia nodded again, as Laura's voice faded. "Yes. Maggie, on the other hand, is most certainly not a believer. Nor is her grandmother. I don't know about any of the rest of her family, but I think we would be wise to pray for all of them."

Laura turned toward Julia and raised her eyebrows. "Then I suppose we'd better get started."

Julia laughed. "I suppose you're right. There's no time like the present, is there?"

✶✶✶

Mei felt herself drawing closer to Zhen-Li by the day, and she didn't like it one bit. It was dangerous to care for others, particularly here in prison. Attachments complicated their already difficult existence, and Mei had long ago insulated her heart against such complications.

Except with her husband and son. Even now, after all the long and torturous days and nights away from them, she was unable to drown out her longing to see them again, to hold them in her arms, to hear their voices and rejoice in their very presence. That longing had driven her from the beginning of her incarceration, causing her to make choices and compromises that nearly engulfed her with self-loathing but that also held out the only hope she had of ever being with her loved ones again.

That hope, however, continued to fade with the passing of time. Even if she survived and got out of this place, would her family still be alive, waiting for her, loving and missing her as she did them? Would they even recognize her if she showed up at their door?

As her cell mate slept beside her through the mild spring night, her breathing light and even, Mei squeezed her eyes shut in a vain attempt to hold back the seemingly never-ending flood of tears that always felt ready to explode at the least provocation. She couldn't help caring for her family, but she could not allow herself to care for anyone else — and that included the gentle soul named Zhen-Li, who now knew about Mei's shame and yet still held her close and sang to her of the Baby Yesu being born at Christmas.

The memories that song evoked were all Mei needed to push the waiting tears over the edge and out from her eyes, dripping hot and wet down her gaunt cheeks and into her hair and ears. As ugly and demeaning as her life had become during the day, Mei decided her daylight hours could never compare to the aching loneliness of the long, bitter nights, spent on a hard cement floor with a companion whose kindness was rivaled only by her illogical religious zeal. For Mei, at that moment, Zhen-Li's beliefs seemed nearly too pathetic and ludicrous even to consider.

It was time to put his ultimate plan into action.

Chapter 19

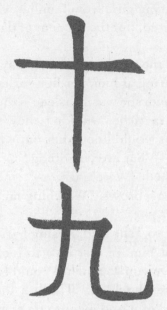

JAKE LAY ON HIS BACK, CONTEMPLATING THE CRACKED CEILING in the afternoon light. He was never more comfortable than when he was lying, satisfied, beside some young, uninhibited girl whose only desire was to serve and please him. Of course, Maggie hadn't been that way when he first met her. Jake remembered the day clearly, when he first ran across Maggie, sitting alone and dejected outside a fast-food restaurant, nursing a soda and nibbling at fries. Her multicolored hair and body jewelry had nearly screamed for attention, and he was more than happy to offer it. After all, it wasn't the first time he had befriended a lonely and vulnerable young girl and eventually lured her into his world...and it certainly wouldn't be the last. Once they were inside his domain and under his spell, he made his move, plying them with drugs and sex until they were soon convinced they could no longer live without him. Then it was time to put his ultimate plan into action.

And so it was with Maggie. She was young and attractive, and apart from her experience with Jake, innocent. He knew he could get more for the girls if they were virgins, but somehow he just couldn't restrain himself from trying the goods before putting them on the market. He also knew that he was flirting with danger by enticing girls from families who would miss them when they disappeared, but the element of danger was part of the game for him.

Jake glanced at the woman-child who lay beside him and discovered she was staring at him, her lips curled into a slight smile. He should have known she wasn't asleep—the drugs he had given her a couple of hours earlier wouldn't allow that, though he had plenty of others that would knock her out when necessary.

"Hey," he said. "What are you doing?"

Her smile widened. "Watching you."

Jake raised his eyebrows. "Watching me? But I'm not doing anything."

"You don't have to," she said, raising herself up on one elbow and gazing down at him. "I just love to look at you. You're so handsome, and I love you so much. I could look at you forever."

"Forever?" Jake chuckled. "That's a long time. You don't think you'd get tired of it and want to do something else?"

She shook her head. "No. Never."

He reached up and pulled her down against his chest. "What if I have something else I want you to do?"

Maggie giggled as he ran his hand through her hair, then closed his fist on a clump of it and jerked her head back so he could kiss her neck, turning her giggle into a gasp. "Anything," she said, speaking in between pants. "I told you...anything."

Jake pushed down on the back of her head until her face was pressed up against his, and then he kissed her roughly, thrilling at the tiny spark of fear he felt run through her body as she resisted ever so slightly, no doubt trying to catch her breath. He wouldn't hurt her enough to do any damage or scare her away, but he wasn't about to let her go without first taking all the pleasure from her that he could.

When he was done, he would make the phone call that would seal her fate.

Zhou Chi lay awake in the predawn light, wrestling once again with his growing desire to leave his sister and son behind and pedal to Beijing to try to find his wife. Perhaps he could even find someone going there by car who would be willing to give him a ride. The neighbor, whose uncle had taken Zhou Chi to Beijing to meet Zhen-Li's parents and request her hand in marriage, had since died, and Chi imagined that the elderly uncle had as well. If only there were someone else...

He sighed, rising from the thin pad that served as his bed, once so welcoming and now only another sad reminder of his absent wife. Zhou Ming and the boy were still sleeping. Chi had been able to bring home slightly more food than usual the previous day, and his rumbling stomach now called him to prepare and eat some of it, despite the early hour. As quietly as possible, he arose to do so, planning to feel his way around the unlit home.

"*Zen me le?* Are you all right, my brother?"

The voice came to him from the darkness, and Chi smiled. He had never been able to sneak past Ming, even when they were children. She slept lightly and awoke at the slightest sound, and this morning was no exception.

"*Hai ke yi,*" he answered. "I am fine. I woke early and could not get back to sleep, so I answered my stomach and got up to fix some breakfast. Will you join me, my sister?"

He heard a slight rustling as he lit the lantern that sat on the table, and shortly a diminutive figure emerged from the shadows. "I will make tea," she announced. Chi considered telling her that he could do so himself and had, in fact, been planning on it before she arose. But he thought better of it. Ming took great pride in being useful and doing her part to keep their household running. Of course, it was her care of little Chan that meant more to Chi than he could ever express. Second only to his concern for Zhen-Li's welfare when she was arrested was what to do with his son while he was at work during the day. Ming's arrival on his doorstep had been an answer to prayer for Chi, though for her sake he was sorry it had come at such a costly price as the loss of her husband.

In the flickering light of the kerosene lantern, it was easy for Chi to imagine that the graceful movements of the woman preparing tea and heating rice were those of his wife, rather than his sister. How many times had he sat at this same rugged table and watched his wife bustle about, preparing a meal for him? *Not enough*, he decided, his heart constricting with the thought of it. *Not nearly enough.*

Blinking away the wetness in his eyes, he asked, "May I help you with anything?"

Without turning toward him, Ming answered quickly. "I can take care of it, my brother. I will have your breakfast ready in moments. And when you are through, perhaps we will have time enough before you leave to pray together."

Though Ming had not mentioned the object of her proposed prayer, Chi knew without asking that they would pray for Zhen-Li. Their concern for her had increased since the earthquake, and though neither had spoken the words aloud, it was obvious they both wondered if she was still alive.

✱✱✱

Tai Tong felt stronger today, and he was relieved to have at last been released from the hospital. If only his dithering wife would stop fussing over him! It seemed the more she tried to please Tong, the more irritated he became. And the boy! What had Tong done to deserve such a cowardly son? The child cringed at the very sight of his father, and though Tong enjoyed the sense of power that gave him, he also despised the quivering excuse for a son who even now clung to his mother as if she could protect him from Tong—which was ridiculous. Tong could squash them both like flies if he so desired. And sometimes he desired that very much.

I must not think about that, he told himself, shifting on his pallet in the corner and watching his family through half-closed eyes. *They are simply necessary pawns in the game—a game that I control, whether they want to play or not. But my energy must be focused on getting better so I can return to work and to my true prey.*

He paused, closing his eyes as he pictured Zhen-Li's frightened face. Why did her fear excite him, while the fear he saw in his wife and son's eyes merely disgust him?

Zhen-Li. Did she think of him often? He hoped so. He hoped she thought of him and regretted her foolish choice to help him, rather than leaving him behind and trying to escape. He hoped she quaked with terror at the thought of what would happen to her when he returned, for her terror only made his returning so much more enjoyable.

"Tong?"

The voice penetrating his reverie was hesitant, and he clenched his jaws at the intrusion. What did she want now?

He opened his eyes. Standing before him, her eyes lowered submissively as she held out a bowl of food in front of her, his wife waited, the boy huddled just inches behind her. The sight sickened him, and he reached up and slapped away the bowl, sending its contents flying across the room and immediately setting off a wailing from the boy, who had wrapped himself around his mother's leg.

Tong's wife stood motionless, speechless, her eyes wide and her face pale. For a brief moment Tong wondered what would happen if he jumped up and grabbed her by the neck, squeezing until her eyes popped and her tongue lolled in death. Would he be sent to prison? Possibly, though he imagined he could concoct some sort of story to escape punishment. But he couldn't be sure, and she wasn't worth taking the chance.

Besides, he had a greater challenge waiting for him, and he couldn't allow himself to get sidetracked. He was so close to being strong enough to return to work...and to Zhen-Li. Nothing would get in the way of his plans for her this time.

Glaring at his wife, he demanded, "Get me another bowl of food. That one is spoiled."

The surprise in her eyes reverted quickly to fear, and she scurried away to comply with his wishes, softly shushing the child as she worked. By the time she turned back to her husband, bowl in hand, the boy's cries had subsided to soft whimpers, and Tong thought that perhaps he would now be able to eat in peace.

She would be so glad when they
could finally be together openly.

Chapter 20

MAGGIE HAD WANDERED BACK HOME LATER THAT AFTERNOON, though she would have preferred to stay at Jake's. But he insisted that he had some business to attend to and she needed to leave. She would be so glad when they could finally be together openly and she didn't have to go home anymore at all. It wasn't that she didn't love her parents, but...well, they certainly couldn't compare to what Jake offered her.

She smiled as she lay on her bed, safely behind her locked bedroom door, watching the light fade as the sun sank behind the horizon outside. Less than three months ago she hadn't even met Jake. What a break it had been when he wandered into her life, befriending her and introducing her to things that were so much more exciting than anything she'd even imagined. And who would have thought it could all be had just a few blocks from her own dreary home? Here she'd been living her dull existence with her parents, wishing there was something more, and then one day Jake popped into her life and everything changed.

Almost from that first day she'd known she would follow him anywhere, do anything for him. No one had ever looked at her the way Jake did—as if he were starving and she was lunch! She grinned at the thought. *If my parents only knew how really wild their daughter is and how easy they make it for me to be that way.*

Her grandmother's face invaded her thoughts, and she frowned. Why did she have to think about her when she'd rather think about Jake? It seemed thoughts of her grandmother and that other old lady with the cane were always nagging at her and ruining her fun. Why couldn't they just leave her alone? And what was the big deal about the old lady's jewelry anyway? At her age, where was she going to go that she'd need to wear it? Like anyone would look at an old hag like that!

Maggie shook her head, determined to dismiss the images of the two elderly women. *Let the one with the cane accuse me all she wants,* she thought. *If they had anything on me, the cops would have arrested me by now. Big deal. So they came to the house and asked me a few questions in front of my parents. At least Mom and Dad defended me, just like they did when Grandma Margaret accused me of taking things from her house before she moved into that old people's home. I can't believe my parents are so lame they actually believe I didn't do any of those things, but I'm sure glad they do.*

She smiled. *I'll just keep on lying to them and sneaking out until Jake can find a way for us to be together, like he promised. Then everything will be wonderful, and I won't have to worry about fooling my parents anymore. And when I need things like new sunglasses or clothes or a ride to the mall, Jake will take me. I won't need my mom or dad for anything anymore. I can hardly wait.*

Margaret was irritated. Not that she wasn't most of the time anyway, but today was worse. It was Sunday afternoon, and Margaret hated that day and time of the week worse than any other.

It's bad enough that those two old hens waste their time all week getting together to pray and read the Bible, she stewed, pushing back and forth in the rocker in her room, *but do they have to inflict their religion on the rest of us? Every Sunday like clockwork, we no sooner get up from our naps than here they come, ready for their so-called service. Ha! What kind of service do you call all that noise going on out there? It wouldn't be so bad if we didn't have to hear that awful singing of theirs! The woman who comes with the pastor who preaches to his pathetic River View Manor congregation every week is one of the worst pianists I've ever heard! I could play circles around her if they'd just let me...not that I want to, of course. The last thing I want is to be invited to join their ridiculous hallelujah club! Who needs it? Weak people, that's who! And I'm not weak. I might be getting old, and this walker sure doesn't help my image, but my determination is as strong as ever.*

Margaret pressed her lips together, wishing she were even harder of hearing than she already was. Some of the home's residents probably didn't even notice all the commotion, but she sure did—and she didn't like it one bit. There should be a law...

She sat up straighter. Wait a minute. Maybe there was! What if there really was some kind of law that she could use to make them stop these pointless meetings? Surely there was some way to find out. And if there was, Margaret would see that it was enforced. Sure, it wouldn't make her very popular among the manor's residents, but they didn't like her anyway, so what difference did it make?

Margaret nodded with satisfaction. Her father had taught her many years earlier that life always worked better when you had a plan. And now that the beginnings of a plan were beginning to form in her mind, Margaret was certain that her life was going to take a turn for the better.

✳✳✳

Zhen-Li struggled against the darkness that enveloped her, sucking the air from her lungs with an evil so intense she could nearly taste it. It wasn't her impending death that terrified her so, but the hatred that accompanied it.

Why? What had she done to make this evil force hate her?

She opened her mouth to voice the question, but no words came. Her chest felt as if it were caving in, decompressing from lack of air, collapsing on itself and crushing her very ribs in the process. It was more than she could bear—the pain, the terror, the hatred . . . the need to breathe!

Fighting, she reached out to push away the darkness, the name of Zhu Yesu on her lips, giving her strength to sit up.

"Zhen-Li?"

The voice came from far away, soft and timid. She wasn't even certain she'd heard it. Then it came again, louder this time, breaking through the night and pulling her back into the dim light of her prison cell.

"Zhen-Li, *zen me yang?* Are you all right?"

Mei. Of course. It was her cell mate, calling her back from her horrible nightmare to her reality, which was only slightly better. But at least here she could breathe; she could speak the name of Zhu Yesu and know that He heard.

Zhen-Li nodded. "Hai ke yi," she said. "I am all right. I am sorry if I woke you."

"You had a bad dream," Mei stated, her hand resting on Zhen-Li's arm.

"Yes. Very bad. I could not breathe."

Mei hesitated before responding. "I have had that dream . . . many times," she said, her voice shaking slightly as she gripped Zhen-Li's arm. "Usually it is very dark. I cannot breathe or speak. Someone—something—is trying to destroy me. Not just kill me, but much worse."

Zhen-Li gasped. Suddenly she understood her dream. It hadn't been for her, but for Mei. God wanted Zhen-Li to understand the depth of Mei's terror—and the very real danger behind it. The source of evil and hatred, which so obviously wasn't satisfied with killing the body but wanted to destroy the soul as well, could not touch Zhen-Li, who belonged to Zhu Yesu. But Mei had never given herself into Yesu's care, and therefore she had no protection. The destroyer could take her at will.

The realization was worse than any pain or terror Tai Tong had ever inflicted upon Zhen-Li. She felt herself begin to tremble at the implications.

Mei's life was in danger, as was Zhen-Li's, but Mei's time to receive the only One who could save her from what lay beyond death was quickly running out. And God wanted Zhen-Li to give herself over to interceding on Mei's behalf. It was the only chance the poor woman had.

With Zhen-Li already in prison, Chi could not risk being arrested as well.

Chapter 21

Zhou Chi was seldom able to break his early morning work routine to attend the local jiao hui, house church meeting, but today he was determined. Though he and Zhou Ming prayed together often, including Zhou Chan whenever possible, Chi felt the need for godly counsel from another man, particularly an elder. Pastor Fu Ho was the perfect candidate.

Chi arose long before dawn and, by foregoing breakfast preparations, managed to creep from the house without waking even the light-sleeping Ming. Pausing at the front door to allow his eyes to adjust to the predawn darkness, he scanned the landscape. There was no visible moon tonight, and though that made navigating his bicycle to Pastor Ho's house more difficult, it also made detection less likely. Their jiao hui meetings had not yet been raided, but Chi imagined the PSB was aware of them and taking note of those who attended. With Zhen-Li already in prison, Chi could not risk being arrested as well, leaving his sister and son to fend for themselves.

All appeared quiet, as if the entire world were sleeping. Chi knew better. No doubt Zhen-Li, if she were even still alive, got little sleep under the harsh conditions she endured. The very thought sliced like a ragged knife through Chi's heart, but he pressed ahead with his plans. Zhen-Li would want him to do so.

With one last furtive glance around, Chi mounted his rickety two-wheeler and proceeded as noiselessly as possible toward his destination, less than three miles distant. When the meeting ended, he would go directly to work, as he would have no time to go back home to eat. He would simply have to endure his growling stomach until he got home that evening.

The cool breeze ruffled his hair as he pedaled, bumping along the dirt road and falling twice when he rode headlong into unseen rocks along the way. Only slightly bruised and disheveled, he continued on, determined to seek Pastor Ho's advice. The elderly man had lived more than seven decades on this earth, and had walked with Zhu Yesu for the vast majority of those years. He would understand Chi's pain because Pastor Ho's wife had died several years earlier and Chi knew the old man still missed her terribly, as he continually talked about "going home" to be with her one day soon. Though Chi's wife had not yet died—at least so far as he knew—the pain was every bit as great as if she had.

Perhaps more, Chi reminded himself. There were times Chi thought he could better endure the agony of missing Zhen-Li if he knew she was safely home with Zhu Yesu. But to think of how she must suffer every day was nearly more than the heartbroken husband could stand.

Qin Ai de Tian Fu, help me, he prayed as he neared his destination. *I am so weak but You are so strong, and Your love is so great. Show me, Zhu Yesu! Tell me what to do! And please, give me the courage and strength to do it.*

As light dawned in China, night settled over Jake's house, and he contemplated what he had done. Everything was set in motion—no turning back now—but first he had to do something about Maggie's appearance. She still looked good to him, but his contact had reminded him that he could get a lot more for girls who came across as young and innocent—even if the latter was no longer true. That meant Jake had to wean her from regular use of the heavy stuff just enough so she'd take better care of herself—eat and sleep more regularly, and maybe even get rid of the multicolored hair and body piercings. She wouldn't like it, but she'd do it if he approached her right. After all, she'd said she'd do anything for him. How hard could this be? If only she knew the reason...

Sitting alone in the darkened living room where just hours earlier the foolish girl had practically signed over her life to him, Jake wondered how bad it would be for her. Not that he cared. He'd done this many times before, and it was a lot more lucrative than selling drugs. But the thought had crossed his mind more than once that the girls he sold would probably never taste freedom again, or see their families, or even live to middle age.

He shrugged. What was that to him? He had a business to run, and they were simply the merchandise. Attractive merchandise, that was true, but destined to the worst possible existence. Still, he couldn't let himself get emotionally involved with them, though it was preferable if they fell in love with him. It made the transaction so much easier. If they weren't completely devoted to him or they began to suspect something wasn't quite right, he was forced to use whatever means necessary to get them to their destination...or abort the transaction. And his contacts didn't like that option at all. In fact, he'd already had to do that twice, and they'd made it clear that a third time would not be tolerated.

He took a swig from a can of lukewarm beer and smirked. No problem getting this one to market. He could put a ring in her nose and lead her down the street on all fours, and she'd go willingly—gratefully, even, thinking she was somehow proving her love for him. If she had even an inkling of the horrors that lay in store for her, she'd run crying for her parents and never look back.

The jiao hui had ended with a simple sharing of Communion, and then the dozen or so worshipers left, wanting to be gone before the sun peeked over the horizon. All except Zhou Chi, who hung back, waiting for a few moments alone with the wise patriarch, Fu Ho.

It seemed the old man hadn't noticed him, as he had gone immediately to prayer when the service ended and the people exited. On his knees at the front of the room, before a makeshift altar, the pastor communed with heaven, his eyes closed and his lips moving silently, as Chi wondered how long he should wait before interrupting Ho's prayers. After all, Chi needed to be at work soon.

A few more moments passed, and at last Chi cleared his throat, hoping to catch the old man's attention. Apparently it worked, for Pastor Ho stopped praying and turned slowly toward Chi.

"If you will help me get up, we will talk together, Brother Zhou," he said, reaching up his hand.

Gladly, Chi took his hand and pulled him to his feet. "*Xiexie*," Chi said. "Thank you, Pastor. I am grateful for your time."

"And I for yours," Ho answered, indicating a backless wooden bench where some of the worshipers had sat earlier.

The two settled down upon it, turning slightly to face one another. Chi was surprised to find himself at a loss for words. What had he expected to say to the pastor? How could he make him understand what he needed from him?

The old man raised his eyebrows questioningly, causing deep rifts in his brow. Chi wondered how someone's eyes could be so dim with age and yet so alive with hope. "It is about Zhen-Li, is it not?" Ho asked.

Chi nodded. "My wife. I wish to speak with you about her."

"As I imagined," Ho answered. "You are understandably concerned about her welfare, particularly since the earthquake."

Chi felt his eyes widen. "How did you know?"

Ho smiled. "From the moment you entered the room, I knew you wished to speak with me. That is why I prayed at the end of the service. Zhu Yesu showed me the concerns of your heart. And the pain."

Hot tears sprang into Chi's eyes, but he wasn't ashamed. He knew Pastor Ho understood and shared his grief.

"I miss her more than I ever imagined possible," he confessed, even as the tears began to spill over onto his cheeks. "I thought it might get easier with time, but it has only gotten worse."

Pastor Ho nodded, slowly, as he did most things these days. "Even in my case, it does not get easier," he said, "though I become more able to cope with the loss of my beloved wife, particularly since I know I am fast approaching the time when I will be with her once again. But for you . . ." He paused, nodding once more. "It must be so much worse, not knowing what she is enduring, whether she is dead or alive, suffering or sick."

He laid a gnarled hand on Chi's, surprising the younger man at the coolness of the pastor's touch. Was it possible that his blood no longer circulated as it once had? Would Chi's one day be the same? He doubted it, only because he doubted he would live that long.

The old man spoke again. "You want to go to her, to look for her and find out how she is. Am I right?"

Chi's shoulders heaved then, and he nodded his answer because he could not bring himself to speak.

"But you do not know if it is the right thing to do." Pastor Ho paused. "What would become of Zhou Ming and Zhou Chan in your absence?"

Chi could not decide if his heart constricted because of the pain or from gratitude that God had shown Pastor Fu Ho exactly what to say, but he was grateful. That someone else understood without being told was a great gift.

"I cannot give you the answer," Ho said. "Only Zhu Yesu Jidu can do that. But I can pray with you to have ears to hear what He says to you. Would you like me to do so now?"

With a final nod, Chi waited, as his beloved pastor began to pray. And somehow he sensed that *Shang Di*, the Most High God, was already moving to bring about the answer.

Julia's heart dropped like a stone, even as tears rushed to her eyes.

Chapter 22

JULIA AWOKE DURING THE NIGHT, SENSING THAT SOMETHING wasn't right. But this time it was obvious that the problem wasn't in some faraway land but rather right here among the residents of River View Manor.

The commotion in the hallway outside her door sprang her into action. As fast as her aging, stiff body would allow, Julia lowered her feet over the side of her bed and slid them into her waiting slippers. Then she lifted herself to a standing position, leaning slightly on her walker with one hand and reaching with the other for her robe at the foot of her bed. As soon as that was securely tied around her, she headed for the door.

The scene that greeted her when she peered into the hallway was not encouraging. Two emergency response firemen were heading into Laura's room, with the manor's two night attendants huddled at the doorway just behind them.

Julia's heart dropped like a stone, even as tears rushed to her eyes. *Laura! No, Lord, not Laura!* Julia knew Laura's heart was failing, but surely not this soon! Oh, if only they had entered someone else's room...

Immediately ashamed, she realized she wouldn't want it to be someone else, but...well, she certainly didn't want it to be Laura.

Her best friend. Her prayer partner. The closest person she had in this life, next to her family, whom she saw only occasionally. What would she do if something happened to Laura?

Convicted of her selfishness, she closed her eyes and prayed silently. *Forgive me, Lord. What a terrible reaction! But please, please let Laura be all right. Show me how to pray, Father.*

Approaching sirens indicated the imminent arrival of an ambulance. By that time all the residents were up and standing in their opened doorways, silently watching and waiting...and, Julia hoped, praying.

The ambulance came to a stop in front of the manor, lights still flashing but siren now silenced. One of the manor's caregivers was already at the front door, ushering the two attendants inside. In seconds they had entered Laura's room, as Julia and the others continued to wait.

Pray for them.

The instruction had come silently, more of a whisper to her heart than actual words, but the direction was clear.

I'm already praying, Lord, Julia answered silently. But she realized God wasn't calling her to pray for Laura, or even for those who were trying to help her, but rather for those who stood in their doorways, mouths and eyes agape, undoubtedly contemplating their own mortality and some with no assurance of where they would spend eternity.

Pray for them.

The loving command echoed once again in her heart, and Julia nodded, forcing herself from the doorway and back inside her room, where she settled into the chair beside her bed and began to beseech God for mercy toward those residents of River View Manor who had not yet received it.

At least, whatever happened to her beloved friend physically, Julia knew beyond question that it was well with Laura's soul. And so, with an aching heart, Julia persevered in prayer for the others.

Zhou Chi was tired, his shoulders aching and his eyes heavy, as he worked his way down one row to the next. The sun was exceptionally warm overhead, and the call to slumber grew louder as the afternoon continued. Only a few more hours and he could lay down his hoe, collect his pay, and climb on his bike to go home. The only good thing about being so sleepy was that it kept his mind off his growling stomach.

But he didn't regret any of it. His decision to rise early and attend the jiao hui at Pastor Ho's house had been a wise one. Missing a meal and a few hours of sleep was a small price to pay in exchange for the peace that had settled inside Chi's heart since praying with the old saint. Though he still had no clear answer as to whether he should try to go to Beijing and find Zhen-Li, he was confident that Zhu Yesu would direct him.

Besides, how dare Chi complain about heavy eyes or an empty stomach when his wife suffered untold deprivations daily? Chi had never been in prison, but he knew some who had. Those who had lived to tell of it seldom spoke of their experiences, and Chi could only imagine that Zhen-Li would react similarly—if she ever had the chance.

My heart yearns for my wife, Father, Chi prayed silently, fighting tears as he labored. *I long to know of her condition—and more than that, I long to hear her voice, to see her face, to touch her soft skin. Will I ever be able to do that again this side of paradise?*

The relentless sun beating down on his head was his only answer. And yet the peace that had seemingly infiltrated his very pores while he sat at Pastor Ho's house continued to sustain him even now. Surprisingly, Chi realized, it was enough.

***

Zhen-Li was surprised at the intensity of the afternoon sun. It was indeed the warmest day so far this spring. And yet she was relieved to be outside, working in the heat with the other prisoners rather than locked away somewhere with Tai Tong, as she had been prior to the earthquake.

How much longer? she wondered, struggling with the load laid across her shoulders as she continued to clear the rubble and rebuild the damaged sections of the prison. *Mei told me just last night that the other guards believe Tong will make a full recovery and be back at work very soon. You know I'm glad he will recover, Zhu Yesu, as You know I wouldn't want anyone passing into eternity without knowing You as their Savior, but I can't help but wonder what his return will mean to me.*

She caught her breath as she nearly tripped over a small chunk of broken concrete. Steadying herself, she continued to commune with God as she worked.

I do not want to complain, Yesu. I want to be willing and obedient to whatever You call me to do. But, Zhu Yesu, if there is any way—

The memory of hearing their pastor read the Lord's prayer in the Garden of Gethsemane nearly stopped her more surely than the uneven ground beneath her feet. How long had it been since she sat in that little jiao hui and listened to those words? Yet they rang in her ears as if it were yesterday. "Not My will, but Yours," Yesu had prayed, knowing the horrible death He would face.

Zhen-Li hung her head. *I am so ashamed, Zhu Yesu—and so weak! I do not want to faint in the face of testing, but I am not strong like You.*

Exactly, came the answer in her heart. *I do not expect you to be. But I will be your strength. And when you are unable to stand, I will be the One to carry you.*

Tears came to her eyes, nearly blinding her to the path in front of her. And yet it didn't matter. Zhen-Li knew more surely at that moment than ever before that God was ordering her steps and upholding her along the way. She would make it—whatever happened, even if Tai Tong returned to torment her once again—not because she was strong or courageous, but because she belonged to the One who was.

At the thought, a smile played on her lips, even as the familiar Christmas song of the Baby Yesu, which she often sang to Mei these days, played in her heart.

***

Breakfast was late at River View Manor, and a much more somber occasion than usual as the residents awaited word of Laura's condition. Julia imagined she wasn't the only one who had lost sleep over the situation, but at least she had done so while praying for the others who were now seated around the dining table. The emptiness of Laura's chair nearly cried out with her absence.

Julia had taken a brief break from her intercession when she overheard the ambulance attendants talking of preparing to transport the patient. As quickly as she was able, Julia had hurried to her door and peeked out just in time to catch Laura's eyes as the gurney rolled past. A smile and a mutual sense of peace had passed between them, and Julia realized her friend experienced no fear as she began what could possibly be her final exit from River View.

As it should be, Julia reminded herself, still staring at her friend's empty chair. *No fear in life, no fear in death, for we know the Creator of the first and the Conqueror of the second. But it doesn't make the pain any less for those who are left behind.*

She glanced around the table. A couple of other residents, who often attended the Sunday afternoon services, seemed relatively at peace with the turn of events. Julia wondered if they might be open to praying with her, though they'd never expressed an interest or willingness to do so before. The expressions on the faces of the half-dozen other residents varied from confusion to disinterest to worry. Julia asked the Lord to use whatever was going on in each of their hearts to draw them to Himself.

But it was Margaret who concerned Julia the most. Her complexion was pale; her long salt-and-pepper hair, usually so neatly swept up on top of her head, hung loose around her shoulders. The lines that crisscrossed her face seemed more pronounced than Julia had ever seen. Apparently Laura's condition was affecting Margaret more than Julia had realized.

Or is it something else entirely? Julia couldn't help but wonder just how much the situation with Maggie was taking its toll on Margaret, though she seemed reticent to admit it. Still, Julia

165

could only imagine how concerned she would be if it were her own granddaughter who seemed to have fallen into such a rebellious and even dangerous lifestyle. With that thought in mind, she offered a smile to Margaret, whose eyes occasionally wandered her way, but there was no response.

Julia sighed and reminded herself to make a conscious effort to continue praying for Maggie in the midst of the crisis with Laura. The young girl obviously had some serious problems, none of which would be resolved without the Lord.

And then there was the woman in China—many in China, for that matter, still digging out from the earthquake—who also needed continued prayer.

Though Julia would miss having Laura at her side, she knew she must continue to pray for all these needs, and she would begin again the moment breakfast was over.

At last, he would see Zhen-Li again.

Chapter 23

TAI TONG WAS SO EXCITED HE COULDN'T SLEEP. THE DAY HAD been long and extremely warm, but the heat hadn't bothered him one bit. He could think only of his return to work the next day. At last, he would see Zhen-Li again, the foolish young woman who had chosen to save his life rather than her own.

Did she think he would be indebted to her? Lying in the darkness beside his dull wife, whose even breathing assured him she did not share his sleeplessness, he nearly laughed aloud. Zhen-Li's sacrifice had not in any way made him feel that he owed a debt of gratitude to this so-called Christian, but instead had served only to fuel his desire to possess her—and ultimately destroy her.

The very thought stirred a longing in his gut that he could scarcely contain. Why did he experience such an overwhelming sense of yearning and power each time he thought of the woman whose name meant truth? Could it be that part of the very reason he wished to conquer her was to teach her that her so-called Truth did not exist, that his truth would defeat hers? Possibly. If so, he knew that was only part of the reason. But there was so much more that even he couldn't clearly define it.

His wife grunted and turned toward him, settling onto her side, her breath warming his bare shoulder. But her nearness didn't excite him as did the thought of being near Zhen-Li. Once again he wondered why. He frowned into the darkness. Surely it wasn't that Zhen-Li was so beautiful. She was lovely in her own way, and perhaps had even been beautiful before her incarceration, but there were others more attractive and sensual. So why did her very presence, her name, her memory, nearly drive him mad with desire?

Perhaps it didn't matter. Perhaps he simply needed to stop worrying about the why and concentrate only on the how. How best would he reestablish his presence in Zhen-Li's life? Should he go immediately to her cell and let her see him in his restored strength and obvious displeasure so that she might be appropriately terrified? Or should he reemerge slowly on the scene, causing her to wonder when he would appear, what he would do, how he would treat her?

Undecided, he grinned. Whatever he did, he would calculate it in such a way as to get the optimum reaction from the woman who already belonged to him, even if she had so far refused to admit it. He could almost smell her fear, and the thought of it turned the passing hours of night into a nearly excruciating trial of endurance.

Just when Maggie thought things couldn't get better, they did. She hadn't even opened her eyes that morning before her cell phone blasted its music in her ear. Dragging herself from the pit she'd fallen into just a few hours earlier, she had fumbled for the phone and finally pressed it to her ear, only to come awake at the sound of Jake's voice.

"Hey, beautiful," he'd said. "Get up. I've got a surprise for you."

Nearly prying her eyes open, she'd sat up on the side of the bed and begged him to tell her what it was. He wouldn't budge.

She would just have to shower and dress and hurry to his house to find out.

And so she had, wondering every moment what in the world Jake's surprise might be and reveling in the very idea that such a great guy cared so deeply for her that he spent his time thinking up new ways to please her. Waiting now on his front porch, her hand extended to knock, she could scarcely stand up under the onslaught of butterflies in her stomach.

Before she could knock, the door opened. Jake stood smiling on the other side, wearing nothing but his faded jeans and staring down at her with obvious desire. "Come in, sexy lady," he said, the husky timbre of his voice nearly knocking her off her feet.

He took her hand and almost yanked her inside, immediately pressing her against his bare chest and running his hands up and down her back. His embrace was so tight that it was almost painful—almost, but not quite. Maggie loved it.

"I have a surprise for you today," Jake whispered into her hair.

Maggie nearly squealed with excitement, struggling to lift her head and look into his face. "What is it? Tell me! I can't wait to see it."

Jake's grin widened. "You won't just see it," he said. "You'll experience it. And I guarantee that you'll love it." He lifted his eyebrows. "Ready to start?"

Fascinated and completely at a loss for what this surprise might be, she nodded eagerly. "Yes," she declared. "I'm ready. Let's do it—whatever it is."

A brief expression of surprise crossed Jake's face, and then he laughed. "You're something else, Maggie girl! Aren't you afraid of anything?"

She shook her head and smiled as sexily as she knew how. "Nothing—so long as you're involved."

His grin lessened but didn't disappear, instead taking on a hint of something that sent a chill down Maggie's spine. But the brief sense of fear and possible danger only heightened her excitement.

"Come with me," he said, lifting her into his arms as she gasped with delight. "I've got someone very special I want you to meet."

***

Margaret was having second thoughts. Not that she still didn't hate the Sunday services that went on at River View Manor, but the episode with Laura had shaken her. Though she wasn't about to admit it to anyone, the thought of death terrified her. She often wondered if that was at least part of the reason she so hated living in this museum. Every human relic in the place had one foot in the grave, and she was no exception.

Still, she wasn't about to back down on what she'd started. She had gone to the caretakers and registered a verbal complaint about the Sunday afternoon services disrupting her peace and quiet, but they had smiled and ignored her. She would have to take it to the next step.

Throughout breakfast she had considered it, as she watched the reactions of the people around the table. She could put up with most of them—even that ancient battle-axe Emily Johnson, who had dared to threaten her and Maggie. Margaret hated Emily for that, even though she knew the cranky old hag was probably right about Maggie taking her jewelry. Still, Maggie was family and she wasn't going to side with Emily over her own flesh and blood. Maggie was another problem entirely, and she couldn't even let herself think about where that worthless girl was headed.

No, it wasn't Emily or most of the other residents who bothered Margaret; it was Julia, the one who was nearly joined at the hip with Laura, who now lay in the hospital no doubt enduring every test known to modern medicine. Margaret didn't really wish Laura ill, but she couldn't say that she'd miss her around the place either. And she surely wouldn't miss Julia. Without those two religious fanatics, the Sunday services might disappear without any further effort from Margaret.

But she couldn't be sure, so she'd better press ahead. While the others waited in the living and dining areas for some word about Laura, Margaret sat in her room, going through the phone book and looking for an organization that might help her. She'd heard there were plenty such groups, dedicated to protecting people from having their rights violated through forced religion. Surely there was at least one of them willing to help out an old woman who couldn't escape the noise of weekly services and the self-righteous attitudes of those who attended those services right there within the very walls of the home where Margaret lived.

She smiled as her eyes landed on a particular legal ad. Yes, this group looked promising. Reaching for the phone by her bed, she eagerly dialed the number.

***

In a million years Maggie wouldn't even have come close to imagining the surprise Jake had arranged for her. When he'd told her there was someone special he wanted her to meet, she thought he was kidding. He wasn't. As she'd gazed dreamily up at him, he'd carried her to the back bedroom, where a heavyset, middle-aged woman in a white smock and loose-fitting slacks smiled at them.

"Hello, Maggie," she'd said. "I've heard so much about you. It's wonderful to finally meet you."

Maggie had been stunned, turning her gaze from the woman to Jake and back again. What was this all about? Who was this woman? Jake's mother, maybe? But why the smock?

Glancing at the portable table next to the bed, Maggie was surprised to see it was covered with all sorts of creams and shampoos and other toiletries. What in the world was going on?

Before she could ask, Jake had kissed her on the forehead and then set her on her feet. "This is Joan," he'd said, indicating the woman, who was still smiling. "She's an amazing beautician, and she's going to fix you up like you can't even imagine."

Stunned, Maggie had turned to Jake, nearly unable to speak. She'd waited a moment to see if he'd start laughing and she'd find out it was just an elaborate joke. But he didn't...and it wasn't. Now, as she sat in a chair next to the bed and the portable table, the woman named Joan fussed with Maggie's hair, while Maggie wanted nothing more than to put her face in her hands and cry. Why was Jake doing this to her? Didn't he like her the way she was? Hadn't he told her she was beautiful? If so, why did he want her to take out her nose ring and belly-button stud? And why would he want her to do away with the color in her hair and go back to its original blond?

Even now, as she sat silently enduring her unwilling transformation, Jake hovered close by, watching every change and constantly complimenting her on how incredible she looked. The couple of times she'd expressed doubt, he'd reminded her that she'd said she'd do anything for him, and now she just had to trust him that he knew what was best for her and she'd like it when it was all done.

Maggie was pretty sure she wouldn't, but she did love Jake—a lot—and she knew he was doing all this for her. She couldn't even imagine how much it was costing him. And if it made him love her and want her more, than she supposed it was worth it. But was there another reason, something else she hadn't figured out yet?

Then it came to her. Hadn't he just told her the day before that he was going to find some way for them to be together? Maybe he thought that by changing her looks to something that would please her parents, they might realize what a good influence he was on her and let her marry him, even though she was only fifteen.

The thought brought a smile to her lips, and she raised her eyes toward Jake. "Thank you," she said. "I know you're doing this for me—because you love me."

Jake's look of surprise changed quickly to a smile, and he winked. "You'd better believe it, pretty lady. I'm doing it all for you...because I love you." He leaned toward her and kissed her cheek. "All for you, baby girl. All for you."

"Not my will, but Yours, Zhu Yesu."

Chapter 24

THE RUMOR SHE HAD SO DREADED HEARING HAD FINALLY reached her ears that morning. Tai Tong had returned. Though Zhen-Li had not yet seen him, she knew it was only a matter of time until he reintroduced himself into her life. She tried to cling to the hope that he would be kinder to her since she had helped him, but she knew it was a slim hope, and highly unlikely. If there was one thing Tong would not react well to it was being shamed in any way, and what more shame could there be than to be rescued by a female prisoner?

As the workday wore on and the sun once again shone hot overhead, she prayed fervently that Tong would at the very least ignore her, allowing her to continue at hard labor with her fellow inmates. But even when she prayed, Zhen-Li concluded her prayers with "Not my will, but Yours, Zhu Yesu."

As she worked, Zhen-Li also thought of Mei. The girl had been included in the labor force immediately after the earthquake, when emergency repairs were most needed, but now she had been returned to her previous assignment of "entertaining" the guards.

Zhen-Li shivered in spite of the temperature. Could there be a worse fate? If so, she could not imagine it. Backbreaking toil was welcome in comparison, and death most certainly so, as it meant she would go to be with her Lord. But to be daily demeaned and degraded by those who held your physical life in their hands, who could beat or torture you on a whim, who considered you less than an animal in captivity, was worse than anything else Zhen-Li could imagine. That Mei had survived such treatment as long as she had was, in Zhen-Li's opinion, a miracle. Surely Zhu Yesu had Mei's eternal welfare in mind and had preserved her life for that reason. And that, in turn, reaffirmed to Zhen-Li that her purpose in meeting and sharing a cell with Mei was to continue to pray for her and to speak to her of her need to receive Zhu Yesu as her Savior. When she was at a loss for words to share with Mei, she sang to her of the Baby Yesu. The song seemed to agitate Mei, and yet she never asked Zhen-Li to stop singing—and so she didn't.

Even now, with the terrifying knowledge that Tong had returned to the prison, Zhen-Li hummed the song as she worked, though she was scarcely aware of it.

★★★

Maggie stood in her room at the end of the day, staring into the mirror and wondering who the strange-looking girl was gazing back at her. She appeared at least two or three years younger than she had the day before, with her hair back to blond, her makeup and body jewelry gone, and her body clad in less revealing clothes.

Jake had assured her that though he loved her just the way she was, he now found her even sexier and more attractive with a soft, innocent appearance. He also told her that he thought her parents would be pleased, and it might help when they approached them about allowing her to be with Jake—permanently.

Though that sounded too good to be true, Maggie was willing to try anything if it meant she could spend more time with Jake, and if it would make him want her more than he already did.

The very thought brought a silly grin to her lips. "He loves you," she said to the girl in the mirror. "He wants to be with you and take care of you—forever! A guy like Jake, handsome and sexy and mature, who could have any girl in the world, and he wants to be with you!" She shook her head, her shoulder-length hair tossing slightly as she marveled at the thought. "It's amazing. And if looking like a nice, innocent kid is what turns him on, then fine. It's the least I can do."

Turning from the mirror, she walked to her locked bedroom door and opened it. Might as well show off the new image to her parents and see what sort of reaction she got. Could be good for a laugh or two.

***

Tai Tong watched her from a distance. He had made it a point to be sure Zhen-Li got the message that he was back, though he wasn't ready to let her see him yet. Better to let her agonize over what was to come, even as he thrilled at the prospect. The anticipation was almost as delicious as he was certain the fulfillment would finally be. Equally exciting was the knowledge that he had complete control over when and how that fulfillment would take place.

She was small and even slightly stooped, though he knew that was due to the difficult work she had endured since coming to this place. If only she hadn't rejected him, he would have spared her from continuing in such menial labor. How much better to preserve her strength to serve him! Why couldn't she see that? It had to be due to her superstitious beliefs in the foreign God she called Yesu.

Standing in the shadows, he snorted in contempt. Did she really think this invisible deity would rescue her and somehow preserve her purity from the inevitable? Tong had already decided that he would own her—in essence, he did already—and there was nothing she or anyone else could do about it. Tong alone would decide how Zhen-Li would live and when she would die. After that she would go the way of all else that had passed before her, into nothingness, for Tong knew there was nothing else beyond this life.

Though the thought fueled his need for power over another human being, in this case Zhen-Li, it also dampened his pleasure and left him feeling irritated. He hated anything that took away from his sense of self-fulfillment, for that was truly all that was worthwhile in this world. And he wasn't about to let anything steal it from him.

★★★

Maggie had nearly laughed aloud at the wide-eyed expression on her parents' faces when she emerged from her room, coming to stand silently in front of them as they sat side-by-side on the couch, staring at their wide-screen TV. Their first reaction had been to ask her to move, as she was blocking their view.

Then, slowly, realization invaded their consciousness, and their jaws went slack as their faces paled. It was several moments before they gathered themselves enough to allow joy to register on their faces and to express it with their words. But as they *oohed* and *aahed* over how wonderful she looked and how happy they were to have their "real Maggie" back, she waited to see how long it would take until they asked the big question.

Her mother blurted it out as she jumped up from the couch and threw her arms around her daughter. "Honey, we're thrilled," she exclaimed, "but what brought about this sudden change?"

Maggie smiled but refused to answer, shrugging instead and murmuring something about how she had just "felt like it." She would wait and tell them the real reason later—hopefully, with Jake at her side. First she was going to go tell him all about it.

As she hurried down the street toward his house, the anticipation of seeing him again brought back the familiar flurry of butterflies in her stomach that seemed to accompany her every meeting with Jake. What was this amazing power he held over her? Surely it was love, but who would ever have dreamed she would discover someone so wonderful while she was still so young? Just a few months ago her life was about as boring as it could get...and now this!

She nearly threw her arms around herself as she picked up her pace. No doubt she was the luckiest girl on the face of the planet!

★★★

Jake hadn't expected Maggie back so soon. Hadn't he made it clear to her that she should call before coming over? It was a good thing he'd glanced out the living room window and seen her coming up the walk before she got to the front door. It had given him time to make sure it was locked and to scoot his newest future victim out the back door.

"I've got a friend coming over," he'd told the unsuspecting girl, just a year younger than Maggie and having been befriended by Jake only a couple of days earlier. Though he hadn't had time to seduce her, he was getting close, and he silently cursed the interruption, as he'd hoped to achieve that milestone tonight. No matter. There was always next time. Meanwhile, he'd have one more fling with Maggie. No telling how many more times he'd be able to be with her before he handed her over to her new owners. It shouldn't take long to finish getting her ready for the transaction.

And besides, she looked so cute now that she had regained her little-girl appearance. Why not make the most of it while he could?

With the girl he was already grooming to take Maggie's place safely out the back door and on her way, Jake called out, "Just a minute," and hurried to the front door to welcome his companion for the night.

Reaching for the doorknob, he shook his head and grinned. *It's a rough life*, he thought, *and I sure am glad I'm the one who gets to live it!*

It grieved her that both her parents despised and rejected her husband.

Chapter 25

ZHEN-LI HAD BEEN THINKING A LOT OF HER PARENTS LATELY, AND also of the baby she had been forced to abort. She knew she would one day see her precious child again, but her parents...

Always her heart ached at the thought that they were so closed to God's love. Their indoctrination along party lines was strong, so much so that they were able to turn against their own daughter and even have her unborn child—their grandchild—murdered. And their only living grandchild, little Zhou Chan, was already four years old and, as far as Zhen-Li knew, they still had not seen him.

Nearly as difficult as dealing with those issues was the fact that Zhen-Li knew her father was furious with her for shaming him and rejecting a loyal party member as her husband, instead choosing a Christian peasant who could scarcely keep a roof over their heads. It grieved her that both her parents despised and rejected her husband. Though he had gone to them with a humble heart to request their permission and blessing to marry their daughter, they had not only denied his request but refused even to acknowledge him as a fellow human being. How was it possible that anyone could refuse to at least give this kind, gentle man who worked so hard to support his family a chance to prove himself?

The thoughts of her loved ones were especially vivid that night, as Mei lay sleeping in the cell beside her. The nights were warmer now, so they no longer needed to huddle together for warmth. Yet whether from habit or loneliness, they often did so anyway.

Zhen-Li was glad. Despite the fact that she now knew Mei often reported to the guards about things Zhen-Li or the other prisoners said or did, Zhen-Li had come to care for the sad-eyed girl as if she were her own sister. And though the two women were fairly close in age, Zhen-Li felt protective of Mei as she would of a helpless child, despite the fact that she knew there would be nothing she could do to help Mei if she really needed it.

Except to pray, she reminded herself, glancing again at the sleeping woman who, even in slumber, did not appear at peace. *Qin Ai de Tian Fu*, she prayed silently, *she needs You so desperately! What will it take to open her eyes and her heart to Your great love?*

At that moment Zhen-Li knew that whatever it was that would cause Mei to see and desire Zhu Yesu as her Savior could ultimately cost Zhen-Li dearly. Instinctively she rolled to her side, pulling her knees to her chest and recoiling at the thought. But even as she lay there, trembling with fear, she heard the voice, echoing in her heart.

Are you willing, My daughter?

Daughter. The word pierced her heart more sharply and exquisitely than any dagger ever could. Tears flooded her eyes, and she nodded, relaxing as she slowly unfolded from her fetal position. "Yes," she whispered, nodding. "I am willing, Tian Fu. But please, make me more so, for I am terribly afraid."

Fear not, came the voice. *For I am with you...even to the end.*

The warm midmorning breeze was of little comfort to Julia as she sat on the front porch of River View Manor and contemplated the immediate future. The news wasn't good. Laura's heart had deteriorated to the point that it was beyond repair; her days were numbered.

But then, whose aren't? Julia reminded herself, trying to put things into perspective despite the fact that she wanted to throw herself on the floor and beg God to heal her friend and give them a few more years together. *None of us will live forever,* she reasoned. *At least, not in this broken-down, sin-sick world. And that's a good thing, Lord! Who would want to? But oh, how I will miss her if You take her home now!*

The words of correction came tenderly but clearly and to the point: *That's the problem, isn't it? It's not that you want to deny your friend her right to come home and be with Me; it's that you don't want her to leave you behind. Who is it that you're really concerned with, My child?*

A sob broke forth from Julia's chest, unbidden and unstoppable. She was usually so careful about keeping her emotions in check, at least where others could see her. But the Lord had spoken the very truth she needed to hear.

"I'm so sorry, Father," she said, her voice scarcely above a whisper. "Truly I am. But You're right. I was only concerned about myself—how I would feel if Laura went on to be with You, leaving me without a companion, a prayer partner."

She waited, gathering her strength before plunging ahead. She had approached the other two residents who attended the Sunday afternoon services at River View, but neither had been receptive to joining her in prayer. Still, she couldn't allow her loneliness to engulf her and make her any more self-centered than she tended to be anyway. "Forgive me, Lord," she said at last. "This is not about me. This is about Laura—and You. Your will and purpose for her life, and Your timing. Father, You know I'll miss her if You take her home. But...not my will, but Yours, Lord. I trust You, no matter what happens."

Glancing up she mustered a weak smile. "But I wouldn't mind if You'd leave her just a little while longer, Lord—or at least let me pray with her one more time. Would that be all right, Father? Just one more time."

***

Margaret hadn't slept well and had scarcely been able to choke down her breakfast. Her nerves were taut and her excitement level high. The group she'd called about the church service invading her right to a peaceful home was sending someone out to talk with her today, and she couldn't think of anything else. When breakfast was over, she decided to head out to the porch to get some fresh air while she waited.

The front door was open, and as she and her walker came to a halt in front of the screen, she heard a voice—soft, hesitant, and if she wasn't mistaken, wrapped in tears. Though she was able to discern only a few phrases here and there, the intent was obvious.

"Sorry, Father...concerned about myself...not about me...about Laura—and You...not my will, but Yours..."

Julia Crockett. Margaret would know that voice anywhere. No doubt the pathetic woman was praying about her equally pathetic friend, Laura, who lay sick and dying at the hospital just blocks from the home. Though Margaret certainly wouldn't wish anything bad on the bedridden woman, her demise was bound to simplify the situation with the afternoon worship services at River View Manor.

Scolding herself for her thoughts, Margaret heard the voice continue, a bit stronger this time. "But I wouldn't mind if You'd leave her just a little while longer, Lord—or at least let me pray with her one more time. Would that be all right, Father? Just one more time."

Margaret shook her head. What was wrong with the woman? How weak must she be to grovel at the feet of an imaginary Sovereign? Worse yet, if there truly were such a God, why would she be foolish enough to expect a favor from Him? All it took was one look around the tragic world they lived in and it was obvious that any deity that might exist was certainly not a kind or benevolent one.

Which is exactly why I have chosen to have nothing to do with Him, Margaret reminded herself as she turned her walker away from the door and pushed it back toward the hallway and the sanctuary of her room. *Let those foolish weaklings spend their time asking Him for favors if they want to, but they're not going to foist it on me! And that includes their noisy services on Sunday afternoons. Whatever it takes, I will see that those are stopped—or at least moved somewhere else so I don't have to hear them.*

★★★

Maggie awoke feeling a bit cranky. Her head hurt, and things just didn't feel quite right.

Then she remembered. Jake had denied her any drugs the night before. He had assured her she didn't have to stop altogether; he just wanted her to cut back a bit so she'd be more alert.

"You'll feel things better that way, experience them more deeply," he had crooned as he lay next to her, sliding his fingers up and down her bare arm.

Maggie had wondered how she could feel or experience things any more deeply than she did right then, with the touch of his fingers and the smile on his face nearly setting her skin on fire.

Confused, she'd wondered why he wanted her to take less of the drugs that he had given her in the first place. But she didn't want to risk upsetting him, so she didn't ask. Maybe he hadn't figured on the two of them falling so deeply in love. Now that they were, he must feel the drugs were infringing on their enjoyment of one another. And if that was the case, then Maggie, too, wanted to cut back—though it wouldn't be easy.

It hadn't been so bad last night, with Jake showering all his passion and attention on her. But this morning, with sunlight filtering through the faded curtains, her craving for the drugs was nearly more intense than her desire for Jake.

She turned her head and looked around. The room was empty. Where was he? Slowly she pulled herself to a sitting position. Somewhere in the distance she heard a voice—Jake's, she was sure of it. But whom was he talking to?

Wrapping herself in a blanket, she tiptoed down the short hallway to the bedroom where just the day before a lady named Joan had given her a makeover.

"Don't worry," she heard Jake say, his voice hushed. "Everything's under control. Trust me."

When he paused, Maggie cleared her throat to let him know she was standing there. Immediately Jake's head jerked up and his eyes widened. Then, almost as immediately, his look of surprise was replaced by a smile.

"Listen," he said into the receiver, "I have to go. Let me call you back." Then he flipped his phone shut and stood up from the bed.

"Hey, Snow White," he said, walking toward her with his arms outstretched, "who woke you up? I thought you'd sleep all day—or at least until your Prince Charming came to wake you."

She swallowed, melting gratefully into his arms as he pulled her close. "My head hurts," she said. "And I feel kind of...funny."

Jake kissed the top of her head. "Don't worry, baby. I'll take care of you. I know exactly what you need, and I'll fix you right up."

He held her away and tilted her chin up with his right hand. "I told you I wanted you to cut back," he said, still smiling, "not quit altogether. I won't let you suffer, you'll see."

When he pressed her against his bare chest once again, Maggie let out a sigh of relief. She should have known Jake would take care of her. After all, he loved her...didn't he?

It was not something he would soon forget.

Chapter 26

WHEN MEI AWOKE DURING THE NIGHT, HER THOUGHTS WERE nearly as troubled as her dreams had been. Glancing at Zhen-Li, who slept silently beside her, she knew her cell mate's fate was the key to her torment. All she could think of when she'd come back to her cell on the previous evening was that Tai Tong was back, and he had made it known to the other guards that he planned to make Zhen-Li pay for shaming him. How he could view the kind woman's self-sacrifice as shameful to the one whose life she had saved seemed incomprehensible, but Mei knew that was exactly how Tong saw it. And it was not something he would soon forget.

Mei's heart constricted as she watched her sleeping friend. Though she considered Zhen-Li a fool for believing in Zhu Yesu, she also admired her for being able to hold on to her faith — unlike Mei, who had relinquished hers so very long ago.

Or had she ever even had it? That was a question she pondered often these days, particularly when Zhen-Li sang that annoying Christmas song. The Baby Yesu! What kind of *shen* comes as a helpless baby, knowing those who were supposed to worship and believe in Him would instead turn on Him and kill Him? If He existed at all, He was either very stupid...or very weak. Whichever it was, Mei could not imagine that He would be of any use to her.

As much as she hated it and would like to believe otherwise, she continued to trust only in herself. It wasn't much, but it was all she had. So far, though it had meant humiliating herself almost beyond imagining in order to please the guards who used and mocked her, at least she had survived. These same guards who abused her also gave her extra food "to keep up her strength," as they put it. Then they would laugh and look knowingly at one another before degrading her once again.

It was a nightmare existence, but Mei clung to it with what little strength and hope she had. To know that Zhen-Li would face an even worse fate brought great sorrow to her heart. It was bad enough to endure the worst humiliation at the hands of your tormentors when you knew there was a good chance you would survive the torture and possibly even be rewarded in some small way. But to suffer through such inhumane treatment only to have the life crushed out of you when it was over was enough to make a quick and painless death sound enticing.

✳✳✳

Margaret was encouraged. The representative from the group had arrived while the other residents were napping after lunch. The meeting had gone well, with the woman spending nearly an hour in Margaret's room, taking notes and asking questions. Before she left she assured Margaret that she would follow up, though she could make no promises. However, she felt it was very possible that the courts might agree that the rights of the residents who did not attend the Sunday afternoon gatherings were being violated.

Now that the woman had gone, Margaret decided to venture out of her room. Leaning on her ever-present walker, she shuffled warily down the hall, not wishing to cross paths with that weak-kneed Julia creature who spent her time whining and imploring a nonexistent God for a chance to see her friend Laura one more time.

Humph, she thought, rounding the corner from the hallway into the family room where, thankfully, the chairs in front of the large, blank television screen sat empty. *As far as I'm concerned, those two were too close anyway. It's just not natural to be that attached to a friend.*

She lowered herself into the recliner directly in front of the television, right next to the end table, where the black remote beckoned her. *Not that I've never had close friends,* she reminded herself, picking up the remote and clicking the ON button. As she waited for the screen to flicker to life, she considered several of the women she'd called "friend" through the years. They'd shared secrets and recipes, watched one another's children, and commiserated over unappreciative husbands. But Margaret couldn't for the life of her imagine caring so much about one of them that she'd get weepy about their welfare and start begging God to fix them! Besides, who needed friends like that anyway? She certainly didn't—wouldn't want them even if they tried to befriend her. Not that they would, of course.

Shifting her thoughts, she smiled as her favorite soap opera filled the screen. With all the other residents off doing something else, she could enjoy her show super-sized, rather than on the small set in her bedroom, and she could do so without interruption. It looked as if it might just turn out to be a good day after all.

Until the sound of a familiar rattle caught her attention. It was the unmistakable noise of a walker, and it was headed her way. Surely not—

But it was. Julia Crockett, her short gray curls framing her only slightly chubby and not too wrinkled face. For a brief moment Margaret found herself wishing she had skin as smooth as Julia's...and then she wished even harder that Julia would just turn around and go away. Unfortunately, it did not look as if she was about to do that.

★★★

The morning light had scarcely begun to invade the tiny cell that the two women called home. They had been awake just long enough for Zhen-Li to take up her daily position in the corner of the cell, on her knees, with her eyes closed and head bowed. She had invited Mei to join her many times, but always she declined. And so Zhen-Li prayed for her instead, as she did for so many others each morning.

When she knew her time was running short and the guards would soon come to take her outside to work with the others, she turned her prayer focus to herself.

"Help me, Zhu Yesu," she mumbled softly, almost inaudibly. "No matter what comes my way this day, do not let me fail You. I am so weak, Tian Fu, but You are so strong, and You have promised to be with me always. Walk with me, Zhu Yesu. Talk with me and hold me close, for I can do nothing without You."

She had scarcely finished putting her thoughts into words when she froze where she knelt. Her heart turned to ice within her, so much so that she imagined she would crack and splinter into frozen shards if she turned too quickly.

But she didn't need to turn. She knew the source of the noise that had interrupted her prayers. She would recognize it anywhere. It was the sound of Tai Tong's heavy boots as they approached her cell and stopped immediately outside. He was waiting for her. And the gasp she heard from Mei told her the recovered guard's visage showed that he had not come to thank her for her help during the earthquake.

Unmoving, she waited for his command—or for the sound of his unlocking the door and coming inside to drag her out by the hair, which she knew he might choose to do whether she obeyed his verbal commands or not. Still, it was easier to wait than to turn and face the inevitable.

No one spoke. Mei's gasp had been quickly followed by faint whimpers, but they were drowned out by the pounding of Zhen-Li's heart. *If only he would kill me quickly,* she thought. *Oh, what a coward I am, but it would be so much easier.*

Never will I leave you or forsake you.

The promise floated around her, as if on invisible wings, and yet it originated from within, flowing strength into Zhen-Li's quaking limbs. As if unseen hands had placed themselves beneath her arms, she felt herself lifted to her feet. Still leaning on the presence that kept her from falling back down to her knees, she turned and looked into the face of the man who struck such fear into her heart.

Evil. That was what she saw as he glared back at her. And hatred. He so obviously despised her. Why? What had she done to so infuriate him? When she could have run for her life, possibly even escaped this horrible place, she had instead called for help and stayed with him until that help arrived, knowing it meant her chance of escape had vanished. But it had been the right thing to do. The right thing . . .

In that instant she understood. He hated her for that very reason—because she did the right thing. Because she followed God and chose His ways and worshiped Him instead of the Chinese government. Because she refused to compromise what she believed, even in the face of persecution. And by Zhen-Li's choice, Tai Tong stood condemned.

Taking a deep breath, she waited, dropping her eyes so he would not think her insolent. Whatever else he thought of her, she would not add that word to the list.

And whatever he had planned for her, she would trust the One who held her in His hands to carry her through it—even if she must pass through the valley of the shadow of death.

The two had become like sisters.

Chapter 27

Laura lay in her hospital bed, watching the evening shadows deepen outside the window, grateful that her family had gone home for a while. She was tired, and so were they.

She smiled. Soon she would be able to rest—really rest—though she imagined that meant more than just lying around listlessly. She envisioned herself dancing and singing and skipping...and the sooner the better! Though she knew it wouldn't be easy for the loved ones she left behind.

Besides her family, that meant the residents of River View Manor, particularly dear Julia. The two had become like sisters. They shared everything, and it would be tough for Julia to carry on their prayer vigils alone.

Maybe she won't be alone.

The thought came to her unbidden, and Laura frowned. Was it possible one of the other residents who considered themselves Christians would join Julia as a prayer partner? It didn't seem likely, but then God could do anything...with anyone. After all, hadn't He saved her and blessed her all these years? Who was to say He wouldn't do the same with someone else at the home?

As Laura pondered the possibilities, a light rap at her open door drew her attention. Nearly astonished at the sight, Laura laughed with joy as Julia came into view, leaning on her walker and looking hesitantly in her direction.

Laura's laugh brought on an instant coughing spasm, but she managed to wave Julia in, motioning her to sit on the lone chair beside the bed. By the time Julia had settled in, Laura had stopped coughing and was working to catch her breath again.

"How...how did you get here?" she gasped.

Julia's pale blue eyes glistened with tears, and the slight lines in her otherwise smooth skin showed her concern. "Rocky gave me a ride," she said, patting Laura's hand gently so as not to disturb the needle that delivered her intravenous feeding. "He said he knew how much we missed one another. But, please, don't try to talk, dear friend. Just rest and get well. I'll talk and pray. You just listen and agree."

Laura smiled. "Still a bit bossy, aren't you?" Her breathing was returning to normal, and she wanted Julia to know how pleased she was to see her. "God bless Rocky...for his thoughtfulness. He always was my favorite employee at the manor." She swallowed, took another deep breath, and continued, feeling a bit stronger now. "And he was absolutely right. We needed to see one another."

Julia's tears began to spill over onto her cheeks, as she nodded her agreement. "Oh, yes! I've missed you so. River View is just not the same without you there. Nothing is the same without you."

Laura used her spare hand to snag a tissue from the box on the stand beside her bed, and then handed it to Julia. Though Laura, too, was fighting tears, she did her best to hold them back.

"This is no time for sadness," she said, smiling to try and encourage her friend. "You and I both knew this day would come; we just didn't know when, or who would be first. Looks like I just might beat you home."

Her words only seemed to increase Julia's waterworks, though she valiantly mopped at her face and managed to return a shaky smile. "I promised myself I wasn't going to do this. When Rocky offered to bring me to see you, I was so glad for the opportunity, so excited at the thought of seeing you again. And what do

I do when I get here? Blubber like a baby!"

Laura chuckled, careful to restrain her laughter so she wouldn't start coughing again and upset Julia. She truly was pleased and grateful to see her dear friend and to have a chance to pray with her one last time—though she resolved not to utter those words aloud. And besides, the doctor had said there wasn't much they could do for her at this point, but he had also said she could rally and have several more months, or possibly even a year, before she passed on. So one never knew...

"Dear Julia," she said, "thank you beyond words for being such a wonderful friend to me these last years. We have certainly had some great prayer times together, haven't we?"

Julia's smile appeared braver than Laura imagined she felt. "And we shall have many more before we leave this planet. Why, just look at you! Your color is much better than I'd expected. How are you feeling? What do the doctors say?"

"I feel fine," Laura assured her. "And who knows about those doctors? I don't pay much attention to them. They can offer educated guesses, but only God knows when our days on earth are finished. It is He who numbers them, you know."

Julia nodded. "That is so true, my dear friend. So true. And we must make the most of them, however many they may be."

"Then we'd better get busy praying," Laura suggested, smiling again. "I imagine you have quite a list for me, am I right?"

"Most definitely," Julia agreed. "And here are the most pressing things, beginning with a very brief visit I had earlier with Margaret. We didn't say much to one another, just sat and watched television together, but I can tell she is really hurting."

Maggie was feeling much better. Not only had Jake supplied her—free of charge—the minimum amount of drugs she needed, but he had allowed her to hang around his place all day and had been quite attentive besides. Now, with darkness descending on the house, she was excited to see that he was making plans for their evening together, as he lit candles and incense and put some romantic music on to set the mood.

Not that he needed to, of course. She would gladly give herself to him anywhere, any time—with or without candles or any other mood-setting enticements. But it was nice to know that he was willing to make the extra effort.

Twice during the day she had noticed that Jake drifted away into his bedroom, though unlike that morning he had been careful to close the door, barring her from following him. She knew better than to open the door without first being invited in, but during his second closed-door escape, she had tiptoed down the hallway just far enough to overhear snatches of what was obviously Jake's end of a phone conversation.

"Nothing to worry about," she'd heard him say. "...under control...ready to fly...a brand new bird to take her place."

What in the world was that supposed to mean? She longed to ask but decided against it. Best to return to the living room and wait for Jake to join her—which he had, several times. And though she had flirted with the idea of mentioning the overheard phone conversation, his kisses always drove the thought from her mind. Now, as she watched this handsome creature who was so obviously and amazingly in love with her prepare for a special time together, she felt her heart soar at her good fortune.

So many girls my age have no idea what real life is all about, she thought. *They're happy with school and homework and slumber parties. The biggest deal in their lives is making the cheerleading squad. I wonder what they'd think if they knew how much better I have it than them? If they took one look at Jake and knew even for a minute what it feels like to be in his arms, they'd fight to trade places with me.*

She smiled as he turned toward her, his preparations complete and the look on his face promising an evening she would never forget. *But what have any of those other girls got that I'd want? I've already got everything any girl could ever need, and I wouldn't trade it for anything.*

Opening her arms to him, she welcomed his crushing embrace as he once again exerted his ownership of her heart, and everything that went with it.

For yet another day Zhen-Li found herself toiling outside under the midmorning sun. Though she was grateful to be there rather than locked away with Tai Tong, she was also confused over this turn of events. Just when she had resigned herself to her final fate on earth, the scowling guard had given her a silent reprieve, walking away without a word and leaving her standing in her cell, head bowed, wondering what to expect next.

For several minutes she had been afraid to move or speak, but at last Mei had stepped up next to her and slipped an arm around her waist.

"He is gone," she'd said, and Zhen-Li felt her shoulders relax as she let out her breath in a sigh.

"But he will be back," Zhen-Li whispered.

Mei did not respond.

"I just wish I knew when," Zhen-Li said, raising her head to look at her companion.

Mei shook her head. "No, you don't," she said. "It is better not to know."

Their eyes locked for a moment, and then Mei released her. "I must prepare for the day," she said softly. "They will come for me soon."

Zhen-Li watched her friend, who did little in response to her announcement of preparation. How could someone prepare for a day of shame and humiliation, particularly if that person did not know Zhu Yesu as Savior? Where could you turn for strength to endure?

Mei stopped in the center of the cell and turned slowly toward Zhen-Li. Just enough light had entered the cell by then that tears were visible in her eyes. "Why do you sing that song?" she asked.

Zhen-Li raised her eyebrows. *The Christmas song? Is that what she meant?*

"Do you mean the song about Baby Yesu—*Ping' an ye, sheng shan ye?*"

Mei nodded.

Zhen-Li hesitated. Why did she sing that song and not some other? She wasn't sure, nor did she have a clear answer to give. She would simply speak what was on her heart.

"I believe Zhu Yesu wants me to sing it to you," she said. "I believe He wants me to pray for you and to tell you about Him...while there's time."

Now it was Mei who raised her eyebrows. "Time? What do you mean?"

"I'm not sure," Zhen-Li answered. "I am only telling you what is in my heart."

Mei turned away, silent, while Zhen-Li waited.

After a moment Mei turned back to her and whispered, "Will you sing it to me again now?"

Zhen-Li was stunned. Though she knew Mei had tolerated her singing of the Christmas song in the past, never had she specifically requested it. *Qin Ai de Tian Fu,* Zhen-Li prayed silently, *there must be a reason. Please, please open Mei's heart to receive whatever You wish for her.*

And then she began to sing, softly and hesitantly at first, a bit stronger as she continued. To her amazement, Mei joined in toward the end, her voice trailing off when they noticed the sound of approaching guards.

"*Xiexie,* Zhu Yesu," Zhen-Li had whispered, just before the guards unlocked the cell and took Mei to her usual activity and Zhen-Li outside to work with the others.

She repeated the words now, as she reveled in the warmth of the sun and even the ache in her back as she worked. Not only had she been spared from spending her day with Tai Tong, but Mei's heart was being turned to Zhu Yesu. Zhen-Li had to restrain herself from opening her mouth and singing once again.

It was time.

Chapter 28

MEI HAD TAUGHT HERSELF TO GO FAR AWAY, TO A PLACE WHERE she no longer felt the pain or humiliation. Today, as the two guards who claimed her "companionship" laughed and abused her, Mei had once again removed herself to that faraway haven. And though she had been there many times before, never had she been so aware of the fact that she was not alone in that place.

Dare I think it? she wondered. *Is it possible that this Zhu Yesu whom my parents talked and sang about all those years when I was growing up is real—and that He truly does love me? But how could He? How can He forgive me for—?*

At that point she seemed to interrupt herself, breaking the carefully constructed shield that protected her from the ugly reality that had become her life. Snapped back to the images of the two men who mocked and humiliated her, she shut her eyes, hoping to return to her safe place. It was the only way to survive from day to day...

But just before drifting away, she resolved to talk with Zhen-Li when they were alone in their cell this night. It was time. Mei would ask her if it was possible that Zhu Yesu could forgive even her. If so, then perhaps there was hope for her after all. In the meantime, she would sing the Christmas song in her mind, the one about the Baby Yesu that Zhen-Li sang to her so often—the one that had begun to sound like a chorus of angels each time Mei heard of that one silent, holy night.

Maggie missed her body jewelry and her multicolored hair. But each time she opened her eyes during the night and saw Jake lying beside her, she knew it was all worth it—everything, including giving up school and her friends and all the things she used to think were so important. And if she and Jake handled things right, Maggie just might get her family back in the process. Her parents were already blown away with her "new old" look, as Maggie thought of it, and she could only imagine what Grandma Margaret would think when she saw her.

A dim twinge of conscience nipped at her heart at the thought of her grandmother, but she ignored it. So what if she'd stolen from her and also from one of the other hags who lived at that disgusting old people's home. Seriously, what were they going to do with jewelry at their age, anyway? And her dad's ivory-handled knife? It wasn't like he didn't have tons of other knives, right?

She smiled in the near darkness of the room. Of course she was right! Everything was right—so long as she was with Jake. Her entire life had changed when she met him, and she wouldn't go back to the way it was before for anything. At last her life was as close to perfect as it could get, and it was all because Jake loved her.

The rest just didn't matter at all.

The long workday had at last come to an end. Zhen-Li's back ached and she could scarcely pull her shoulders out of their hunched position, but at least she had been spared a little while longer.

Trudging back to her cell under the watchful eye of a guard, she wondered if tomorrow would be the day Tai Tong came for her—not just to announce his presence or to frighten her, but to actually take her away with him where he would no doubt finish what he had started before being interrupted by an earthquake.

An earthquake, she mused as her cell came into sight and she felt herself smile when she saw that Mei was already there, waiting for her. *Who would have thought Zhu Yesu could take advantage of such a huge natural event to deliver me from the hand of my tormentor? But He did. Is it possible He might do so again?*

Considering what Mei and so many others had been through, Zhen-Li saw no reason that she should be singled out for special treatment, but she also knew that God could do anything, anywhere, at any time—if it was His purpose.

May I always be found in the center of Your purpose, she prayed silently, stepping through the unlocked door into her cell and waiting silently until the door clanked shut and was locked behind her.

She smiled down at Mei, who sat on the floor, leaning against the wall, looking up at her. Zhen-Li thought she detected a spark in her cell mate's dark eyes, something she hadn't seen before. Tilting her head slightly to one side, she studied Mei for a moment.

"What is on your mind, my friend?" she asked, smiling as she joined her, sitting on the floor beside her and leaning her back against the wall. "Do you have something to tell me?"

Mei raised her eyebrows, appearing surprised at the questions. "How did you know?"

Zhen-Li widened her smile. "I saw it in your eyes. A question. A curiosity."

Mei dropped her gaze before she spoke. "I have a question for you, but..."

Zhen-Li waited. When Mei didn't continue, Zhen-Li laid her hand on her arm. "What is it, Mei? Are you afraid to ask?"

Mei nodded her bowed head slightly before raising it to look into Zhen-Li's eyes. "It is about Zhu Yesu. About the song you always sing. About the things you believe, and..." Her voice seemed to trail off for a moment before she continued. "And if it's

207

true that . . . He could love me." She dropped her head again, and Zhen-Li had to strain to hear her final words. "Even me."

Zhen-Li felt the hot tears pool in her eyes as she gathered her friend in her arms. "Mei," she whispered, "of course He loves you—very much. So much that He gave His very life for you. That same baby I sing about, the One who came on that holy night so long ago, is the same One who willingly offered His life for you—to pay for your sins and mine."

She lifted Mei's chin with her finger and waited until the trembling woman made eye contact. "He took your sins, Mei," Zhen-Li said, "and He also took your shame. All of it."

At those words, Mei's face crumpled and she broke into sobs, burying her face on Zhen-Li's shoulder as she wept. "Can He forgive me?" she whispered between her sobs. "Can Zhu Yesu ever forgive me?"

Zhen-Li smiled as she caressed the woman's hair. "He already paid the price for your sins," she crooned. "He's just waiting for you to come to Him and receive His forgiveness. Are you ready to do that now, my friend?"

As the early morning light began to peek its way into Julia's bedroom window, she lay on her back, staring at the ceiling and going over her visit with Laura. They had spent as much time in prayer as they could before the nurse came in and shooed Julia away, telling her Laura needed to rest. Julia knew that was true, but she had resisted leaving her friend behind.

Much of the night after she returned home had been spent praying for Laura. If only God would spare her for a little longer! Julia knew her request was a selfish one, as Laura was completely ready and even anxious to move on and leave this old world behind. But Julia was still too close to the situation to be objective about it, and life without her beloved friend and prayer partner just wasn't something she was ready to consider at this point.

In addition to praying for Laura, Julia had continued through the prayers that she and Laura had started at the hospital—

praying for the woman in China, and also for Margaret and Maggie. Laura, like Julia, seemed to sense an urgency about Maggie's situation, and Julia found herself thinking of the girl often throughout the night. What was going on in her life? How was it possible that such a lovely young girl could so obviously be drifting through life with no direction or goals? What would become of her without the proper supervision or guidance? And what was the girl's relationship with her parents?

So many questions, so few answers. Julia shook her head and sighed, offered up a final petition for the girl named Maggie, as well as Maggie's grandmother, and then pulled herself from bed to start another day.

She wondered if he just might ask
her to marry him.

Chapter 29

Tʜᴇ ᴅᴀʏ ʜᴀᴅ ʙᴇᴇɴ ᴀɴ ᴇxᴄɪᴛɪɴɢ ᴏɴᴇ ꜰᴏʀ Mᴀɢɢɪᴇ, ᴀs sʜᴇ ʜᴀᴅ spent it entirely with Jake. When she had ventured to mention their future together and asked how they would handle the situation with her mom and dad, he had smiled and assured her that things were about to change, and very soon her parents would no longer be a problem. Maggie sure hoped he was right because she knew that any day now the school was going to manage to get in touch with her parents, despite Maggie's efforts to intercept their messages, and then the game would be over.

Well, maybe not over, she thought, as she strolled home in the late afternoon sunlight, glad that Jake had given her just enough drugs to hold her over until she saw him again. *But the rules will sure be changed. Still, I've always managed to handle my parents before. And besides, I have Jake on my side now. I can't wait to see what he has planned.*

Smiling at the thought, she wondered if he just might ask her to marry him. Sure, she was young, but Jake said their age difference wasn't a problem. In fact, he said it was actually a good thing because then he could "train her" the way he wanted her.

Maggie laughed out loud. She wasn't sure exactly what Jake had in mind when he said that, but she liked what he was doing so far. How could his future plans for her be anything but wonderful? And according to him, he would begin to reveal those plans to her tomorrow night.

***

Leo closed his shop a few hours early. And why not? Customer traffic was up, and he had turned a nice profit today. But that wasn't the reason he was smiling as he flipped the OPEN sign to CLOSED on the front door.

Tomorrow night he would receive some merchandise that was worth substantially more than any of the used trinkets that made their way in and out of his shop. Jake was going to deliver the goods he'd promised, and Leo would then pass them on to his buyers, receiving enough to cover all of Leo's overdue bills and leaving him with a little left over besides. Though the nature of the transaction niggled at his conscience on occasion, it wasn't enough to make him turn down such a lucrative opportunity. The only thing he needed to do was act as a middle man. Jake caught all the fish and passed them to him, and Leo held on to them until the details of the sale were completed and the merchandise delivered to their final destination. How hard could it be?

Leo grinned as he scanned his now closed pawnshop, thinking about the empty room upstairs that awaited the precious cargo. Jake had cautioned Leo that, as usual, he couldn't promise "undamaged goods" to the buyers—but close. She was young, fresh, and only "slightly used," so she should still bring a good price.

Leo chuckled. However slightly used the girl might be, she would be more so by the time he delivered her in a few days. It was just one of the perks of the job, a fringe benefit that made whatever dangers might be involved more than worth the risk.

Still grinning with anticipation, he climbed the stairs to take one last look at what served as a holding room for the various "packages" that passed through his hands. He wanted to be sure he hadn't forgotten a thing.

★★★

Mei awoke feeling lighter than she'd ever imagined possible. The weight of guilt and shame had lifted from her shoulders, and her heart sang, even in the predawn darkness. Glancing to her side, she saw Zhen-Li sleeping peacefully beside her, and everything came back into focus.

"Qin Ai de Tian Fu," Mei whispered. "Dear heavenly Father, You are real." She closed her eyes and placed her hands over her heart. "And You are here. Right here, with me. Oh, Zhu Yesu, xiexie! Thank You, thank You!"

She wanted to wake Zhen-Li to thank her as well, but she knew it would be kinder to let her sleep as long as possible. The poor woman had seemed so weary when she returned from her many hours of labor the previous evening. But, oh, how glad Mei had been to see her cell mate walk through the door! She had been waiting, anticipating the moment ever since she herself had returned from her day's duties, having already made the decision that she was going to ask Zhen-Li about Yesu. Was He real? Did He truly love her? Could He forgive even her?

The answer to all her questions had been yes, and Mei had felt hope explode in her chest, birthing joy and excitement right along with it. Though she and Zhen-Li still languished in their dark, empty cell, with no reasonable expectation of deliverance from their pitiful circumstances, Mei knew that everything had changed. As she had prayed with Zhen-Li, asking Zhu Yesu Jidu to forgive her for her sins and to become her Lord and Savior, it was as if everything dark and heavy had fled in the light of His presence.

Oh, how my parents would rejoice to know of this day, she thought. *Zhu Yesu, if they are still alive, somewhere on this earth, please let them know somehow. And if they are with You, then they must already know.*

She smiled then, as she realized that wherever her parents were at this moment, there was no doubt that she would one day see them again. Oh, what a glorious promise! How many years had she buried the pain that had come from being separated from her mother and father—first because she had rejected their

213

faith and second because they were arrested for it, leaving her in shame and poverty. But now everything had changed; everything had become new! And she was certain that somehow, some way, Zhu Yesu would draw Mei's husband and child to Himself as well.

Zhen-Li stirred then, and Mei could restrain herself no longer.

"Good morning, dear friend," she said, her voice soft as Zhen-Li opened her eyes and turned toward her.

The women smiled at one another, their faces visible now in the growing light. "My dear sister," Zhen-Li said. "Truly now you are my sister, for we have the same Father."

Mei's heart soared at the thought. Of course that was true! Shang Di, the Most High God, was now their Father, and she and Zhen-Li were eternal sisters because of it.

"It is an amazing thing," Mei whispered, taking Zhen-Li's hand, and her cell mate nodded her agreement.

"Amazing and wonderful," Zhen-Li concurred. "It is so far beyond our understanding! I know that we have brothers and sisters all over the world because true believers everywhere have the same Father... but it is too difficult for me to comprehend."

Mei pondered her friend's words, unable even to think of an adequate response. Zhen-Li was right. Everything about God was so far beyond anything they could imagine, and yet they knew what really mattered: that He loved them and had made a way for them to be born into His family.

Rattling cell doors and pounding footsteps snapped their attention back to their present surroundings. The day was about to begin. Mei knew Zhen-Li prayed that once again she would be allowed to work outside with the others, rather than be taken away by Tai Tong. Mei prayed silently that God would grant that request to her beloved cell mate and sister, for she couldn't imagine what horrors might await Zhen-Li if she were forced to spend the day with the malicious guard who sought revenge on a woman who had done him such a great favor.

And then the realization of what she herself faced as the day progressed washed over her like muddy, sludge-filled flood-waters. God was now her Father! How could she possibly shame

Him by giving herself to the guards as she had been doing all this time in an effort to preserve her life?

Wide-eyed, she turned to Zhen-Li, whose gaze was already locked on hers. It was obvious Mei wasn't the only one who had realized the choice that lay ahead of her.

"What shall I do?" Mei whispered, nearly frantic at the sound of the approaching footsteps.

Zhen-Li appeared almost as panicked as Mei felt, as tears invaded their eyes and they quickly clasped hands. "I do not know," Zhen-Li answered. "But I know the One who does. And you now know Him too. Let us ask Him quickly what to do and then ask Him for the strength and courage to do it."

So many things about Jake were
mysterious to her, and in some ways
she liked that.

Chapter 30

Even though Jake had given her enough drugs to help her sleep, Maggie was restless. She had quickly become accustomed to waking up and finding Jake sleeping beside her. It was lonely now without him, and the loneliness made for a very long night.

"I miss you," she whispered into the darkness. "Are you thinking of me right now? Why couldn't you let me stay over tonight? I know you said you had some business, but why couldn't you do it with me there? If we get married, you'll have me around all the time then, so . . ."

She sighed and let her whispers fade away. So many things about Jake were mysterious to her, and in some ways she liked that. It made him that much more appealing. And yet it also made her wonder, when she lay alone in the dark as she did tonight. He said he loved her, and she had no reason not to believe him, but what if—?

No. She shook her head, as if to drive out the treasonous thoughts. Jake was as devoted to her as she was to him. They were going to be together—soon—and forever. She had no reason to doubt that.

Her makeover with the woman named Joan should have proven that, shouldn't it? Why else would Jake spend money to change Maggie's looks except to convince her parents that he was a good influence on her, that he loved her and would always take care of her? Surely her parents would see that and agree to let her marry him, wouldn't they?

Well, if not, she would do it anyway. One way or another, Maggie was determined to find a way to be with Jake all the time. No more nights away from him, lying in the dark all alone and wishing he was beside her. He had promised that the very next night he would begin to show her his plan for them to be together, and she could hardly wait.

They had come for Zhen-Li first, so she had no way of knowing what had happened when they took Mei from her cell. Yet even as Zhen-Li labored in the warming rays of the morning, she prayed for her friend. To be so new in the faith and to be tested so stringently was more than Zhen-Li could imagine. She at least had been able to spend time with other believers, as well as time with her Lord in prayer and Bible study, before being arrested and thrown into prison. It seemed Mei was experiencing a trial by fire before she'd had time to grow as a believer.

I know You don't make mistakes, Zhu Yesu, Zhen-Li prayed, struggling up an incline with a load over her shoulders, *but it is difficult for me to imagine how little Mei will stand strong under such persecution. Oh, Tian Fu, be her strength when she has none! Sustain her, Yesu. Hold her close.*

Zhen-Li remembered then how she had prayed for comfort and encouragement, for a visible reminder of God's faithfulness even behind prison walls. And she smiled.

Qin Ai de Tian Fu, Mei is that reminder, isn't she? The comfort and encouragement I prayed for. What better way to be reminded of Your faithfulness and power than to see a heart and life changed before my very eyes? Oh, Tian Fu, forgive me for doubting You! Of course You hold Mei in Your hand, even as You hold me. And there is no safer place to be in all the world. Thank You, Zhu Yesu. Thank You for Your love and faithfulness!

✳✳✳

Julia couldn't seem to fall asleep. Long after everyone else had drifted off, she found herself pacing—as much as someone on a walker could pace—back and forth in her room. She knew it was ridiculous; she should just plop herself down in her chair and pray, as she usually did. But tonight was different.

Oh, if only Laura were there to pray with her! But she wasn't. In fact, Laura was one of the reasons Julia felt so anxious. She was praying for her friend, for the woman in China, for the girl named Maggie. There seemed to be no end to the prayer needs that swirled around her.

"What is it, Lord?" Julia asked, speaking out loud, since she knew there was little chance any of the other residents could hear her now that they were all in bed and had removed their hearing aids. "What am I missing? I'm praying for all the people You've put on my heart and mind. Is there something else? Someone I've missed or forgotten?"

An image of Margaret Snowden filtered slowly into view, and Julia raised her eyebrows questioningly. "Are You trying to tell me something, Father? I've prayed for Margaret. You know I have! And I've tried to befriend her too. But, well, You know how impossible that is."

But the image remained, and Julia could no longer deny what she knew God was speaking to her heart. Not only did she need to pray for Margaret and continue to try to befriend her, but she also needed to ask God to forgive her for her attitude toward the woman. The truth was that Julia simply didn't like her, but she realized she could no longer use that as an excuse for her underlying animosity toward her. It was time to get the issue straightened out between Julia and her Lord, even if Margaret wanted no part of it.

Determined to do so, Julia at last made her way to the chair beside her bed, and then sat down to do some serious business with God.

***

Mei wanted nothing more than to die—except that she now wondered if God would still receive her. Just last night He had forgiven her and welcomed her into His family, and she had experienced a depth of joy she had never even imagined existed.

And then she had betrayed Him. She hadn't wanted to. She had tried not to, had tried to resist, to stand strong, but the pain had been too great, and she had yielded to the pressure to do whatever was necessary to make that pain go away.

Now, bruised and heartbroken, she waited alone in the cell for Zhen-Li to return from her day's work in the fields. How would Mei tell her brave friend that she was a coward who had denied Zhu Yesu and made a mockery of His sacrifice for her? Would Zhen-Li turn away from her when she knew? Would she offer words of condemnation or healing? Was there still hope for someone so weak as Mei, or had she failed the test and doomed herself to an eternity apart from Tian Fu?

With tears as her only companions, Mei waited, believing her soul hung in the balance.

Margaret knew Julia had gone to the hospital a couple of nights earlier to visit her friend. Curiosity nagged at Margaret to find out how their visit went and if there was anything different or more positive about Laura's prognosis. Nevertheless Julia hadn't said anything to anyone that Margaret had overheard, and she wasn't about to ask.

Right now, as she prepared to leave her room and go into the dining area for breakfast, Margaret was more concerned with Emily and her confounded continued harassment about Maggie and the jewelry. Though Margaret had little doubt that her granddaughter was a thief and had probably taken the old biddy's baubles, she wasn't about to admit it to Emily or the police or anyone. At this point it seemed to be a closed case except that each time Emily and Margaret crossed paths, which was often since they lived in the same house, Emily pounded her cane on the floor and demanded her jewelry back. Margaret managed to ignore her most of the time, but occasionally her temper got the best of her and she told Emily exactly what she thought of her, loud and clear. At least that seemed to shut Emily up more often than not, but it certainly didn't make for a pleasant living environment.

Blasted granddaughter, Margaret fumed as she fussed with her hair, trying to get it to stay in place on top of her head. Why was it giving her so much trouble these days? Didn't anything go right anymore? *Kids, grandkids, all of them—worthless. And now even my hair won't behave.*

She tossed her hairbrush back on the dresser and gave up. Her hair would just have to hang down until it decided to cooperate again. Meanwhile, she'd have to hope that the lady who had stopped by to see her would have some news soon about what could be done to stop the Sunday afternoon gatherings. That at least would make Margaret's life a lot more bearable.

Her first glimpse of her friend did
not bode well.

Chapter 31

Zhen-Li was exhausted by the time she stumbled back to her cell, but she was also anxious to see Mei and learn how she had fared during the day. Her first glimpse of her friend, huddled in the corner, head bowed and resting on her bent knees, did not bode well. She did not even look up at the clanking of the key in the lock when the guard opened the door for Zhen-Li to reenter.

"Mei?"

Though Mei still did not raise her head, Zhen-Li noticed a slight tremor in the woman's hunched shoulders. No doubt she was crying. Zhen-Li moved silently toward her and dropped down on the floor, just inches from where Mei sat in self-imposed exile.

"I am back," Zhen-Li said, laying her hand on Mei's shoulder.

She waited, and at last her friend lifted her head. Zhen-Li wasn't surprised at the redness of her eyes or the wetness of her cheeks, but she was shocked at the fresh bruises and swelling that marred her face. It was obvious Mei had paid a price today for her newfound faith.

"Zen me le?" Zhen-Li asked, resisting the temptation to touch Mei's injuries. "How are you? What happened? Are you all right?"

Mei opened her mouth, but no words emerged, only a strangled sob as she shook her head and dropped it again to her knees. Her shoulders shook violently then, as she nearly wailed with anguish when Zhen-Li pulled her close and rocked her while she cried. What could have happened to make her weep so deeply?

The night shadows had begun to invade their cell by the time Mei's tears stopped falling. Only an occasional shudder disturbed her otherwise still form, as Zhen-Li continued to stroke her hair and whisper words of comfort, even as she prayed that Zhu Yesu would give her the wisdom and encouragement her beloved friend so obviously needed.

At last Mei raised her head and fixed her puffy eyes on Zhen-Li. "I am not worthy to be called a follower of Zhu Yesu," she whispered. "You are so brave. You have followed Him so faithfully. But I"—she squeezed her eyes shut and held her breath for a moment, undoubtedly repressing another onslaught of weeping—"I failed Him."

Her brows drew together, intensifying her words. "I tried," she said. "Truly I did. I told the two guards that I could no longer participate in...in their activities, but...they just laughed and said I had no choice. When they began to hit me and kick me, I—"

Tears burst forth again and she buried her face in her hands, her final words muffled as she cried. "I did what they told me to do. I did it just so they would stop hurting me. And now I am so ashamed!"

Once again Zhen-Li gathered Mei into her arms and rocked her as she cried. At least now Zhen-Li understood the problem, and she prayed Zhu Yesu would help her lead Mei back to a place of forgiveness and peace. *Qin Ai de Tian Fu, help her to understand,* Zhen-Li begged silently. *Help me to know what to say and do!*

Without words the assurance came, and Zhen-Li knew her faithful Zhu Yesu was there to minister to Mei's broken heart and to reassure her that His love for her had not changed because of what she perceived as her failure. Zhen-Li knew she, too, would have to cling to that truth in the very near future.

Maggie was so excited that she was having trouble remembering everything Jake had said to her when he called. She knew tonight was the night he was going to tell her about his plan for them to be together, but she'd been surprised when her cell phone rang and he told her to be sure to bring a few extra things when she came over that evening.

"Just throw a couple of extra things in a bag or something," he'd said. "Enough to last you for a few days. I'll take care of everything else."

A few days? What did that mean? Was Jake planning to take her on a trip somewhere? And what was the "everything else" he planned to take care of? He must be taking her somewhere romantic, maybe to a beach somewhere.

Her heart raced as she tossed some extra clothes and a toothbrush in her backpack. What else should she take? Some makeup, of course, and—

Oh, she could hardly think! It was a good thing Jake was handling all the details, because it was all she could do just to gather what she needed for a couple of days away.

Satisfied that she had done the best she could and that if she needed anything else, including drugs, Jake would no doubt take care of it, she slipped out of her bedroom window into the afternoon haze and nearly skipped down the sidewalk toward Jake's house and freedom, her heart singing all the way.

After years of lying next to her husband each night and listening to him snore, Yin Xei thought she would go mad from the silence. She had been lying there through the long night hours, wondering whether sleep or morning would come first, but so far neither had arrived.

Who would have thought that a man who one day seemed so healthy and strong could the next day be gone, dead of a heart attack? Even more amazing, who would have thought she would miss his presence, even slightly, when she had so resented it while he was still alive? These were questions Xei had never considered, but now they had become her reality. The only person with whom she shared her life was no longer at her side. What was left for her now?

Even as the tears dripped slowly from her eyes and down her face into her ears and hair, she wondered why she was crying. Was it that she had cared for Yang Hong after all? Did she truly miss him now that he wasn't here? Or did his absence simply highlight the emptiness that already consumed her miserable life?

Xei had no answers, nor did she expect to find any as she fired them into the darkness of her room, aiming at nothing as she wallowed in despair. Hong was gone. The man who had slept at her side for so many years and who had fathered her only child and then kept her only grandchild away from her had slipped into nothingness without so much as a warning. Now Xei had no one. Her daughter was in prison, and her grandson was a stranger to her. The pain was so great she wondered if it might crush the life from her as well.

Tai Tong stood at Zhen-Li's cell door, waiting for the two women inside to awaken. It was disgusting the way they clung to one another, as if they truly cared. Five minutes alone with either of them and Tong knew he could turn one against the other without a second thought.

But Tong had no desire to be alone with Mei, though he had been so in the past many times. He had heard she offered resistance for the first time yesterday, which made her a bit more enticing, but then she had yielded to the pressure and returned to her compliant ways. She simply was no challenge to Tong. Her cell mate, however, was an entirely different matter.

Zhen-Li lay to the left of Mei, whose head was cradled on Zhen-Li's outstretched arm. He doubted they would be sleeping so peacefully if they knew what lay ahead of them.

Sounds of prisoners being awakened in other cells drifted their way, and soon the two women began to move. Tong watched without a word. The reward for his patience came when Zhen-Li opened her eyes and sat up, only to lock her gaze on her adversary, who stood over her in power, his very presence a promise of things to come.

Tong took pleasure in watching the woman's eyes widen, as did Mei's when she, too, awoke and realized they were being watched. He wondered at their thoughts, relishing the fear that no doubt dominated all other feelings.

No expression, he told himself. *Just watch. Let them wonder, worry, even pray. Most of all, let them realize that there is no escape for them. Their lives are in my hands. I will decide if they live or die, as well as how and when.*

With that silent promise spoken through his iron stare, he turned and walked away, leaving the two women to ponder his next move.

Even when Zhou Chi played with little Chan, it was obvious his mind was elsewhere.

Chapter 32

Zhou Ming was concerned. Her brother was more distracted than usual. Even when Zhou Chi played with little Chan, it was obvious his mind was elsewhere.

Zhen-Li. It had to be. Ever since the earthquake it seemed Chi could think of nothing else. Ming knew that his desire to see his wife, to confirm that she was all right, was driving him. She knew also that it was only his concern for Chan and herself that kept him from going to try to find her.

As Ming puttered around making tea and heating rice for their breakfast, she watched Chi kneel in prayer in the corner, and she knew he wept for Zhen-Li as he petitioned Tian Fu for her safety. It was obvious that Chi's commitment to Zhu Yesu had intensified since Zhen-Li's arrest.

What should Ming do? If it were just her, she would insist that Chi go to Beijing, however he must get there, and search until he found Zhen-Li. But it was little Chan who made the difference. Truly she and the boy might starve if Chi's absence were extended, for who knew how long he could be gone on such a difficult and even dangerous journey? That he might not return at all was a possibility she could not bear to consider.

Qin Ai de Tian Fu, she prayed silently, *surely there is a way! Will You please show it to us? Direct my brother and give him peace about his decision, whatever it may be. Assure him that You will care for us if he is to go to Beijing, and assure him that You will care for Zhen-Li if he is to stay here. And whatever he is to do, Tian Fu, please let me be a help to him. Let me know what I am to do in this situation to ensure Zhou Chan's safety.*

Ming glanced at the little boy who didn't cry for his mother as often anymore but who carried a permanent sadness in his eyes that seemed so much worse than tears. Her heart wrenched within her. Chan was her nephew, and she had grown to love him as if he were her own child. She knew she would give her life for him if need be, but would that be enough? Their situation in life was very hard, and if the boy was to going to live long enough to grow into manhood, he would need the care of Shang Di to do so. Neither her protection nor Chi's would be enough.

May I never cease to pray for Zhou Chan, she thought. *May I daily teach him of You, Zhu Yesu, and may he see You in my life. If that is my only purpose on this earth, then it is enough...*

She sensed the answer then, and she knew what she must do. Stepping across the room to the spot where her brother knelt in prayer, she laid her hand on his shoulder. He did not look up, but his lips stopped moving and she knew he listened.

"Go," she said. "Find Zhen-Li. God will provide for little Chan and me."

For a moment Chi did not answer. Then his head bowed in a slight nod, and Ming knew the decision had been made.

Julia was determined to break the proverbial ice that separated her and Margaret. But she knew it wouldn't be easy.

"We need a miracle here, Lord," she whispered, as she prepared to leave her room and walk the short distance down the hall to Margaret's room. Julia knew Margaret was there, as she had seen her leave the dinner table earlier that evening and disappear down the hall and behind her door. Julia had gone to her own room immediately after and prayed for clear direction, keeping an ear open in case Margaret left her room. But Julia hadn't heard anything to indicate that Margaret had done so, and it was time to put her plan into action.

She stopped her walker in front of Margaret's door and knocked. The television volume was quickly muted, but no one spoke. Julia knocked again.

"Margaret? It's me, Julia," she called. "May I come in?"

She waited another moment and was about to knock yet again when the door opened slightly and Margaret peered out, her hair askew and a puzzled frown on her face.

"What do you want?"

Julia took a deep breath. She had known this wouldn't be easy, and Margaret certainly wasn't making it so.

She smiled. "I just thought it would be nice to visit a bit before turning in for the night."

Margaret's eyebrows shot up in surprise, and her dark eyes appeared confused behind her glasses. Then her eyebrows drew together and her frown returned.

"Why would you want to do that?" she asked, opening the door an inch or so wider.

Julia shrugged and smiled. "Oh, I don't know. It just seems we're both sitting alone in our rooms with nothing to do and no one to talk to. So I thought we should sit and talk together for a little while — get to know one another a bit."

Margaret's frown deepened, and she appeared to study Julia as if looking for some ulterior motive. Just when Julia thought the woman was about to open the door and ask her to come in, she drew up straight and pushed her glasses back tight against her face.

"I don't think so," she said. "You're just lonely because your friend is in the hospital, and I don't feel like filling in for her. So if you're looking for someone to take her place, forget it. I don't pray, I don't believe in God, and furthermore, if I have anything to say about it, your obnoxious church services here at River View Manor will soon come to an end." She raised her eyebrows as if for emphasis and added, "And the sooner, the better."

The next thing Julia knew, the door slammed shut in her face, the TV volume had resumed inside Margaret's room, and Julia's attempt at reconciliation had become a complete disaster.

Vacillating between tears and anger, Julia turned her walker around and stomped back to her room, arguing with God the entire way. It was one thing to ask God to forgive her for her bad attitude; it was quite another to be expected to reach out to someone like Margaret Snowden. No wonder the crabby old woman had no friends and even her family didn't like her. She was insufferable! And as far as Julia was concerned, she had made her last attempt at befriending the miserable wretch. She had better things to do with her time.

Jake had welcomed Maggie with open arms, pulling her into the house before she could even knock and then locking the door behind her. "Now you're mine," he whispered as he held her close, tossing her backpack to the floor. "Say good-bye to that world out there. You've got a new life ahead of you now."

Maggie's heart fluttered at the realization that whatever Jake's plans included, she was now going to be able to stay with him all the time. She was thrilled, though she wondered how he was going to pull that off with her parents. But as he kissed her neck and ran his hands over her shoulders, she decided it didn't really matter. Jake was the wise one, the mature one with the plan, and all she needed to do was trust him to carry it out. The important thing was that she was finally going to get to be with him every day, every night—no more climbing in and out of her bedroom window and hiding behind her locked bedroom door, wondering how long it would be until her parents figured out she wasn't even going to school anymore. School was a thing of the past now. No more homework or tests or annoying teachers. From now on it was just Jake and Maggie...forever.

The thought weakened her knees, and she clung to Jake as he continued to hold and kiss her. She had nearly forgotten about his plan until he nudged her away from him and looked down at her with his dreamy eyes.

"So," he said, "you ready for the surprise?"

Maggie thought if she were any more ready she would burst, but she just giggled and nodded her head. She knew this was going to be more fun than anything she'd ever experienced in her life.

"Good," Jake said, smiling as he kissed the tip of her nose. "First, let's get you nice and relaxed with just the right chemicals."

Maggie raised her eyebrows. Chemicals? Drugs? "But I thought—"

Jake's smile widened. "I know, sweet cakes. You thought I wanted you to cut back. And I do! But like I told you, cutting back doesn't mean quitting. We're still going to do whatever it takes to have a really good time, right?"

Maggie nodded, hesitant but slightly reassured. Something didn't seem quite right, but she wasn't about to question the man who had just taken control of her life. She trusted him to take care of her, so whatever he wanted her to do, she knew she had to comply.

"Are you going to get relaxed too?" she asked, hoping his answer would be the reassurance she needed.

Jake laughed. "You mean, am I going to get high with you? Of course I am! You don't think I'm going to let you have all the fun, do you? Hey, baby doll, we're in this together, remember?"

Maggie felt her shoulders relax. How could she have doubted him? She nodded excitedly. "We sure are," she said, standing on her toes to kiss him again. "I love you so much, Jake."

"I love you too," he answered, his voice husky. "Now come on. Let's get this party started."

Within the hour, Maggie found herself floating in a cloud of unreality, drifting in and out of consciousness and wondering vaguely who Jake was talking to when she heard his voice in the distance. Was he on the phone? Was someone else there with them? Was he talking to her and she just couldn't understand him? Nothing seemed to make any sense. But when two strong arms lifted her from the floor, she used what little strength she had to loop her arms around his neck and then rested her head against his chest. She had no idea where he was taking her, but she knew she could trust Jake to take care of her, no matter what.

She knew neither of them would
be able to withstand the pressure in
their own strength.

Chapter 33

Zhen-Li awoke early and found Mei already on her knees, crying softly and asking God for strength to honor Him that day. Zhen-Li immediately rose from her spot on the floor and went to kneel beside her, slipping her arm around her friend's waist and joining her in prayer.

After leading Mei in prayer the previous evening and explaining to her that God still loved her and had not abandoned her, they had rejoiced together before falling into a peaceful sleep. But now the harsh realities of a new day were bearing down upon them, and she knew neither of them would be able to withstand the pressure in their own strength.

"For God has not given us a spirit of fear," Zhen-Li declared, calling to mind some of the Scriptures she had memorized before her arrest, "but of power and of love and of a sound mind." She felt Mei lean against her and knew God's words were impacting her. "Be our strength today, Zhu Yesu," she prayed. "Grant us Your power and love and a sound mind. We acknowledge that apart from You we can do nothing, but through You we can do all things. All things, Zhu Yesu! You can cause us to stand when we have no strength. Oh, Tian Fu, may we be found faithful this day, whatever it may bring!"

"Thank You," Mei whispered. "Thank You, Zhu Yesu!"

The women continued in prayer until they heard the sounds of approaching guards, the unmistakable noise of keys opening doors and heavy boots on cement. It was time to face the day, and despite the fear that swirled around them, they clung to the promises of a faithful God and stood to their feet to await their assignments.

***

Yin Xei moved as if on wooden feet, going through the motions of preparing for the day without thinking through her actions. The only thing she knew for sure was that more than ever she wanted to be near her family at this time, and that meant her daughter and grandson. Yet it was almost impossible to see Zhen-Li and nearly as impossible to see Zhou Chan.

And so she would do the next best thing. She would visit people who believed as Zhen-Li did. Yin Xei knew of several in her surrounding neighborhood, though she had heard that most of them gathered for worship in secret, usually late in the night when everyone else was asleep. But there was one home in particular where she was sure she would be welcome because the couple had greeted her on several occasions and more than once invited her to come to their home, though she had never done so. Now she was determined to go there. Perhaps they could help her understand why her daughter believed as she did. Perhaps they might even be able to help her find some meaning in what was left of her lonely life.

Making her way briskly down the still-quiet morning street, she was encouraged to see the door open and a bit of activity in and around the house that was her destination. She was pleased that the old couple who lived there was already awake. She imagined it would make her unexpected visit more palatable to them.

Xei and the elderly couple exchanged customary greetings, and to the couple's credit, neither husband nor wife showed surprise at her arrival but rather invited her inside. Within moments she was seated at their table, sipping tea and trading pleasantries about the weather. At last the old man known as Brother Wu, or Wu Dixiong, folded his hands and engaged Xei with his eyes.

"*Ni hao ma?*" he asked. "How are you, Yin Xei? I sense there is a burden on your heart."

Xei dropped her eyes, hoping to hide the tears that refused to be kept back. "It is my husband," she said. "Yang Hong. He...died just yesterday. A heart attack. I see the news has not yet reached you. But I have no one else, no other family I can go to, and—"

Her voice broke and a sob shook her shoulders. As she buried her face in her hands, the man's wife dropped to her knees beside the chair and pulled Xei into her arms, calling on the name of Zhu Yesu and holding Xei close as she wept. For the first time in all her years, Xei did not recoil at the name of her daughter's God, as the very sound seemed to soothe her aching heart, and she knew she had come to the right place after all.

✦✦✦

Maggie tried so hard to concentrate, to figure out where they were going, but her mind kept drifting away. She was awake, but everything was so fuzzy. This drug was different from anything Jake had given her before, and she hoped it would wear off soon, as she really wanted to be aware of all the details of this new life she would share with the man she loved. She especially wished her thoughts were clear now, as she wanted to see where they were going. Not long after the drug had started to take effect, Jake had carried her to his car, which was unusual since he'd hardly ever taken her anywhere before. They'd nearly always spent their time together at his house because Jake said he didn't want anyone to see them and alert Maggie's parents before they were ready to tell them in person. Apparently secrecy in their relationship was no longer necessary, and Maggie was thrilled. Just wait until those silly girls at school saw what a handsome, wonderful boyfriend she had! They'd understand then why she wasn't interested in any of their silly social stuff.

Slumped in the front seat, Maggie alternated between peering out the window to try to pinpoint their location and glancing at Jake, who sat beside her, driving. She tried several times to ask him where they were going, but she couldn't seem to get her mouth to work right. Each time she uttered a sound, however, Jake peeked at her and smiled before returning his eyes to the roadway.

"Don't you worry about a thing, baby cakes," he said. "You'll find out where we're going soon enough. We don't want to spoil the surprise now, do we?"

She supposed he was right, and she knew whatever he had planned would be great, but she just wished she could concentrate better. Whatever new drug Jake had given her she sure wouldn't take again! She could scarcely sit up, let alone think or talk. She wondered briefly why it hadn't affected him the same way, but she decided he was just more experienced and knew how to handle it. How else would he be able to drive?

When the car pulled to a stop in a dark alley, she frowned, once again squinting her eyes to try to establish her location. But nothing came into focus. There were no signs or lights to help her figure out where they were or why they had stopped.

Turning to Jake, she concentrated all her efforts into asking him where they were, but before she could speak he kissed her and said, "One last kiss for the road." Then he smiled and pulled back, opening the door and stepping out before coming around to the passenger side. Maggie watched his movements as if they were in slow motion, realizing he was opening her door and reaching in to lift her into his arms. She wanted to protest that she could walk, but she sensed that wasn't true. Besides, she liked being carried.

Smiling up at him, she clasped her hands behind his neck and leaned her head against his chest as he made his way down a dark walkway and stopped at an unmarked door. Balancing her carefully, he fished some keys from his pocket and unlocked the door, then carried her inside.

The room was stuffy and dimly lit, with the unmistakable odor of very old food predominant over other even more unpleasant smells. Wrinkling her nose, she hoped Jake would get her out of here quickly and on to wherever it was he was taking her. Why was he stopping here anyway?

The next thing she knew he was carrying her up a stairway at the far side of the room. Maggie wanted to protest, wanted to tell him that she just wanted to get out of this awful place. But she still couldn't speak clearly, and they were already more than halfway to the top.

When they reached the landing, Jake once again balanced her in one arm while he unlocked another door and took Maggie inside.

What was this? Her vision was blurry, but she was able to see that they were in a small room, furnished with a four-poster bed. In the corner was what appeared to be a doorless bathroom, not much larger than a closet. A single, dim lightbulb hung from the ceiling, and there were two doors—the one they had used, and another one across from it. Where did it go? What was this room supposed to be? And why in the world had Jake brought her here?

Maggie was more confused than ever. Was this the surprise he'd promised her? It had to be, or they wouldn't have come. But somehow she had expected something...well, nicer. A lot nicer. And she wished more than ever that she hadn't taken the drugs so she could think clearly and better understand what was going on.

Lifting her head to look at Jake, she smiled up at him. She wanted to say something to reassure him, but she was still having trouble forming words. She would have to tell him later, when the drug wore off. For now she would just have to show him.

Certain he was about to lie down next to her on the bed, she continued to smile and cooperate as he gently laid her on the mattress. Her first jolt of alarm came when he clamped a set of handcuffs on her wrists and then used another set to attach them to one of the bedposts. She felt her eyes widen, struggled some, and opened her mouth to say something, but Jake covered her lips with his, kissing her gently before whispering, "Don't fight it, baby girl. You're mine, remember? You trust me, don't you?"

Somewhere between confusion and panic, Maggie remembered hearing of this sort of thing, and she was certain Jake wouldn't hurt her. That thought, combined with her drug-induced stupor, stifled the scream that ached to burst forth from her heart. Jake continued to kiss and reassure her that this was just part of his wonderful surprise he had for her, and that if she truly loved and trusted him as she said she did, she wouldn't fight him. But instead of joining her on the bed, he leaned down and kissed her forehead and said, "Just roll with it. Cooperate and it'll go easier on you." Then he stood beside the bed looking down at her for a moment before turning away.

What was he doing? Where was he going? Struggling to call out his name, to convince herself that he was just teasing and testing her, Maggie watched him cross the room, turn one last time and give her a wink, and then disappear out the door, which she heard him lock before he descended the stairs.

How was it possible that anyone could be so evil as to delight in another's suffering?

Chapter 34

Z HEN-LI COULD SCARCELY CONCENTRATE TO PRAY, LET ALONE work, as her heart cried out to know what was happening to Mei. But did she really want to know? No doubt she would find out at the end of the day when she returned to her cell.

The morning's scene replayed in her mind, over and over, as the door had opened and the sneering guard had yanked Mei out into the passageway, shoving her in front of him as he ordered her to move. The anguished woman had managed one last glance over her shoulder at Zhen-Li, who had tried her best to give her an encouraging look, even as in her heart she wondered if she would ever see her beloved friend again.

How was it possible that anyone could be so evil as to delight in another's suffering? Zhen-Li knew such behavior was rooted in unbridled rejection of God, and yet it was still difficult to fathom that human beings could sink to such levels of depravity.

Help me to remember that You died for them as well, Zhu Yesu, she prayed silently. *At times my mind seems unable to comprehend that. And yet You died for me—even me! How then can I doubt that You would do the same for anyone else? Do I truly believe that my sin is any less evil than theirs? Forgive me, Father. Help me to see these guards, our tormentors and captors, as You see them. Remind me that it was for their very souls that You willingly bled and died—and rose again! Thank You, Zhu Yesu, for Your faithfulness and mercy.*

The sun was almost directly overhead now, causing sweat to trickle down her face and back. And yet she knew how blessed she was to be toiling outside, rather than being locked away with one or more of the guards, as poor Mei was even now.

At the thought, Tai Tong's face swam before her eyes, and she closed them, hoping the vision would go away. Still there, it taunted her, warning her that it wouldn't be long until she, like Mei, would be put in the position of compromising her faith and shaming her Lord—or suffering the consequences.

May I be found faithful, Zhu Yesu, she prayed, *even as I pray little Mei is at this very moment.*

***

Maggie's thoughts were becoming more focused as the night wore on, and as her mind cleared her terror increased. What had Jake done to her and why? Where was he? Was this some kind of crazy joke? Was he testing her to see if she loved him, trusted him? She did; surely he knew that! But she sure wished he'd come back and uncuff her from the bed so she could sit up and stretch. Her arms hurt and she needed to go to the bathroom. So far this surprise was not turning out to be fun at all.

And then she heard a noise coming from the door she and Jake had not used to enter the room. Someone was using a key to open it. Jake had come back! Maggie almost cried with relief as she shouted his name.

"Jake! Jake, where have you been? Why did you leave me here? I hated being here by myself. Please don't do that again. Please don't..."

Her voice trailed off as the door opened and a man who was most certainly not Jake stood looking at her, grinning, his dark eyes gleaming. Who was he? And why did he look vaguely familiar?

"Who are you?" she screamed. "Get out of here! Where's Jake? I want Jake!"

The man laughed as he closed and locked the door behind him and neared the bed, never removing his eyes from her for a moment. "I'm sure you do," he said, his voice smooth and low. "Everyone wants Jake. All the girls love Jake. But you can't have Jake anymore. He's gone. Now I'm here, and whether you want me or not, you've got me."

He sat down on the side of the bed. "Or should I say, I've got you? Yeah, I think that's more like it. I've got you, whether you like it or not. As for me, I like it a lot."

He leaned closer, his hot breath reeking of garlic. Struggling against the cuffs that held her, her wrists protesting in pain, she screamed at him to leave her alone, but he only laughed.

"Let's not pretend you've never done this before," he said, fixing his dark eyes on hers. "Jake's told me all about you, and I know you're not new at this. So let's just cut the screaming, shall we? Nobody's going to hear you anyway. You might as well just shut up and enjoy it, because it's going to happen whether you want it to or not."

He grabbed a handful of her hair and yanked her head back until she yelped with pain. "Do you understand me, little lady? You're mine for two days, until your new owners come for you. What they do with you after that, I really don't care. But I'm sure going to have fun with you until then. Understand?"

Maggie's breath was coming in short gasps by then, and she kept thinking—hoping—that Jake would come in the other door any minute and tell her it was all just a bad joke. But he didn't. The realization exploded inside her then that he wasn't going to come back at all...ever. He had left her there with this horrible man, and somebody else was coming for her later. What did that mean? What was going to happen to her? Why had she ever let Jake bring her here in the first place?

The tears began to pour from her eyes then, and she heard herself calling for her father. Oh, if only he were here, he would protect her! He would rescue her from this awful person and—

Wait a minute. The man's familiarity was swimming in her mind, taking shape slowly, and...

Her dad's ivory-handled knife. Now she knew where she'd seen this guy before. The pawnshop! Leo's Pawnshop. This was the man who had bought her dad's knife not too long ago, and the jewelry before that.

Without thinking she spoke his name. "Leo? You're Leo, aren't you?"

The look of surprise on the man's face was followed by an explosion of profanity, as he backed away from her and stood to his feet.

"Who are you?" he demanded. "How do you know me?"

Relieved that he had taken his hands off her and moved away, Maggie waited, watching to see what he would do next. When she didn't answer, he cursed again, spun on his heel, and rushed from the room, locking the door behind him.

Maggie wondered why he'd bothered since she was still cuffed to the bed. But she was so relieved to see him go that she let her tears flow, crying for Jake one minute . . . and for her parents the next.

Julia had never felt so agitated. She tried to sit in her chair, tried to lie down, but she couldn't be still. She paced with her walker, praying and complaining and wondering if things were ever going to settle down.

"If You don't stop keeping me up praying all night, Lord, I'm going to drop dead from exhaustion," she threatened, and then laughed at her outburst. "I'm sorry, Father. Forgive my impatience, please. It's a privilege to pray for all these needs, but I must admit that I do get a bit tired at times."

Laura had taken a turn for the worse that evening, and Julia had been praying for her for several hours. In between, she included prayers for the lady in China and also for Maggie and Margaret, though she was still struggling with the Margaret issue. But there was no doubt in her mind that Margaret's granddaughter Maggie was in trouble. That prayer need had loomed large throughout the night hours, and still seemed to take preeminence, even over Laura.

"What is going on with that girl?" Julia asked, sitting down once again on the side of her bed. "Lord, how much trouble can a young child like that possibly get into? Is it boyfriend trouble? Drugs? What is it?"

No answer came, but the continued call to intercede beckoned, and Julia heeded the call, lying down to rest her back but continuing in prayer for a young girl she had seen only a few times, but who quite obviously was extremely important to God. And with each word of prayer she uttered for Maggie, Julia prayed for the child's grandmother as well. Margaret Snowden might be one of the most cantankerous women who ever walked the face of the earth, but God loved her and sent His Son to die for her, so it was up to Julia to pray for her.

It was time to deal with Zhen-Li.

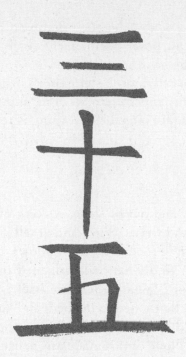

Chapter 35

Tai Tong grew more impatient by the hour. Even watching the two guards humiliate and beat the suddenly resistant Mei didn't assuage his thirst to conquer Zhen-Li. If anything, it increased his passion, particularly when he realized Zhen-Li must now be influencing Mei in her thoughts and convictions. From a mousy little weakling who subserviently did whatever was demanded of her, Mei had suddenly become almost defiant in her attitude toward her captors, though not haughtily so. Tong imagined a few more blows would knock that out of her, but her resistance could come from nowhere but Zhen-Li's influence.

It was time to deal with Zhen-Li... before she grew stronger and began to infect others around her.

Turning on his heel, he left Mei in the capable hands of two of his fellow guards, ignoring her cries as he stomped down the passageway toward Zhen-Li's cell. He wanted to be sure she heard him coming. The more fear, the better.

Disgusted with himself when he found her cell empty, he considered going outside to locate Zhen-Li, which shouldn't be difficult since he knew the area where she would be working.

But then he had a better idea, one that would be so much more effective for his purpose, particularly since he knew Zhen-Li would be returning soon.

Unlocking the cell door, he let himself inside and sat down in the corner, drew his knees up to his chin, and waited. He wanted to be sure that his face was the first thing Zhen-Li saw when she arrived.

✶✶✶

Maggie drifted in and out of sleep, waking often because of the pain in her arms and wrists. She couldn't tell if it was day or night in this closed-up little room with no windows. She had completely lost track of time. And what had happened to that horrible man from the pawnshop? What if he came back? What if he didn't? Would she just lie there, tied to the bed, and starve to death?

The drugs had completely worn off by now, but she was as confused as ever. None of this made any sense! Why would Jake bring her to this horrible place and then leave her? He had said he loved her. He had said they were going to be together, that he'd always take care of her. And now he was gone.

The sobs started again, though she choked them back when she heard the key in the lock. It was the door Leo had used, though she still hoped it was Jake coming back for her. The minute the door opened, her hope was gone. The horrible man with the mustache who had ripped her off more than once at the pawnshop now stood in the doorway, glaring at her.

"How do you know me?" he demanded. "Tell me! How do you know who I am?"

Maggie caught her breath. Should she tell him? What would happen if she did? Maybe the only reason he had left her alone so far was because he thought there was some connection. If she told him it was just the pawnshop, he might rape her...or worse.

She swallowed, deciding to take a chance and offer a bluff. "I just do, that's all. I know you, and so do my parents. We know who you are. And when I don't come home, my parents will send the police here to look for me."

The man's eyes narrowed, and his face reddened. "You're lying! No one knows where you are—only Jake, and there's no way he's coming back for you. Haven't you figured that out yet? He dumped you! Sold you, actually, just like I'm going to do." He pointed his finger menacingly. "And believe me, little girl, you won't talk so big once your new owners get hold of you."

Once again the man turned and exited the room, slamming and locking the door behind him. Maggie felt herself go limp with relief that at least he hadn't attacked her. But what did he mean about Jake selling her? This was the second time she'd heard something about "owners." What could it mean? What had Jake done to her, and what was going to happen when these so-called owners showed up?

Terror and frustration exploded in her as she began to kick her legs and scream, bellowing out her rage at not being able to get loose and escape. "Oh, God, help me!" she cried. "Get me out of here! Help me!"

It wasn't until her throat became too hoarse to scream that she finally settled into a quiet sobbing that eventually lulled her to sleep.

Throughout his long workday Zhou Chi had not been able to stop thinking about his sister's words. It was as if God Himself had spoken to him, giving him the direction he had been seeking. He was still concerned about Zhou Ming and Zhou Chan, of course, but he sensed that God had released him to go in search of Zhen-Li, and he knew he could trust Zhu Yesu to care for his sister and his son.

Now he had only to make his plans and to clear the time off with his employer. He had never made such a request before, and he had no idea how the man would react, but he knew he had to try. He lay on his mat in the dark now, the little house quiet except for the steady breathing of those who slept.

Zhu Yesu, go ahead of me, he prayed silently. *Prepare the heart of my employer to be gracious and understanding, to grant me the time I need to go to Beijing and find my wife. I believe that is what You are direct-*

ing me to do, Zhu Yesu. Please make a way, even where there seems to be no way.

Already it appeared God was answering his prayer, as the last few days Chi had been able to earn slightly more than usual and had therefore purchased extra supplies of rice and tea, and even a few vegetables. His sister and son would be fed for several days during his absence. If the food ran out before he returned, Chi would have to trust God to somehow provide what they needed.

How is it that I was so hesitant in my faith before, Zhu Yesu? Chi wondered. *Unlike Zhen-Li, I was raised in a Christian home, with parents who knew and loved You and prayed that I would do the same. Yet I took my faith for granted. So many other cares of life seemed more important. But now that my beloved wife has been taken from me, and I know how deeply she must be suffering for her faith, I understand that there is nothing more important than You. Forgive me for not recognizing that sooner, and please help my son to see it while he is yet young, before he wastes his life on other pursuits.*

With a fresh appreciation for his parents' faithfulness, Zhou Chi drifted off, wondering if he just might see his beloved Zhen-Li soon.

Zhen-Li's feet dragged as she was led back to her cell. It had been a long day, and her shoulders ached, though not nearly as much as her heart as she wondered about Mei. How was she? How had she handled the challenges of the day? Would she be waiting for her in the cell? If so, what condition would she be in?

A few feet from her cell, in the dim light of the passageway, Zhen-Li spotted a figure sitting in the corner, leaning up against the wall. So, Mei was there after all. And at first glance she seemed to be sitting upright and doing fairly well. Zhen-Li was relieved.

And then she stopped in front of the cell door, close enough to discern the figure more completely. As her escort unlocked her door to allow her entrance, her heart nearly stopped from the fear that swept over her. It was not Mei at all, but Tai Tong who stared back at her through the bars, waiting for her to join him.

The feet that moments before had dragged now refused to move. Even as the guard grabbed her arm and shoved her through the open door, she seemed unable to comply, stumbling instead onto the floor and landing just inches from the man who terrorized her every waking moment and haunted her dreams.

Tong. He was there, waiting for her. And there was nowhere to run. The end had finally come, and now it was she, rather than Mei, who would be put to the ultimate test of her faith.

Head down, she lay still, trying to summon her strength, but there was none. "Zhu Yesu," she whispered, even as Tong grabbed her hair and pulled her head back so she would be forced to look up at him. "Help me."

The kindness of the two old people had been the healing balm she'd needed.

Chapter 36

Yin Xei was back home, and though the emptiness still rang out to her as she passed through the front door, the pain wasn't quite as sharp. Somehow the hours she'd spent with the Wu family in their modest little home had given her hope, however faint it might be.

It had been so soothing to allow herself to be rocked in the old woman's arms, to cry on her shoulder, listen to her soft words, and relish her gentle touch. The kindness of the two old people had been the healing balm she'd needed to survive this first full day since her husband's death. She knew she could not go back there every day and hide from all that needed to be done, but it had been the few hours of peace and comfort she had so desperately needed just to believe she could keep breathing now that she was so utterly and completely alone.

The Wus had told her she could come back anytime. They had assured her they would pray for her, and they had even done so right in her presence. Rather than being offended by it, as Xei would have expected to be any time before Yang Hong's death, she was drawn to it. She only wished she'd had the courage to ask them to pray more, as their words of concern and petition had washed over her like warm water.

The words they recited to her from their *Shengjing* had produced a similar effect, causing her to feel light and carefree, as if someone were lifting her out of herself, above the burdens that threatened to crush her. How could that be? She had always believed the words of the Christians' holy book to be so much foolishness, though her own daughter believed they were from the one and only true *shen*—so much so that she now endured a prison sentence that could easily kill her.

Xei imagined Zhen-Li as she had been when she was a child, laughing and playing in this very room where she now sat. How cheerful the house had been then, with their family all together! Now it was just she, Xei, alone with her pain.

She tried to recall some of the words the Wus had spoken as they recited their memorized verses or prayed to their God, but the only thing that came to her memory was the name Zhu Yesu.

Zhu Yesu. It echoed in her mind...or was it her heart? She couldn't be sure, so she spoke it aloud. "Zhu Yesu." The words on her tongue were like warm honey, and she began to weep, though for the first time in many years she felt no sadness. She sat there in that place, unmoving, even as the night shadows began to make their way through the window.

"So," Tai Tong hissed, still holding her hair in his tight grip, "you call to your imaginary God to help you." He raised his eyebrows. "Where is He? Why hasn't He come in response to your cry? Is it because He does not exist and therefore cannot hear you?" He leaned closer to her face and whispered, "Or is it because He does not care?"

Releasing his grasp with a jerk, he leaned back, his dark eyes still boring into Zhen-Li as she struggled to pull herself to a sitting position. Was it possible that Tai Tong had become even more hateful than before? She had thought he was as evil as any human being could be, but he seemed more so now. If she'd had even a shred of hope that he might be grateful for her help after the earthquake, it was gone now. Even knowing that she had done the right thing at the time did little to ease her terror. She was going to pay dearly for her choice, even before he allowed her to die. Zhen-Li only hoped she would be faithful to the end.

And then she thought again of Mei. Where was she? Why hadn't she returned to the cell ahead of her, as she usually did? What had they done to her? Was she even still alive?

The questions nearly crushed her with agony, and she folded in on herself, burying her head in her hands and weeping aloud. Where was Shang Di? Why did He not show Himself and rescue them when He was more than able? Was Tai Tong right that perhaps Zhu Yesu did not care? If that were true, she would rather die now, right here on the spot. There would be no reason to live on.

Tong's laughter brought her back. He was mocking her. More than that, he was mocking her Yesu. And she heard it in his laughter—not human, but otherworldly. A hatred so intense it could only be demonic. No wonder Tong hated her so! It was a hatred directed at her not because of who she was, but because she belonged to Zhu Yesu. It was Zhu Yesu Jidu that he hated so intensely.

Suddenly her heart broke free, and she felt herself soar above the dark, putrid prison cell to a place where angels sang and joy offered strength beyond measure. Wrapped in that joy, she raised her head and locked her eyes on the man whose laugh still bounced off the surrounding walls. At the sight of her lifted head, his laughter stopped, and his jaw clenched.

"Tomorrow," he said. "I will come for you tomorrow. There will be no more waiting. Tomorrow you are mine."

With that he rose up and strode from the cell, leaving her on the floor to ponder her fate.

Maggie wondered if she was having flashbacks from the drugs when she opened her eyes and saw Joan standing by her bed. Did this mean Jake had sent the woman to rescue her? For the first time since he'd left her in this horrible place, she felt hope leap to life in her heart, and she cried out with relief.

"Thank God! Finally, somebody came to get me out of this place!" She yanked her still-bound wrists and begged, "Oh, hurry, please. These handcuffs are killing me!"

Joan didn't respond, but instead sat down on the bed beside her. "I'm going to unlock the cuffs this morning," she said, "but just long enough for you to use the bathroom. Do you understand?" She held out her right hand, and for the first time Maggie saw that she was holding a gun. "This is to make sure you don't try anything stupid. The doors are both locked, so you're not going anywhere, you understand?"

Maggie couldn't remove her eyes from the gun. What kind of crazy nightmare was this? Joan was Jake's friend. She had done her makeover just the other day. Now she was sitting on the bed waving a gun at her and telling her not to try anything stupid. Had everyone lost their minds? What was going on?

"I don't get it," Maggie said, raising her eyes from the gun to look into Joan's face. "I thought you were my friend...Jake's friend. Why are you doing this? Why is everyone doing this? What's that pawnshop guy got to do with all this? And where is Jake? Why did he leave me here?"

"You sure ask a lot of questions for somebody who's not in a position to demand answers," Joan said. "Listen, I'm just here to do my job, that's all. I can't answer any of your questions. But I can tell you this, kid. It'll go a lot easier on you if you just cooperate with everybody. Understand?"

Maggie frowned. She didn't understand at all, and she wasn't about to cooperate with anybody. But maybe if she talked nice to Joan, she'd help her get out of here.

"Listen," Maggie said, forcing a smile, "I don't want any trouble. I just want to go home. That's all. Just uncuff me and let me out of here so I can go home. Please. I won't tell anyone about this—any of it."

For a moment the woman hesitated, and Maggie held her breath. Then Joan shook her head. "Can't do it," she said. "I need the money. And besides, they know where I live. Sorry, kid, but I just can't help you. Now, do you want to go to the bathroom or not? Because that's the only reason I'm going to unlock those cuffs, and then it's right back here where you can't cause any trouble. Got it?"

Maggie felt the tears coming in a torrent. Joan wasn't going to help her. No one was going to help her. She didn't know what was coming next, but she knew it wasn't good. Oh, why had she trusted Jake . . . and why had he betrayed her?

Margaret seemed unable to think of anything or anyone but Maggie.

Chapter 37

IT WASN'T OFTEN THAT MARGARET SKIPPED MEALS, BUT HER stomach was in knots and there was no sense going to the dining room and putting up with those insufferable old fogies if she wasn't going to be able to eat. She'd gone in for breakfast and hadn't been able to eat then either, so there was no sense trying to force lunch down now.

Nervously nudging her rocker back and forth with her right foot, she wondered why she wasn't more excited about the visitor she expected today. If all went well, she would find out that the group had decided to take her case and help her shut down those ridiculous hallelujah gatherings that went on every Sunday afternoon. But instead of feeling hopeful at the possible outcome, Margaret seemed unable to think of anything or anyone but Maggie.

What has gotten into that girl? She was such a sweet little thing in her early years, she thought, remembering how her namesake had brought her flowers from the garden and marveled at her grandmother's ability to bake cookies. But somewhere along the line she'd become as selfish and thoughtless as the rest of them, and

Margaret had told herself she'd written them all off and no longer cared what happened to any of them. Now she wasn't so sure.

God, help her, she prayed silently...and then stopped her rocking chair in midmotion, stunned at the words that had passed through her mind. Had she just prayed? Surely not! Why, she didn't even believe in God; why would she pray to someone she didn't believe existed?

But the realization that she had done just that shook her to the core. Worse yet was the thought that she wished she had the nerve to go to that pesky religious nut, Julia, and ask her about it.

About what? she thought. *What would I ask her? Why I prayed if I don't believe in God? If maybe I really do believe in God and just don't realize it? If God is real, and if so, how do I get Him to help my grand-daughter, even though I don't know what's going on with her?*

She shook her head and began to rock once again. Maybe she was just getting senile, like the other old people at River View. After all, hanging around with dimwits was bound to rub off after a while, wasn't it? She knew she should have fought harder when her family tried to put her here. This mausoleum for the decrepit was no place for her! She should be back in her own home, where she could eat when and what she pleased and never have to put up with a bunch of noisy holy rollers disrupting her peace and quiet.

But instead she was here, stuck with the lot of them. And now things had become so bad that she was actually resorting to talking to an invisible, nonexistent deity. What in the world would happen to her next?

★★★

Zhen-Li had scarcely slept the entire night, not so much because she was worried about what she would face when Tai Tong came for her in the morning, but because she had been doing her best to care for and comfort poor Mei. When the fragile woman had returned to their cell, soon after Tong had departed, Zhen-Li had nearly fainted at the sight of what the guards had done to her beloved friend. How depraved and evil could someone be to do such a thing to a helpless woman?

Blocking out the thought that Tai Tong meant to do the same to her and more once he got his hands on her in the morning, she had spent the night hours holding and rocking Mei, and singing the Christmas song that seemed to bring comfort to her. Zhen-Li was certain that Mei's right arm was broken, and possibly some of her ribs, but she also knew there was nothing she could do for her except to pray and assure her that she was not alone. Mei's face was nearly unrecognizable from the beatings she had endured, but what seemed most difficult for the wounded woman to bear was the fact that despite her attempts to resist, she had been repeatedly raped. Zhen-Li wondered silently how much more of this abominable treatment her friend could sustain before she passed on to be with her Savior.

Qin Ai de Tian Fu, Zhen-Li prayed silently as the first sounds of morning began to invade the darkness of their cell, *do not let her suffer anymore. Deliver her, Zhu Yesu, or take her home to be with You. Let her suffering fall upon me instead, dear Yesu!*

Mei's pitiful whimpers were interspersed with occasional moans, and Zhen-Li knew every movement—even breathing—caused her nearly unbearable agony. To think that they might come back for her today was unfathomable.

"Please, Yesu," Zhen-Li whispered, holding her friend's head gently in her lap. "Please."

The heavy sound of boots approaching in the passageway alerted Zhen-Li to the fact that she would be the first to leave the cell that day, for she would recognize the steps of Tai Tong anywhere. When he stopped outside her cell and waited, she slowly raised her head and leveled her eyes on him, his outline visible in the waning darkness.

For a moment neither of them spoke. At last Tong broke the silence.

"Your friend is a fool," he said, the venom in his voice slicing through the stillness. "But you are an even bigger fool for not realizing how much greater your own punishment will be for poisoning her mind. She was quite cooperative before and able to avoid the type of suffering that has now been inflicted upon her because of your influence. I should think she will be more careful in choosing friends in the future."

263

Zhen-Li swallowed. How was it possible not to allow the terror of the moment to overwhelm her? How would she stand strong, knowing what Mei had endured and that Tong had promised her much worse?

I am weak, Zhu Yesu, she confessed wordlessly, *but You are strong. You must hide me in Your strength or I will fail You.*

The sound of the key in the lock told her the waiting was over. Tong had come for her, and she must go. Gently she removed Mei's head from her lap and laid it on the floor. Then she stood to face her captor, once again placing her soul in the nail-scarred hands of her Savior.

Maggie tried hard to keep track of time, though it wasn't easy in this windowless room. The woman named Joan had brought her a couple of meals, calling the last one supper, so Maggie assumed it must be late afternoon or early evening. Each time Joan came now she uncuffed Maggie so she could use the bathroom and eat, but then relocked her immediately. It wasn't much, but Maggie was grateful even for the brief respites. And though she had told herself she wouldn't eat anything Joan brought, she had wolfed down every bite, amazed at how ravenous she felt. How could she be concerned about food when she was trapped in this horrible place? And yet she argued with herself that it would be wise to keep up her strength in case she had a chance to escape.

Lying on her back and once again alone in the room, she glanced up at her arms, still held firmly in place. Escape! Who was she kidding? She was stuck here, and they could do anything they wanted with her—even sell her to "new owners," whatever that meant. She'd heard of people being sold as sex slaves or free labor, but she'd always thought that took place in other countries. Now she was beginning to realize that it happened right here in her own backyard—to her. And if what she'd heard about this business was true, the slaves almost never escaped alive.

Tears once again began to leak from her eyes as she realized that not only had Jake lied to her and betrayed her, but he had actually sold her into a lifestyle that would no doubt include a miserable existence and a very early death. How could she have been so stupid? Why did she listen to him? Oh, what she wouldn't give to be back at home once again, safe and sound with her parents and living a normal life like other girls her age!

Zhen-Li was shocked when the soft,
trembling voice stopped her.

Chapter 38

TONG'S GRASP ON HER ARM WAS PAINFUL AND ROUGH, AND completely unnecessary. Zhen-Li knew she had to go with him and resistance was futile. Yet he grabbed her, she knew, as a tactic to reinforce his power over her. If she didn't know that ultimately she belonged to Zhu Yesu and that He, not Tai Tong, controlled her destiny, she would be crying and cowering on the floor, begging for mercy. She knew, too, that there was nothing Tong would like better, though he would never grant such mercy.

Taking a tentative step toward the open door, Zhen-Li was shocked when the soft, trembling voice stopped her, turning even Tong in his tracks.

"Do not take her," Mei pleaded, gazing up at them from her spot on the cell floor. "Please. Take me instead. I will go with you. I will do whatever you wish. Just please do not take Yang Zhen-Li."

Zhen-Li caught her breath and her eyes widened, as she dared to peek at Tai Tong. The man's face was close enough that she could see it redden with fury, even as his jaws twitched in response.

Oh, Mei, she cried silently, too terrified to speak, *do not say any more! Please!*

Trembling now with obvious fury, Tong tossed Zhen-Li aside and reached down to grab Mei by her broken arm. The scream that tore from the wounded woman's throat nearly burst Zhen-Li's heart, as she, too, cried out in protest.

"Mei, do not say any more, please," she begged. "I am fine. I will go with him. Zhu Yesu will go with me."

But Tong already had his face buried inches from Mei's, as he bellowed, "What did you say to me? You dare to defy me, to question my decision?" Still clutching her injured arm, he shook her, evoking yet more screams of agony from the defenseless woman. "You want me to take you instead? What good are you? You are broken and defiled, nothing more than worthless trash. What are you to me?" Loosing her, he tossed her violently to the floor, and Zhen-Li watched in horror as her already-injured friend took more punishment upon impact.

Instinctively she tried to crawl to Mei, but the toe of Tong's boot in her ribs sent her sprawling. "Don't you move unless I tell you to," he ordered, glaring down at her. Then he turned his attention back to Mei. "I should kill you for your insolence," he snarled. "But I will leave that to the others who will come for you shortly." Reaching down, he yanked Zhen-Li to her feet, nearly knocking her breath from her in the process. "I have better things to do."

Turning from Mei toward the still-open cell door, he shoved Zhen-Li in front of him just as Mei uttered yet another cry. "No," she screamed, and Zhen-Li turned to see her friend throw her good arm around Tong's boot and nearly topple him as he, too, snapped his head around in Mei's direction.

"You no-good scum," he snarled, kicking her from his leg. "How dare you touch me!"

"Please," Mei cried again, "do not hurt her. Kill me, but leave Zhen-Li alone!"

"Kill you?" Tong reached down and grabbed Mei by the throat, lifting her up and shaking her as if she were no more than a pile of rags. "Yes, I will kill you. I will grant you your last wish!"

"Mei!" Zhen-Li threw herself at her friend, trying to gather her into her arms and support her weight as Tong continued to strangle and shake her. In moments she knew it was pointless. Mei no longer twitched or moved on her own. Tong had, indeed, granted her final wish.

As the realization that Mei was dead washed over Zhen-Li, she let go of her friend's body and collapsed to the floor, burying her head in her hands and weeping. In seconds she felt the weight of Mei's lifeless body drop next to her.

"Here is your friend," Tong spat. "This is what happens to people when you tell them about your religion." Cuffing her head, he knocked Zhen-Li onto Mei's body. "When I return, you will pay for this."

Zhen-Li heard him step out of the cell, lock the door, then stride purposely down the passageway. Carefully she lifted Mei's head into her lap and stroked her hair while she crooned her friend's favorite song into her now-deaf ears.

✷✷✷

As morning broke over their humble home, Chi hugged his sister and son and prayed with them for God's protection and provision for them while he was gone. Ming prayed that Zhu Yesu would guide Chi in his search for Zhen-Li and then bring him home safely once again.

Leaving little Chou behind was the most difficult part. The boy clung to his neck, somehow sensing that his father's leaving was more than his usual trip to work in the fields each day. Though the child had no idea where Beijing was or even what it was, for that matter, he had been told his baba was going there, and he seemed none too happy about it.

Nevertheless, Chi's mind was made up. He had cleared it with his employer to be gone for a few days, and he had laid up as much extra supplies of food for his sister and son as possible. He also had supplies of food and water for himself, which he carried in a sack over his back. It was time to go, even as the day broke on the horizon. Zhen-Li's welfare was the most important thing on his mind at that moment, as he climbed on his dilapidated bicycle and began the arduous trek toward the city.

Guide me, Zhu Yesu, he prayed silently as he pedaled away. *You know where she is. Please, please,* Tian Fu, *take me to her before it is too late.*

Leo tried to focus on the shop, but it was hopeless. People drifted in and out, buying or selling worthless trinkets, while the only treasure he was interested in lay captive upstairs—and he was afraid to take advantage of it.

Why? What was wrong with him? So what if she knew his name? It's not like he was ever going to see her again once he made the transfer. And he knew for a fact the girl would never live to come back and identify him. Still, the idea that she knew him from somewhere bothered him.

He racked his brain, methodically trying to review each and every customer who had come into the shop over the last weeks or months. But there were so many, and they all ran together. If a young, innocent-looking blonde like the one upstairs had come in, he would have remembered. No, she must know him from somewhere else. But where?

It doesn't matter, you idiot, he told himself. *So what if she knows your name? Big deal. Who's she going to tell? Her new owners? Like they'll care!*

He shook his head. *You're getting paranoid,* he scolded silently. *Whoever she is and however she knows you, forget about it. She'll be gone tomorrow, and you'll never have to worry about her again.*

He knew that was true, but he couldn't get past the questions in his mind and take advantage of what was waiting for him upstairs. He'd never had that problem with any of the merchandise before, and that's what bothered him most of all.

What a waste, he thought. *What a complete and total waste.*

Tai Tong had been angry many times in his life, but never had he felt quite like this. First one woman and now two had defied him—and he had lost control and killed the second one. He would have to explain that to his superiors, something he had not had to do before. Tong took great pride in his ability to control his actions, and he hadn't meant to go as far as he did. Threatening to kill the prisoners was one thing, but actually doing it was another. It happened, of course, and he certainly wouldn't lose his position over it, but he didn't like any marks against his name. And he knew the officials preferred to preserve the prisoners alive until the last moment of their usefulness, especially if there was a chance of harvesting healthy organs, a lucrative income in the Chinese underground.

Ah well, the woman was weak and sickly anyway, and likely wouldn't have survived long after the previous day's beatings. Still, Tong would have preferred that she'd died at someone else's hands besides his.

Yet wasn't that what he planned for Zhen-Li? He had always told himself that was the case. He would conquer her, use her, humiliate her, and then eliminate her. Wouldn't he? Wasn't that ultimately what he desired?

He sat now in the shadows of the rising sun, hidden in a quiet area of the prison yard, contemplating his next move. He could not afford to lose control again. He must plan his steps carefully. That he would have Zhen-Li for himself was without doubt at the top of his list, but how he would handle her after that was something he must still contemplate.

What was it about the woman that drove him nearly mad? Certainly not her beauty, as there were others more attractive than she. True, her refusal to yield to his attempts to turn her from her religion, whether through force or kindness, had failed and he was determined to wear down her resistance. But there was something more, something that nagged at him and nearly boiled in his gut like a poisonous cauldron.

Recognizing his true adversary, he lifted his head and squinted his eyes, glaring into the rising sun. Of course, that was it. The woman wasn't what drove him, but the god she claimed to worship. This Zhu Yesu she spoke of and claimed to belong to needed to be disproved, exposed for the sham He was, if ever they were to finally stamp out these religious followers of His.

Zhen-Li was the worst. Look what she had done to Mei! A perfectly good prostitute and slave, now dead because she listened to Zhen-Li's lies about her worthless religion.

Tong shook his head. The dead woman's courage at the end was surely fueled by stupidity and stubbornness, but why had she been so adamant in changing her behavior over a religious belief? Why not just abandon her belief and accept the privileges she had enjoyed all these years? Those privileges may have been meager at best, but they had at least kept her alive and in relatively good standing with prison officials.

And now she is dead, Tong thought. *Dead! Why? Why would anyone, particularly someone as weak and compromising as Mei, hold fast to such a belief, even in the face of suffering and death?*

His jaw went slack at the thought that formed slowly but clearly in his mind. His eyes widened momentarily, and then he closed them against the brightness of the morning sun.

There is only one reason, he thought, his heart racing at the implications. *Only one. And it is not a reason that pleases me.*

Knowing that a generous payday
loomed, they approached their task
with silent relish.

Chapter 39

THE TWO MEN HAD THEIR ORDERS. NIGHT HAD FALLEN OVER THE city hours earlier, and even the seedier neighborhoods were now still and quiet. Their job was a simple one. Together they would drive to the pick-up spot where they had received other merchandise many times in the past, use their key to unlock the pawnshop door, climb the stairs and unlock yet another door, uncuff their package, gagging her in the process to be sure she didn't alert anyone with her screams, and then transport her to the drop-off point. What could go wrong?

Knowing that a generous payday loomed, they approached their task with silent relish. They would live well until the next assignment on what they earned for a couple of hours of menial work. Even now, as they climbed into the dark sedan, the younger of the two felt a jolt of excitement shoot up his spine. It was always like this. A simple job, a mega-payday, and the bonus of transporting some unsuspecting young chick to a fate she would no doubt consider much worse than death. Some lucky guy some-where was going to get first crack at her in the next few days. He just wished it could be him.

***

Maggie awoke to the sounds of someone inserting a key in the door, the one Leo and Joan had used since she'd been there. She wondered briefly which one it might be, though she expected Joan since she was the one who came most often. In fact, she hadn't seen Leo since the time he'd confronted her about how she knew his name.

When the door cracked open, however, she was disappointed and even apprehensive to realize he had returned. Why would he suddenly appear after staying away until now? Whatever his plans, she imagined they couldn't be for her good.

Cursing the cuffs that held her, she waited as Leo approached. Should she say something? Scream? Accuse or threaten him? Unsure, she remained silent, watching his every move.

He stood over her now, silently gazing down into her face, and she shut her eyes as tight as she could, wishing she could make him disappear. At the same time she resigned herself to what was to come. How could she even fight him if he decided to rape or beat her? She was helpless, completely at his mercy...and she hated him for it. But not as much as she hated Jake. If she could somehow get loose and escape this hideous place, she would personally track him down and kill him for what he'd done to her.

She felt the man's hands on her wrists then, and she began to cry. How could she even think about getting away and going after Jake? She was trapped here like an animal in a cage, and there was nothing she could do about it. They could kill her, and no one would ever know.

Or sell her, she reminded herself. That seemed to be the plan. Either way, Maggie knew her life was over.

Then she realized Leo was fumbling with the key to her cuffs. Why would he unlock her if he was going to rape her? Did he want more of a challenge?

She clenched her jaw. Well, if that's what he wanted, that's what he'd get! Raising her leg, she lashed out at him, nearly catching him in the head. Ducking just in time, he cursed and jerked on her wrists, which he still held in his hands.

"Knock it off," he growled, trying again to fit the key into the handcuffs. "Can't you see I'm trying to help you? But you'd better cooperate, or we'll both be dead. They'll be here any minute, so shut up and quit fighting me."

Maggie had been ready to try kicking him again when it occurred to her that maybe he was telling the truth, though she couldn't imagine why. "Who's going to be here any minute?" she demanded. "And why would you help me?"

His job of unlocking the handcuffs completed, he looked at her in disgust. "Because I'm an idiot. Because if I don't clear out of here and keep going as far and as fast as I can, I'll be road kill before the night's over. Now get out of here, kid. You hear me? There's no time for questions. Just run and don't look back!"

Dazed, Maggie stared up at him, speechless. None of this made sense. Was it a trick? Why would this no-good scumbag help her? What if—

Before she could ask herself another silent question, the man had turned and fled out the door and down the stairs, leaving her alone in the unlocked room, free for the first time since Jake had fastened her to the bed. And suddenly she knew that whether Leo had told her the truth or not, the only chance she had was to run out the door and down the stairs behind him. Where she would go from there, she had no idea, but she would follow Leo's advice and do it as quickly as possible.

✱✱✱

The call had come just before Julia turned in for the night. She was sitting in the family room, visiting with a couple of other residents, but her mind was on Laura. The latest reports had not been good, and Julia had spent most of the day praying for a miracle. This evening, however, once they'd finished dinner, she'd decided to stay out of her room for a while and to interact with some of the others. She had hoped it would help her concentrate on something other than Laura, but it hadn't worked. And then the phone rang.

From where she sat, she could see Rocky as he picked up the receiver. By the quiet, subdued way he spoke, holding the receiver close and turning his back to the residents, Julia's first thought was that it was about Laura—and the news wasn't good. When Rocky ended the call and turned back to face them, focusing first on Julia, she knew her suspicions were right.

She swallowed. "What is it?" she asked, scarcely able to squeak out the words. "Is she...?"

Rocky nodded. "I'm afraid so. Less than an hour ago."

As the others gathered around to ask questions and comment on how much they would miss Laura, Julia hoisted herself onto her walker and went straight to her room—to cry and to pray, and to ask God why He couldn't have spared her just a little longer.

"You know how much she meant to me, Father," she whispered. "Did You really have to take her so soon?"

Then reflecting on what she'd just said, she continued, "Forgive me, Lord. I know You don't make mistakes, and I know Laura is so happy at this very moment. How could I possibly wish she were still here in this broken-down old world? I'm sorry, Father. Truly I am."

A sob escaped, even as she cried, "But, Lord, I'm sad too. Brokenhearted, really. You know that. You know I loved Laura like she was my own sister. What am I going to do now? I know I can still pray alone, but...it's not the same, Father. It's just not the same!"

Similar cries from her heart eventually lulled her into a fitful sleep, but one that wouldn't last for long.

★★★

The driver circled the block before deciding all was well and parking the car a half block away from the pawnshop. The vehicle's front doors opened simultaneously, and the two barrel-chested men, wearing almost identical dark trench coats, exited the sedan as if on cue. In moments they were in front of the store.

Reaching in his pocket for the key, the driver put it into the lock, stunned when the door pushed open at his touch. Alarmed, he turned to his partner, as they exchanged glances and then silently drew their weapons. The lights were off, just as they always were when they came for their packages, but they hesitated, listening for any sound that might hint that they were being set up. After a moment, the driver ordered, "Stay here and watch the door. I'll check on the girl."

Creeping stealthily up the stairs, he paused at nearly every step, but still he heard nothing. By the time he was within the last few feet, he could see the door. It was open.

Gun at the ready, he burst into the room, only to find it empty. The cuffs were still attached to the bedposts, but the girl was gone.

Running his hand over the rumpled sheet, he felt the lingering body heat and knew his package hadn't been gone long enough to get far. And he had a pretty fair hunch where the no-doubt vengeful girl might be headed.

"How much longer until I can come home to You?"

Chapter 40

ZHEN-LI HAD SPENT THE DAY CURLED UP IN HER CELL, NO longer able to weep, not even curious as to why Tai Tong had not come back for her nor had the other guards come to take her to work. Once they had come and taken Mei away, she had just crawled toward the wall where she and Mei had slept and leaned up against the corner, thinking of how her friend was now with Zhu Yesu Jidu.

"Thank You, Tian Fu, that Mei is no longer suffering. Thank You that she is with You. And forgive me, but I wish only that I could be there too. How much longer, Yesu? How much longer until I can come home to You?"

She thought of her beloved Chi and little Chan, and even of her parents, though she hadn't seen any of them in so very long. True, she still missed them and longed to see them again, but not enough to want to remain here in this world any longer. Her desire to go home had now overcome any lingering desire to remain in her current life.

"Have mercy on me, Zhu Yesu," she whispered. "Please, take me to be with You. There is nothing left for me here."

I have work for you, daughter, came the reply to her heart. *You are not finished yet.*

Her eyes widened at the silent words. Zhu Yesu had work for her—even here in the prison, even now that Mei was gone. How was that possible? She had come to believe her purpose was to pray for her friend and to tell her of Zhu Yesu Jidu. But she had done that, and now Mei was with Him. What more could she possibly have to do?

But Zhu Yesu had spoken. It was not for her to question. She would pray and wait to see what would come as the day passed once again into night.

Maggie stumbled along as fast as her bare, sore feet would take her, wondering if she could make it to her parents' home before she was caught. No, it was too far, and she had no doubt that whoever these "new owners" were, they would already be looking for her. She had to go somewhere safe, somewhere they wouldn't think to look for her. That ruled out Jake's, as that would be the first place they'd look, and besides, she knew now that she wasn't safe there.

Grandma Margaret! Of course. Maggie was only a few blocks from the old people's place, and no one would expect her to go there. Hobbling on bruised feet, she increased her pace and set her sights on the only place she could think of that might provide the refuge she so desperately needed. She didn't imagine that anyone would hear her knocks on the door and let her in, but surely at least one of those old fogies would have left a window open so she could slip in unnoticed, the way she had when she'd stolen the jewelry from the cranky woman with the cane.

Yin Xei had made up her mind. She had spent far too many years avoiding her own flesh and blood. Now that Yang Hong was no longer alive to forbid her, she was going to go see her grandson. Though her heart yearned to go to Zhen-Li, she knew that would be much more difficult. To visit her grandson, however, was a simple matter of finding a ride with a neighbor. As a new widow, she should have little trouble finding someone who would take pity on her and drive her.

She was right. The Wus explained that they no longer drove, as their eyesight was too poor, but they had prayed with her that she would quickly find a ride and have a nice visit with her only grandchild. Xei decided that the Wus' prayers must be very powerful, as it didn't take her long to locate neighbors who not only had a car but offered to take Xei to meet her grandson that very afternoon. At last Xei would lay her eyes on the child whom Zhen-Li had birthed into the world. Xei only hoped that her son-in-law would be understanding about the visit.

Hurrying to find some appropriate gifts for the boy, Xei picked out several items from her daughter's long-unused toy box, including a tiny, multicolored top that had been one of Zhen-Li's favorites when she was little. Tucking them inside a large sack, Xei hurried to the neighbors' home to begin the two-hour drive.

Julia's sleep was restless, and she finally gave up after a few hours of tossing and turning, deciding a cup of warm milk might help. Making her way as quietly as possible down the hallway toward the kitchen, she stopped outside Margaret's door, certain she'd heard the sound of crying inside. Yes, there it was again! Rapping softly on the door, she waited. When nothing but silence echoed back at her, she knocked a bit harder.

"Margaret, it's me, Julia. Are you all right?"

When still there was no answer, she tried the door. The knob turned, and Julia nudged it open. "Margaret? Are you awake? May I come in?"

At last she heard a sniffle. "If you must."

Julia took that as a yes and pushed the door the rest of the way, then followed her walker into the room, pausing to let her eyes grow accustomed to the dark. Just when she thought they had, Margaret flipped on the bedside lamp, and Julia blinked in response.

"What do you want?" Margaret demanded. "You have a lot of nerve coming to someone's room in the middle of the night."

Margaret was glowering at Julia by then, and Julia wondered if she should turn around and leave. No, she was tired of retreating from this grouchy woman, and tonight she was going to stand her ground.

"I heard you crying," she said, leaving no room for doubt in her tone of voice. "I wanted to make sure you were all right."

Margaret's eyes narrowed. "I should think you'd be the one crying, with your friend dying and all."

The knife had found its mark, but still Julia pressed ahead. "You're right. I did plenty of that earlier and will undoubtedly do much more. But right now I'm concerned about you. I assume you're not crying because of Laura."

Margaret frowned. Touché! Julia had found her mark as well, though she took little pleasure in wounding the already-miserable woman.

And then Margaret's face crumpled, and tears came in torrents. Stunned, it took Julia a moment to react. Gathering her wits, she closed the door behind her, made her way toward the weeping woman, and sat down in the rocker next to her bed. Wisely, she waited, praying silently as Margaret cried. When the tears slowed, Julia handed her a tissue from the bedside table. Margaret blew her nose and then turned to Julia with the saddest eyes Julia had seen in a very long time. For a moment Julia wondered if Margaret's eyes had always been like that and perhaps her glasses had hidden them. Before she could decide, Margaret spoke.

"I think my granddaughter is in trouble," she said, still mopping her face with tissues. "Very serious trouble. I didn't think I'd care, since none of my family seems to care much about me. But"—she shook her head and shrugged—"I know she looks terrible, with her crazy-colored hair and all that body jewelry. But to me she's still that sweet little girl who used to sit on my lap and..." Her voice trailed off and Julia thought she was about to start wailing again, but then Margaret seemed to regroup.

"I hate to admit it, but deep down I'm sure she's the one that took Emily's jewelry, just like...just like she took some of my things before I moved here. No doubt she sold it for drug money or something." She shook her head again, looking at Julia as if she expected her to be able to give her an explanation. "I just don't understand how she could have gotten involved in such a lifestyle." She paused and dropped her glance before raising it again. "No, that's not true. I do understand. What I don't understand is how her parents could have allowed it to happen. They let her run the household from the time she was little. I told them they'd be sorry, that they were making a mistake, but—"

Tears pooled in her eyes then, interrupting her comments. When she spoke again, there was a note of defeat in her voice. "But who am I to tell anyone how to raise their children? I made such a mess of things with my own. Tried to give them everything I never had, and look where it got them. All they can think about is money and what it can buy them—bigger houses, better clothes, nicer cars, more exotic trips—and their kids are all headed for hell in a handbasket!"

Julia felt her eyebrows raise, thinking perhaps Margaret had just spoken a more profound truth than she'd realized. She longed to tell her it wasn't too late—for her children, her grandchildren, or herself—but she sensed God's restraining hand. It wasn't time, not yet. Soon? She hoped so.

But even though she felt it wasn't time to speak to Margaret about her need to accept Jesus as her Savior, she did feel free to ask if she could pray with her. She did, and to her surprise, Margaret readily agreed.

"Yes, please," she said. "Pray for me and my family—especially Maggie. I just wish I knew where she was right now. I'd feel so much better if I knew she was all right."

Taking Margaret's hands in her own, Julia began to pray, first for Maggie's safety at that very moment, and second that God would give Margaret a peace about her granddaughter. Before she could move on to pray for the things that were really on her heart, she heard a noise and stopped, opening her eyes at the same moment Margaret opened hers.

"Did you hear that?" Margaret asked.

Julia nodded. "I did. Do you think someone else is up?"

Margaret frowned. "I know this sounds crazy, but it sounded

like it was at my window. Listen! There it is again. It sounds like someone is removing the screen."

Even as the two women focused on the white lace curtain that covered the open window, it moved, as a hand pushed it back and a blonde head poked its way into the room. Wide-eyed, the girl looked at Margaret and Julia and said, "I saw your light on, Grandma, and I didn't want to wake anybody else. I didn't know you had company, but—"

Before any of them could say another word, a beeping sound interrupted Maggie, continuing as the three of them stared at each other, stunned. At last Julia said, "I believe you've set off the alarm, Maggie dear. The one they installed after you broke in and stole Emily's jewelry."

With that Maggie began to cry, and the two women did their best to help pull her inside, even as the other residents started pounding on Margaret's door.

Silent, she waited.

Chapter 41

DARKNESS HAD INVADED ZHEN-LI'S CELL, BUT STILL SHE SAT IN the corner, praying and asking Zhu Yesu to take her home, despite His assurance that she still had work to do here on earth. She barely noticed that the day had ended and night had arrived without her having been summoned to work. So caught up was she in her sorrow and intercession that she didn't even hear the familiar sound of Tai Tong's boots as they arrived outside her door. He had opened the lock and entered before she realized she was no longer alone.

Raising her head, she recognized her adversary, even without light to show his face. His very stance was enough to identify him, and yet she felt no fear. Perhaps this was Zhu Yesu's way of answering her prayer to go home. Strangely, though she knew it would be a painful passage, she welcomed it.

Standing to her feet, she stood in front of the man, more than a head shorter than him and at least a third lighter in weight. Silent, she waited, eerily peaceful at the prospect of enduring what he had planned for her.

Without a word he turned and exited the cell, with Zhen-Li following mutely behind. Would they go to one of the two rooms he had taken her to before—the one where he first beat her as he attempted to get her to renounce her faith, or possibly the one where he had plied her with food and drink and whatever sense of false kindness he could muster? Was either of those rooms still standing? Certainly the second one had sustained considerable damage from the earthquake, as she remembered so well.

She sighed, matching her footsteps to his so she wouldn't lag behind. It didn't matter where he took her, she decided, or what he did to her when he got her there. What mattered was that soon she would be free of this horrible place, free to rejoice in the presence of her Savior and to await the arrival of her husband and child. Though she would never again see them here on this earth, their reunion in heaven would be that much sweeter.

After a few moments Tong stopped, with Zhen-Li nearly running into him. She did not recognize the room when he opened the door, but it looked similar to the one they had been in when the earthquake hit. A couch with a small table in front of it and one overhead light made up the room's furnishings. So, he planned to rape her after all. Even that didn't bother her as much as it had before, because she knew when he was done he would kill her, and then the pain and shame would finally end.

Stepping inside, she waited until Tong indicated that she should take a seat on the couch. Without further urging, she obeyed, her eyes downcast as she waited again. Whatever he did, he would have to do without her cooperation or consent, though she knew to fight him would be pointless. She would simply endure to the end. The only thing she knew she would not do was to deny Christ. If Tong insisted on that, she would surely take a beating before her death.

He was sitting beside her now, their legs nearly touching on the couch, but she did not pull away. There seemed to be no point. What would happen would happen. Her lips were pressed together in preparation, as she determined again never to deny her Lord, regardless of the price.

"I have decided to make you an offer," Tong said, and she lifted her head slightly to listen. "I know you are a stubborn woman—and a stupid one. I can beat you anytime I like, and there's nothing you can do about it. I can rape you, too, as you well know. But the one thing I have been unable to do is to get you to deny your false shen. That makes me very angry."

Zhen-Li suppressed a shudder. It was coming, the beating and torture and rape. She was sure of it. *Help me, Zhu Yesu. Don't let me deny You! Be my strength!*

"Here is my offer," Tong said.

Zhen-Li stiffened. What would it be?

"Your family," he said. "Your husband and son. Zhou Chi and Zhou Chan."

She jerked her head up, fixing her eyes on him. Why would he mention her family? What did they have to do with her? She was the one in prison, not they. Surely Tong wouldn't...

His smile was cold. "Ah, I see I have your attention now. Just as I thought. Perhaps you will not deny your faith when it is only your life at stake. But your family's? A different story, I believe."

Zhen-Li's heart raced at the implications. What was he saying? What did he plan to do to her beloved Chi, her precious little Chan? *Oh, no, Zhu Yesu, not that! Don't ask that of me!*

Tong's eyebrows rose questioningly. "So, you are no longer so confident or so stubborn, I see. I see also that I have found the right offer to help turn you from the error of your ways. Your religion and your Yesu, do they still hold first allegiance in your heart if it means your husband and son will suffer as you have suffered?"

He leaned closer, until she could feel the warmth of his breath. "You know I can make it happen, don't you?" He paused and then continued, even as she fought to hold back the scream that threatened to burst from her lungs. "What do you say now, Yang Zhen-Li? Do you still spurn my advances and confess your shen as Lord? Do you still insist you did the right thing in teaching religion to children and printing and distributing forbidden material? Or are you ready to sign a confession, admitting your wrongdoing and promising never to do it again? Will you finally speak the words that deny your imaginary god and admit that I,

Tai Tong, am your lord and master? If so, then my offer stands. Your husband and son will remain free and unharmed. If not, perhaps I will be forced to obtain the signature of your confession in red ink — the blood of your family, which will be on your hands. But one way or another, you will sign it."

Once again he paused and then whispered in her ear, "What do you say, Zhen-Li? What is your answer?"

★★★

Yin Xei's heart pounded in her ears as they neared the area where her son-in-law and grandson lived. Though she had never been there, she had long ago memorized the address "just in case of an emergency," she had told herself. Did this qualify as an emergency? Her husband was dead, her daughter was in prison, and she was all alone. It certainly seemed like an emergency to Xei.

As the car pulled up in front of the shack that matched the address, Xei felt hot tears sting her eyelids. There, directly in front of her, was a little boy, his clothes nothing more than rags but a smile on his face as he dug in the dirt next to a meager garden. A few feet away stood a woman Xei did not recognize, hoe in hand as she stopped her work and gazed with obvious curiosity at the car that had stopped in front of her.

The couple who had driven her waited in the front seat while Xei opened her door and climbed out. Moving slowly toward the child, she heard his singsong voice as he played, and her heart turned over at the reminder of the child's mother when she was small. How could Xei have let so many years pass without trying to see her grandchild or heal the rift between their families? Oh, if only Zhen-Li were here...

The boy stopped singing and lifted his head, dark eyes curious as he spotted her. The woman in the garden came to stand beside him, laying a protective hand on his head.

I am not here to hurt him, Xei thought, struggling against the tears that yearned to burst forth. *Please understand that!* But how could they? After all these years with no communication...

"I am Yin Xei," she said, surprising herself that she could speak. "I have come to see my grandson."

The look of surprise on the woman's face changed quickly to a smile, and she nodded her head in a slight bow. "Welcome," she said. "I am Zhou Ming, sister of Zhou Chi. Please, come inside. I will make tea." She glanced at the car. "Your friends are welcome."

Yin Xei's smile was hesitant, but her heart soared. She had done the right thing in coming.

✳✳✳

Julia's head was still spinning the next morning. What a night it had been! By the time the police arrived and Maggie had at last told her whole story, it was obvious that not one resident of River View Manor would get a wink of sleep before dawn.

Even Maggie's parents had arrived soon after Margaret called them. Stunned at the tale they heard from their daughter's lips, they were obviously ashamed that they hadn't even realized she was gone, as they explained it wasn't unusual for her to slip in and out of her window to visit friends, and she had forbidden them from entering her room uninvited. Julia could only hope and pray that there would be major changes in that household after this near-disaster. The police had assured Margaret that would undoubtedly be the case, since Child Protective Services would also be brought in to ensure that Maggie's parents weren't involved with or aware of the human trafficking ring.

Armed with the information Maggie had given them, the detective who had questioned her assured the girl and her family that an all-points bulletin would be put out immediately on all involved and that they would keep Maggie and her parents apprised of the results. Once the suspects were captured and brought to trial, Maggie would be called on to testify in court. First, though, Maggie would have to be examined by a doctor and complete reports had to be filed before any decisions would be made on what would happen with her next, much of which would hinge on what was decided by Child Protective Services.

The large house had seemed exceptionally quiet once everyone had gone their separate ways. Julia had just returned to her room when Margaret knocked on her door and asked if she could come in. "I have something to confess," she said. "It's about your Sunday afternoon services."

Julia couldn't imagine what Margaret might have to say about the meetings, but she welcomed her in to find out.

How could Zhu Yesu ask this of her?

Chapter 42

Z HEN-LI'S HEAD SWAM, THE PRESSURE OF CHOOSING BETWEEN her family and her Lord nearly crushing the breath from her. How could Zhu Yesu ask this of her? It was one thing to give her own life for her faith, but the lives of her family? Chan was only four years old!

This is impossible, Father, she prayed silently, even as Tai Tong waited so close she could feel his breathing. *Please do not ask this of me, Zhu Yesu! Please! How can I betray my husband and son?*

The answer held no condemnation, but rather wrapped her in an all-encompassing love that birthed a new sense of courage and conviction in her heart. *You do not betray your family by refusing to betray Me; rather, you honor them. What you must not do is betray the blood that I shed for the sins of the world. For that is the true red ink, the blood that signed My confession of love for you.*

As the truth of those words began to burn, even in her bones, Zhen-Li raised her head and fixed her gaze on Tong. "I cannot sign what is not true," she said. "For it is written that those who love husband or wife, children or parents, more than Zhu Yesu are not worthy to be His disciples." She lowered her eyes before continuing. "May I be found worthy in His eyes."

Zhen-Li waited for the blow that was sure to come, resigning herself to whatever Tai Tong should choose to do—to her or to her family. They were in the hands of Shang Di, and she knew she could trust Him to do what was right.

"Look at me," Tong ordered, the tone of his voice softened slightly.

Obediently Zhen-Li raised her head. Tong still sat beside her, though he no longer leaned in toward her menacingly. He seemed to be studying her, and so she waited, not knowing what he wanted. And yet her fear was gone, and that made the waiting so much easier.

"I believe you," he said. "I no longer have a choice."

Zhen-Li was confused. What was he saying? What was it he believed?

Tong turned away, dropping his head slightly as he shook it from side to side. "I did everything I could not to believe you. I hated you with every ounce of my strength. I wanted to punish you and possess you and prove to you that you were wrong, especially after you gave up your chance to escape so you could help me. But when the woman named Mei began to listen to you, I saw her changing. At the end, the one who was once a simpering coward became a fearless follower of your Yesu. I asked myself how that could be. I tried and tried to find an answer, but there was none...except that what you said was true."

He lifted his head and looked at her again, this time with a hint of wetness in his dark eyes. "When she was willing to give her life in place of yours, I tried once again to destroy the faith you profess. I realized I was able to kill Mei's body, but her faith, and yours, lived on."

Zhen-Li could not speak. It was as if her heart had stopped— as if all time had ceased and nothing existed but the words of Tai Tong, speaking Truth into a listening universe. Reason told her it was a trick, that she couldn't believe his words, yet faith told her he could not speak in such a way if it did not come from his heart.

Tears pricked her eyes then, and for the first time she felt compassion for the man who had tormented her and killed her beloved friend. Zhu Yesu had died for him, she realized, even as He had died for her. Her Lord and Savior desired to write Tai Tong's name on the list of the redeemed in the red ink of His blood.

"It is too late for me, I know," Tong said. "But I had to be certain, and so I made you this final offer. When you refused, I knew you could never have done so in your own strength. One much greater than you—or I—was sustaining you. I only wish..."

His voice trailed off then, and he dropped his head into his hands and wept softly. In a gesture Zhen-Li would never have imagined she would make without revulsion, she laid her hand on the prison guard's shoulder and began to pray that God would help her show him that it was never too late—not even for him.

***

Julia was stunned. She'd had no idea that Margaret had been planning to file a lawsuit to force them to stop holding their Sunday afternoon worship services at River View Manor. Now, however, Margaret had assured her that she would drop the action completely. In fact, by the time she left Julia's room that morning, the woman had actually promised to at least consider attending one of those meetings herself.

"I do play the piano a bit," she'd confessed. "Maybe I could even learn some of those hallelujah songs I hear you people singing every week."

Julia had laughed in spite of her heavy heart and told Margaret they would love to have her do just that. Margaret had then reminded her that she hadn't made up her mind yet and went off to her room. But her visit had left Julia with a lot of new thoughts to mull over.

As she waited for lunchtime, Julia remained in her room, praying and thinking about the many events of the last twenty-four hours. Her beloved friend Laura had "graduated" to heaven and now rejoiced with the Lord and all the saints who had gone on ahead of her. It was hard not to be envious, but at least Julia was moving past her initial resentment of having her prayer partner taken from her. Who knew? Perhaps God was grooming Margaret Snowden to be Laura's replacement! The idea nearly caused Julia to laugh out loud, but then God had been known to do much bigger miracles than that, so anything was possible.

She nearly laughed again at the memory of Margaret's granddaughter poking her head through the bedroom window and setting off the house alarm. What a commotion that had brought about! Before they knew it, the house was crawling with police and detectives, a weeping teenager and her stunned parents, and an entire crew of befuddled senior citizens who were beginning to think their quiet little home had become a gathering place for all sorts of misfits and miscreants.

At least the media didn't show up, Julia mused, smiling as she sat in the chair beside her bed. *Though I wouldn't rule that out as news about Maggie's harrowing experience begins to spread.* She shuddered. Imagine such a thing going on in their own little town!

A knock on the door interrupted her thoughts. Had lunchtime arrived and she missed it?

"Come in," she called.

The door opened and Rocky poked his head in. "How are you doing?" he asked.

"All right." She smiled sadly. "Considering."

He nodded and came inside, closing the door behind him. "That's what I thought." He approached her and held out an envelope in front of him. "I brought you this. It's from Laura. She left specific instructions that it be delivered to you immediately after . . . well, after she was gone."

Julia felt her eyes widen. Her hand trembled as she reached for the envelope. So Laura had left her a note before she graduated! Her heart raced as she tried to imagine what her friend and prayer partner had written.

When Rocky slipped out, Julia opened the envelope and pulled out the flowered stationery. Her eyes blurred as she began to read:

My dearest friend and sister in the Lord:

As I lie here in this bed, praying and thanking God for your friendship, I realize afresh that my days are numbered. But so are yours. From the day we are born, God holds our lives in His hands. His love is so faithful. Soon I will be in His presence, and my heart yearns for that moment. But I know it will be difficult for you, dear Julia. You must remember that you were left behind for a reason. However many days you have, use them to fulfill His purpose. Continue to pray for Margaret and Maggie, for everyone at River View, for our families, and for the precious people in China. By His mercy, we will meet many of them in heaven one day. Until then, know that I am waiting for you.

Clutching the note to her breast, Julia whispered, "Thank You, Father. And thank you, my dear friend. I will see you soon."

***

Yin Xei returned home with a joy in her heart that she hadn't felt since Zhen-Li was a little girl. Though she still yearned to be reunited with her imprisoned daughter, she now had the memory of her grandson's face to comfort her. She had even taken pictures of him and his aunt, Zhou Ming, a pleasant woman who had been very kind to her. Xei wished their time together had been longer, but because her neighbors insisted on waiting in the car while she visited, she felt compelled to leave quickly.

And yet in that time she had learned much. She now knew that the man she had believed unworthy to marry her daughter had risked everything to go to Beijing to try to locate his wife and to confirm that she had not been injured in the earthquake. Xei chastised herself for not insisting that her husband use their party ties to learn of Zhen-Li's welfare, but now she was free to do so, though she would wait until Chi had time to locate Zhen-Li first so as not to jeopardize him. She wished she had made the trip sooner so she could have stopped Chi from going at all, but she had been unable to when her husband was still alive.

"It all works together for a reason," Ming had told her when Xei had expressed her regret at not having come sooner. "Zhu Yesu knows what He is doing. We need only to trust Him for the outcome."

Xei had thought the woman quite brazen or even foolish to speak to her of her religion, knowing that both Xei and her husband had not been receptive to Zhen-Li or Chi's faith in the past. But perhaps Ming had sensed the softening in Xei's heart to such things, for truly Xei had to admit that such a softening was taking place. She had even decided that she would visit the Wus again, soon and often, as she had many questions for them about this Zhu Yesu and their religion.

Before leaving to return home, Xei had made a point to stress to Ming that if Chi ran into trouble and did not return as expected from his trip to Beijing, Ming was to bring little Chan to Xei's home. She would care for both of them, for as long as need be. Ming had smiled and promised to do so.

He had left the prison feeling lighter
than he'd ever imagined possible.

Chapter 43

AFTER AN EMOTIONAL TIME DISCUSSING THE FORGIVENESS OF Zhu Yesu, Tong had humbly prayed to receive His forgiveness. Then he had escorted Zhen-Li back to her cell, promising to come for her again soon so they could spend more time together, talking about this new life that even now washed over him in waves. He had left the prison feeling lighter than he'd ever imagined possible, even as a desire to laugh and cry did battle in his heart.

Tong was thrilled with the knowledge that God was real and had forgiven him—him, Tai Tong!—for his sins and that he would one day leave this earth and go to be with Zhu Yesu forever. And yet he was devastated at the knowledge of all the pain and destruction he had wrought before coming to this new life of faith. He had hurt many people in his lifetime, no one more permanently than the courageous little woman called Mei, who had laid down her life for her friend.

True, Tong had killed others in the course of his lifetime, but never so cruelly and needlessly as with the frail form he had strangled and shaken to death. He tried to console himself with the fact that Mei was in heaven with her Lord, and that Zhu Yesu Himself had already paid the price for the terrible sin Tong had committed in snuffing out her life, but the responsibility for such an act was not easily dismissed.

As he walked through the darkness toward home, he wondered how long he would have to live with his sin before paying the price. But what would that price be? Even if he confessed the entire story to his superiors, rather than the self-serving version he had already given them, he would receive little more than a reprimand. She was, after all, a mere prisoner, while he was a faithful servant of China with a clean and honorable record. His punishment would certainly not fit his crime.

Even as he considered this dilemma, the outline of his house came into view in the moonlit night. Tong stopped and stared for a moment before approaching. The woman and child who lived there were his family, and yet they were terrified of him because of the horrible treatment he had inflicted upon them over the years. Perhaps he could at least assuage some of his guilt by showing them a little kindness.

Stepping into the house, he saw by the one dim lamp that his wife had left lit for him that both she and their son were sound asleep. Tiptoeing toward the boy, he knelt down beside the child's sleeping mat and stroked his hair. The boy sighed in his sleep but did not move. Tong berated himself for having been so cruel to the little one and resolved to do better should God grant him the opportunity.

Then he rose to his feet and crossed the room to where his wife lay still, her eyes closed. Her uneven breathing told him that she was not asleep after all, though she no doubt hoped he would believe she was.

Undressing, he lay down beside her and put his arm over her, pulling her close. He felt her stiffen, and he knew she feared he would force himself on her and even beat her in the process, as he often did. Instead he lay quietly beside her, waiting several hours before he finally felt her body relax and her breathing become deep and even. Allowing her to go to sleep in peace was the first real gift he had ever given her.

***

The day was drawing to a close, as the residents of River View Manor gathered together to hear from the detective what had happened regarding the case with Maggie and her kidnappers. Julia was surprised that they had all been included, but the woman investigating the case explained that she believed it would be easier to keep the facts straight and set all their minds at ease at once, rather than allow rumors and suppositions to spread.

"Before you hear any of this on the news, let me assure you that Maggie is fine," Detective Mallory explained, her short red hair bobbing as she talked. "I know you're all relieved to hear that."

Julia sat next to Margaret on the sofa, and she reached over and squeezed the woman's hand at the announcement. She noticed Margaret nodded her head in appreciation, even as she blinked away a few stray tears.

"Without going into any details that might jeopardize the case," the detective continued, "I will tell you that we captured one of the primary suspects, a man who owned the pawnshop where Maggie was being held. It seems he was the one who, for whatever reason, decided to set Maggie free. He was trying to catch a plane out of town when we caught him.

"We also arrested a woman who worked closely with this trafficking ring, and we are actively searching for several others."

She took a deep breath and glanced around the room before continuing. "Another suspect, Jake Holder, was found dead in his home early this morning. Apparently the other suspects thought he was the one who let Maggie go, and they didn't take kindly to that. Though he wasn't the one who actually set the girl free, he was the one who lured her in. He paid the ultimate price, I'm afraid."

Her announcement produced a few gasps and whispers and much head-shaking around the room, and once again Julia took Margaret's hand, this time hanging on as the detective wound up her report.

"The investigation continues," she said, "and I haven't told you anything you won't hear on TV in the next few hours. But I wanted to tell you personally, as you were all involved to one degree or another." She glanced at Margaret with a thin smile and then asked, "Are there any questions?"

When no one spoke, the detective excused herself and walked out the front door, leaving the residents of River View Manor wide-eyed as they turned to one another and at last began to discuss what they had heard, showing deference to Margaret by restraining their comments.

Julia focused only on praying for the woman who sat beside her. No longer was it an effort to pray for Margaret, as she had truly begun to care for her and wondered if she might one day become the friend and prayer partner to fill the gap left by Laura's departure.

★★★

Tong left his sleeping wife and child and returned to the prison long before the morning light pierced the skyline. He hadn't gotten any sleep himself, but he felt refreshed in spite of it.

As he neared the prison walls, he spotted a figure in the darkness, though it was obvious the individual had seen him as well and was trying to hide. At one time Tong would have pounced on the hapless person and beat him within an inch of his life. This morning he approached slowly yet cautiously.

"Who is it?" he called softly. "Who are you, hiding in the shadows? Come out where I can see you."

Hesitantly, a man stepped from his hiding place. Thin and haggard, dressed nearly in rags, he stood with his head bowed, waiting.

Tong stepped closer. "Who are you?" he repeated.

"I am Zhou Chi, husband of prisoner Yang Zhen-Li. I have..." His voice trailed off, and Tong heard him take a shaky breath. "I have come to see if she is all right. I was worried about her after the earthquake."

Stunned, Tong nearly fell backward at the man's words. Zhen-Li's husband! How could it be? Only Zhu Yesu could arrange such a meeting. Nothing else made any sense.

"I am Tai Tong," he said. "I know your wife, Yang Zhen-Li. She is well. I can assure you that she was not hurt in the earthquake."

The man named Zhou Chi raised his head, his eyes wide as he stared at Tong in obvious amazement. "You know Zhen-Li? She is all right?"

Tong nodded. "She is fine. I saw her only a few hours earlier. She is well." Then he continued in a barely audible whisper, "And her faith is strong."

It was too dark to be certain, but Tong imagined that he saw tears glistening in Zhou Chi's eyes. Tong smiled, speaking without thinking, shocked at his own words as he heard them. "Would you like to see her?"

The man gasped. "You...you would do that? You would allow me to see her?"

"I will try," Tong answered, wondering even as he made the statement how he would accomplish such a thing. "I will show you where to wait."

With that, he led Chi back into the shadows.

Zhen-Li had wondered through the sleepless night when Tong would arrive for her. He came earlier than expected, the darkness of the night having not yet retreated, and when he did, he seemed agitated—or was he just excited? She certainly was, and she couldn't wait to speak with him more about Zhu Yesu.

As she followed him wordlessly down the passageway, she wondered at the mercy and faithfulness of Tian Fu, who would take the very man who was her tormentor and turn him into her brother. When they entered the room and Tong locked the door behind him, he gently took her arm and turned her toward him.

"Listen carefully, Zhen-Li," he said, his voice low. "I have to tell you something, but you must not cry out or make any unnecessary noise. I do not think anyone can hear us, but we cannot take chances. Do you understand?"

Zhen-Li felt her eyes widen with apprehension. What had happened in the past few hours that would make Tai Tong behave in such a way? She had thought their time together would be a joyous one, but now she was not so certain.

"What is it?" she asked, her voice hushed in response to Tong's subdued tone.

Tong's eyes darted around the room, and then he quickly escorted Zhen-Li to the couch. Once seated side by side, he turned to her and took her hand. "Something has happened that is almost as amazing as what happened to me last night," he said. "I met someone."

Zhen-Li frowned. What was he talking about? And what would his meeting someone have to do with her?

"I do not understand," she said. "Please explain. I am very confused."

Tong's eyes locked on hers, and at last he said, "I have met Zhou Chi. Your husband. He is outside, waiting for you."

Zhen-Li sat perfectly still, unable to move or speak. What did he mean? How could he have met Zhou Chi? He was at home, caring for Zhou Chan. Even if Chi had somehow found his way here to the prison, how would he then have known to contact Tong? Zhen-Li wondered for a moment if Tai Tong had become so emotional over his experience of the night before that he had lost his mind. It was the only explanation that made any sense.

"Zhen-Li," Tong said, squeezing her hand, "did you hear me? Your husband is here, outside the prison, waiting to see you. I told him I would try to get you to him. Do you understand what I am saying?"

At last his words began to make sense to the dazed woman, and she realized Tong was telling her the truth. How it could be so she could not imagine, but quite obviously it was. What, then, was she to do? How could Tong get her outside the prison walls to see Chi? Surely they would all be caught and killed. Was it worth the risk?

An image of Chi's kind face swam in front of her eyes then, and she thought of how it had been when they first met. She had been attracted to his gentle spirit and sweet nature, and it hadn't been long until she had also adopted his Christian faith, though it ultimately came between herself and her family. Did she regret it? Not at all. And she prayed continually that her parents would one day come to know Zhu Yesu Jidu as she did—as Tong now did as well.

And then the memory of her last moment with Chi before she was taken away came crashing in on her heart—the way they had cried out to one another as she was forced into the PSB car by a vengeful Han Bai and driven away, while Chi held little Chan in his arms, both of them weeping. Was it worth the risk? Oh, yes! To see Chi again would mean so much. Yet did she have the right to risk both Chi and Tong's lives in the process?

"It is not fair to you," she said, still looking into her friend's eyes. "If you are caught—"

"It does not matter," Tong said, interrupting. "You have given me the greatest gift anyone can ever receive. You forgave me and introduced me to Zhu Yesu and His forgiveness as well. I owe you everything—even my life. As for Chi, he would not have come if he were not willing to risk his life to see you again."

Tong was right about Chi, though she still felt uncomfortable about putting Tong in danger. And yet...

"There is no more time to think," Tong said. "Come. I have a plan, but you must act as if I am forcing you to come with me. Do you understand?"

No longer hesitating, Zhen-Li nodded. To see her beloved Chi again had now become a yearning that emboldened her to move ahead at any cost. She would follow Tong and trust him, whatever he said or did.

Exiting the room, Tong made a show of bullying her to walk ahead of him; she turned when he said to turn, stopped when he ordered her to stop. But the deeper they went into the passageway, the less Tong spoke. At last he said, "Here. There is a seldom-used entrance just a few feet ahead. I have the key. Chi is hiding nearby."

Stealthily they crept the last few yards to the gate, which Tong unlocked quickly. Glancing first at the still-dark area surrounding the gate, he urged Zhen-Li toward a large clump of bushes. "He is here," he whispered, continuing to glance over his shoulder. "I will wait by the gate and watch."

"No need for that," said a voice, snapping both Tong and Zhen-Li to attention. As their heads swiveled as one, they found themselves staring into the glowering face of another guard. "I noticed you behaving strangely last night," the man declared, "so I've been following you. When I saw you earlier, outside the gate, talking with some good-for-nothing countryside peon, I knew you were up to something." His gaze swept over Zhen-Li before returning to Tong. "She is a piece of trash, a traitor, a fanatic. And now you have joined her in her treason, trying to release her. Is this how you show your allegiance to your country, by betraying your own people to help our enemies?"

A noise from behind caught Zhen-Li's attention, and she turned in time to see Chi emerge from the bushes. Her heart leapt at the sight, even as a jolt of fear and regret shot through her at the realization that now her husband would also be imprisoned—or worse. What would happen to little Chan?

"It is my fault," he said. "I asked him to help me. Please, let him go and punish me instead."

Before anyone could respond, Tong took the opportunity to jump on the guard while his attention was turned. In a moment they were grappling on the ground, and Zhen-Li was sure Tong would get the best of the smaller man. But then the gleam of a knife in the darkness caught her eye, as the guard managed to pull a weapon from the sheath on his waist and plunge it into Tong's stomach, resulting in a grunt of pain from Tong and a loosening of his grip on the man.

As Tong rolled off the guard and onto the ground, the man pulled himself to his feet. With his back to Tong, he confronted the stunned couple. Zhen-Li suppressed a gasp and Chi slipped his arm around her as they watched Tong slide the knife from his body and pull himself to his feet before throwing his entire weight at the guard, knocking him to the ground once again. Before the man could react, Tong plunged the weapon into the man's throat, silencing him almost immediately. Then Tong rolled off onto his back once again, as Zhen-Li and Chi hurried to his side.

"Oh, Tong," Zhen-Li cried. "I will run for help while Chi prays for you."

"No!" Tong grabbed Zhen-Li's arm, surprising her with the strength he still possessed. "Not this time," he gasped. "You saved me once. It is too late now. This time you must save yourself.

You and Chi will be killed if they catch you here with two dead guards. Do not worry about me, my friend. You have already given me the best gift possible. I will be with Zhu Yesu in minutes. There is nothing anyone can do to keep me here. Do you understand, Zhen-Li? Think of your son. You must go, quickly. Please!"

Though her heart burned at the thought of leaving Tong behind, she knew he was right. If she and Chi were to have any chance at all, they had to leave immediately.

Wiping tears from her eyes, Zhen-Li asked, "But, Tong, where shall we go?"

Struggling with the effort, Tong spoke one last time. "Wherever...Zhu Yesu...leads you." With a final, raspy breath, his head rolled to the side and he was still.

After a moment, Zhen-Li felt Chi behind her, as he placed his hands under her arms and gently lifted her to her feet. "We must go," he said, his lips close to her ear.

The reminder that she was once again with her beloved husband momentarily drowned out her regret over Tong's death. She gazed up at him, her eyes flooded with tears of both sadness and joy, until Chi kissed her forehead and spoke again. "Just as Tong said, we must go, Zhen-Li, quickly...wherever Zhu Yesu leads us."

Blinking away her tears, she nodded, and, hand in hand, they turned and ran into the silent night, even as the first faint rays of morning promised to light their way.

People of the Book

Book Four of the "Extreme Devotion" Series
Kathi Macias

Prologue

Farah Mohammed Al Otaibi lay bruised and bloody on the floor beside her bed. The image of her soft mattress floated in and out of her consciousness, but she had no strength to drag herself from her current position. Even the slightest movement brought stabs of excruciating pain, so she tried to remember to keep her breathing shallow and her body still.

How long had she been here? Hours, certainly. Days? She couldn't be sure. Her father and brother had covered the windows with heavy, dark cloth, blocking out any light that might help her keep track of time.

Hunger wasn't an issue, for who could think of food when the pain was so intense? But thirst? Oh, how she longed for just a sip of cool water! Surely her mother would sneak in soon and bring her some. She had always taken care of her before —

Before...

The memory was back, though she tried desperately to block it out. Impossible. She could never forget that moment in time, for it was the dividing line between the before and after of her life. Before the tragedy that led to her brother's discovery. Before her father had flown into a rage over what he considered his daughter's betrayal and treachery. Before they had threatened to kill her in order to preserve the family's honor. Before her mother had tried to intervene.

Hot tears pricked the back of Farah's eyelids as the vision of her mother's face before — and after — swam in front of her eyes. The pain in her heart at that moment far exceeded anything she felt in her body. Then suddenly, inexplicably, the meaning of her name — Farah, "joy and cheerfulness" — burst into her consciousness. Despite her agony and sorrow, Farah was unable to hold back the brief burst of laughter that exploded from her aching chest. How absurd that her parents had given her a name that implied happiness, and yet she now wondered if she had ever truly understood or experienced any of it in her not quite sixteen years of life.

But then she had met Isa, and everything—both good and bad—had changed forever.

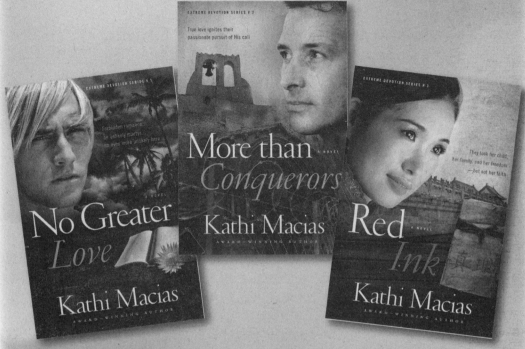